Inanna Drew has a problem, and, of course, that problem is a boy. Though she's quite content to read her books and excel in school, he bothers her and seems incapable of taking a hint. Thus this is a journal, nay, a chronicle that she must put to paper to explain, in her own voice, why he doesn't deserve the time of day.

All of this changes after a sudden upheaval in her life, making Hadrian Marshall less of a pain in her side and more of a friend to be counted on.

# Running Out of Air

K.T. Swift

A NineStar Press Publication

Published by NineStar Press
P.O. Box 91792,
Albuquerque, New Mexico, 87199 USA.
www.ninestarpress.com

# Running Out of Air



Printed in the USA
First Edition
July, 2018

Print ISBN: 978-1-949340-16-7

Also available in eBook, ISBN: 978-1-949340-08-2

Warning: This book has depictions of the death of a parent.

# September

**9/1 SATURDAY**
*(Scratched in a worn notebook)*

I am a self-admitted fool, which probably jettisons me out of the category by virtue of the self-admission. Foolishness, to me, always seemed to be a want of realisation more than anything else, but I am still foolish, and foolishness always leads to trouble. That is why I'm writing this all down. Maybe someone can help me if I can show them that it started here or perhaps there, later on.

Anyway. To the point. I don't think I can finish school, not here, not under these circumstances. I mean, well, I'd really rather not. After two weeks of nerve-racking, nail-biting stress, I am about to reach the end of my rope. Why, you may ask. Why is this straitlaced, straight-A mathlete about to toss herself into the nearest lake with stones in her pockets? (Oh, poor Virginia Woolf) A boy, that's who. How damn trite.

And I'll try to warn you before I drown you in allusions (if you will forgive me the pun).

He's just so damn annoying. He refuses to leave me alone, insists on talking to me, tries to insinuate himself into my life. What on God's green earth is he doing? Is he trying to badger me to death?

I mean, I do like people, but not when said people are parading themselves before me so incessantly that I would rather die than see another sickeningly false-friendly face. I like my space, thank you very much. Perhaps I should start at the beginning, so you may fully comprehend this boy's single-minded quest to bother me to death.

All right, the first day of school is usually more uninspiring than sugar-free fudge unless the senior class plays an opening prank, which they did not because my class is full of washed-out ne'er-do-wells without a handful of brain cells to share amongst them. At least, when it comes to actually breaking rules and sowing chaos like proper teenagers.

So life goes on the way it always does. The smooches from boyfriends to girlfriends who haven't made out in school since, like, the end of summer school; the fist-pumps and giggly hugs from the jocks and fashionistas respectively; the loners gravitating to the new loners transferred in from other schools to impart their invaluable knowledge of where to best hide when "expressing your sorrow" (i.e.: whining under a stairwell listening to loud "musak" and writing insufferably angsty poetry about the colour black and the joys of leaving their confining mansions/obscenely wealthy but damningly inattentive parents behind).

Losers, the lot of them. I can't wait to escape this chasm of anti-intellectualism for the greener pastures of university. That is where I shall go far, where I can correct the teachers and have them respect me for it, not give me a detention or send a letter home. I shall be an award-winning essayist whilst teaching at Harvard, my future alma mater. I'll show those idiotic "teachers" when I have my PhD in the time it took to finish their sissy education licence... Anyway, I digress.

The only thing really interesting in those moments, because trust me the AP classes were not riveting in the least, was watching the new students flounder in our labyrinth of a school. I swear the thing is built to pen in a Minotaur—

Let's just head off that digression before it can fully mature, because believe me, I can ramble about Greek myths for ages.

First period had some sniffling girl who arrived earlier than *me*. Which I had thought was patently impossible until that moment, I assure you. Second period had some new student from Dubai with a smartly be-suited translator in tow (Health, why must I take you?). Third period was absolutely soulless, very little surprise there. When has anything interesting happened in a sociology class? Fourth period was where the action was. That was where I met my first and only enemy in all of high school.

"Marshall, Hadrian."

"Please, Miss Roughy, call me Hade."

He was leaning back in his chair, languid and sure like a cat in a room of exceptionally fat and stupid mice, which it might as well have been. I disliked him instantly. Well, maybe not *exactly* instant of course, but it sounds dramatic, and thus must not be scratched out. Ms. Fish, as I secretly call her, softened her brows, hardened by years of public school teaching (She only transferred here on the good graces of her second cousin, Mr. Collins, the principal of Jackson Academy of the Sciences), and shocked the rest of us to actual quiet.

"All right, Hade." What the flipping heck. I just stared at her for a minute, but...she was just the very image of a lovesick teenager, two seconds away from spouting love poetry she didn't understand to impress a boy so out of her league as to be pitiful.

Ms. Fish, one of the nastiest, cruellest teachers I have had the misfortune to pretend to learn from, had bestowed the fainted glimmer of a smile on a student. A student who had only said, what, six words to her, and she was already wrapped around his finger. What kind of child is that adept at manipulation? I had no idea, but I surely did not approve. I should be that child, not this impudent upstart! I have forgotten more psychology than he will ever learn, I am sure.

Ms. Fish shook herself and returned to the roll. I returned to my book. It was new, a promising doorstopper about a poor Victorian girl picked by some sadistic count to play *Pygmalion*, (otherwise known as *My Fair Lady* for the film and musical lovers out there) only to rip her apart, bit by bit. At least, that was my guess. Sometimes, good books surprise you.

In any case, I was finishing up the introduction by a modern author when the lesson began. God, math is so tedious when your father's a mathematician. Class finally ground to a halt, and I waltzed to the only class I cared a modicum about, drama.

I may not seem it, but I have an incredible soft spot for the arts. The only reason anyone in the student body knows my name is because I played Puck in *A Midsummer Night's Dream* last year. I'm rather proud of it, actually. It took two years to prove that I was good enough for a role that didn't also double as a techie.

In any case, our teacher always tells us the fall and spring lineup on the first day so that we may prepare for the roles and pick out parts to practice. I had sent in a request for a Shakespeare play I like (*Merchant of Venice*) and a musical no one would understand, let alone recognise. Acting is the only thing outside of books that really gets me excited about school anymore. Everything else is excess.

That smooth talker from statistics had to go and ruin it all by winding his way to the front row of the auditorium, smiling and winking through the crowd of giggling no-talent prima donnas. I sighed and rolled my eyes, waiting for Mr. Tucker—part drama teacher, part wrestling coach—to make an appearance. He did not disappoint. In he stalked from stage right, looking outright menacing and sending the entire audience into a dead silence.

"Most all of y'all know the rules, but for those that forgot: No fu[dge]ing around (I patently refuse to swear in this volume). This is my theatre, and I'll throw you in my workouts as tackling dummies for the team if you stop payin' attention. You get me?"

"Yes, sir," we chorused. Some people were cringing and regretting their decisions, but those in his good graces just enjoyed their discomfort (myself and Araz, really). I looked for the self-possessed jerk in front, to see if he was wetting himself in terror and sprinting toward the doors. I couldn't see his face, but it didn't seem like he was ready to bolt at any second. Drat.

"Good, the fall play sheet is in the scene shop. Be back in four minutes."

I made the arduous journey four yards to the door from my seat (the closest chair to the shop from the auditorium). On the other side of said door, a slip of paper:

FALL
*Twelfth Night* (Ah, well. Yay-worthy, still)
*Phantom of the Opera* (Dammit)

SPRING
*Dracula* (Spectacularly unimpressed)
*TBA* (!!!)

That last one deserved a little concern and attention. When had Tucker ever written TBA or changed his mind about a play? Never, that's when. I slipped away before I ended up trampled by the stampede and ventured forward to find my teacher sitting on the stage, reading the paper.

"You're wondering what the spring musical's gonna be, right?" He hadn't even bothered to look up.

"Yes, sir. I'm on tenterhooks of anticipation."

"I really liked your idea," he admitted. "If you can translate it and get the music, we'll do it."

I nearly fainted with joy.

"Mind, if you don't get it in before winter break, we'll do *High School Musical*."

Oh, double hell. If that isn't an incentive, I've no clue what is. Even the utterance of such a foul creation of Disney sent shudders of disgust down my spine.

"It will be in your hands before October, I promise!"

He granted me a rare half-smile before whistling the rest of the group back to their seats. "Here are the parts for Shakespeare. I expect them to be memorised and ready by tomorrow. Start practising." He slapped down a pile of papers and walked back to the black curtains. He was pretending to give the group privacy while they practised to see if they actually used the time wisely, as always. I sequestered myself in a corner with all the audition pieces. I already knew Viola's bit, the ring soliloquy, but trying out Sebastian's part could have proven fun. I memorised the part (all five lines of it) before lunch bell (Honestly, Shakespeare was so damn lyrical, it's child's play to remember his works).

Hadrian spent his time laughing and chattering with the many and varied girls of the drama department: those that dyed their hair fabulous colours, those that looked utterly meek unless placed in the limelight and fed after midnight, those that simply must be excellent in everything, and those that thought their calling was to strut upon the stage, all sound and no fury.

Needless to say, I did not participate in the meet-and-greet.

Instead of eating, I exited the school and pulled out my cell phone. The thing is a lifesaver, always there when I need it most. Now with unlimited international minutes! I looked up a few numbers on the internet and then called a few proprietors and middlemen (I'll spare you the mind-numbing details). Thus, I secured myself a quick Skype meeting with the actual writer and copyright carrier of my current musical obsession, *Traum* (*Dreams* in English).

Five minutes before the next bell (to send some people back to class and some to lunch because we believe in intimate dining experiences at Jackson Academy of the Sciences), I finished my final call. My tasks done, I ended up leaning against the brick wall for a moment. I was smiling in relief. That's important, because it was wiped off my face not a second later.

"So, you're bilingual?" The new kid was leaning all cool-like with his shoulder against the brick facing me, arms crossed. Was he trying to channel James Dean? Please. James Dean impersonations were so 2009. He smiled faux-charmingly and continued, "I've always respected those who could master multiple languages."

I rolled my eyes and walked back to class.

"Wait. Inanna, isn't it?"

*"Was? Ich sprechen nicht so gut Englishe. Entschuldigung."* Feeling quite proud of myself for the quick retort, I stalked back to the stage. I turned before entering the building to find him looking quite uninjured by my snark until he caught my ill-advised glance. Then he smiled and waved. Damn, so much for the dramatic exit. I still have to work on that.

"Anyone ready to audition today?" Tucker was glaring down at them from behind his Clipboard of Judgement.

"I am." It was like clockwork. For the last three years, he would ask, I would answer, then audition and whatnot, and I would pay absolutely no attention to anything until rehearsals started.

"Then get up and read Viola's soliloquy."

I jumped upon the stage and turned, stared down my captive audience, then began. I finished to vague applause, really just from the new boy. Was he trying to be nice or trying very hard to start a trend of positive reinforcement for the moment he popped on stage?

Everyone knew I would earn a substantial role because I am the only one left on campus with the patience and grasp of language for big Shakespeare parts. Our last Intense Shakespeare Lovers had left when I was a sophomore. Coupled with seniority and commitment, I was sure to get all the best roles regardless of gender this year. I made to exit the stage, but Tucker stopped me.

"No, stay there. The fresh meat's next."

Did I not notice that he raised his hand with mine? Well, I must have had a rather intense case of tunnel vision. I sighed and sat on the edge with legs dangling, waiting for the strutting peacock to waltz on stage. He performed Sebastian's part flawlessly and without prompt. Well, beat me with a self-effacing stick; he was actually good at something (even if that talent is hoodwinking others into believing him talented).

Well, you can guess what such a performance yielded; Tucker threw us together with a fresh audition piece and had us play off of each other. Please let him end up as Malvolio (i.e.: unimportant and unloved), regardless of his acting chops. I don't want to pretend to be anything but indifferent at best or cruel at worst to him. That's what I hoped at the time—in vain, of course. I always have the darnedest luck with this kind of thing.

In any case, the bell rang, and I was out to sixth period, mercifully free of any new students, then seventh, which was infested with infantile intellectuals who thought they understood the English language. The fools wouldn't understand Chaucer if the book pranced across the floor in a NASCAR jersey and nothing else.

I spent the night writing up a lovely little speech for Mr. Leitmotif (writer and producer of *Traum*), which I ended up tossing before I made a fool of myself with flowery words and sycophantic grovelling. I had added him to my contact list using the name his assistant read me and spent the time I should have used to slog through some James Joyce staring blankly, yet earnestly, at the computer screen. He wasn't even calling until the morning, at 5:00 a.m. to be exact. Right before lunch. For him, at least.

I wanted to be early, so I woke up at an ungodly hour to get ready. I actually prettied myself up a bit, in the strictly professional sense. I riffled through the YouTube to divine how to make a "professional eye look," so dedicated was I to making a good impression. He had a red wine stain on his shirt. I just wanted to shoot myself during the entire interview. He asked me who would translate the play from German to English, and I told him the honour was mine. He laughed at me, so I corrected the English translations in the Special Edition DVD of one of their performances.

I promised that I was perfectly capable of writing within the meter and scope of the play and would send him any changes I felt necessary to make without detracting from the whole experience. I spent an hour and a half wheedling him, before he granted rights on the grounds that I hand over my translation of the lyrics only to him. I managed to get him to split potential publishing rights with me (Note to my readers: never try to out-weasel the scion of an academic and athlete, for we know our way around confounding and swindling contracts). We made another appointment for December, where we would touch base, and he would give the final green light.

Why am I telling you? Well, I was almost late for school because of this meeting. Thus I had no time to change or imbibe a healthy breakfast. I blame my behaviour on that. I actually *skipped* part of drama, but I'll explain that in a moment.

In the morning, the plaza that exists within the three wings of our beloved institution is always filled with ambling students, enjoying the last hot days before autumn forced us all into sweatshirts and rain jackets. I passed the garish science wing, striding quickly across the lawn to the entrance of the humanities wing. Between the two, sitting across from one another, are the offices, which are separate from the main building, and the gymnasiums and theatre. Sara Jane, an old acquaintance, was sitting with Regina, another former acquaintance, and Hadrian on one of the wrought-iron benches lining the plaza.

"No, no." Sara Jane smiled, blindingly bright. "This one's even better!" She scrolled through her laptop, and the others burst into laughter.

"'My skin is a scale of teeth.' Are you serious? Who writes this shi[z]?" Hadrian's voice carried far and wide.

I couldn't help to overhear even as I kept my head down and rushed my steps. Realising, of course, what they were reading made my heart sink.

He put on an overwrought tone. "Bones rattle and burn; Chimes out of my innards; Music out of my guts!"

"Let me," Regina cut in, pulling the laptop onto her legs. "Streaming notes like banners." She giggled. "My castle is a...forge?"

"Let Hade. He's much better," Sara Jane said gently, pulling them all closer to the screen. "Read the rest?"

*Horrible little girl.* I sprinted out of the plaza. How dare they mock my poetry. Granted, it wasn't very *good*, but that gave them no right to laugh and jeer like some Greek chorus twisted out of its proper configuration. And why did Sara Jane have to trot it out whenever she added a new member to her clique? I tried to put it out of my mind, not to remind myself how she'd found that poetry in the first place as I walked to class.

First and third period were homework hours and second was "reading room." Fourth period should have been another hour in that same vein, but the newest addition distracted me. The entire class had reconfigured itself. Every girl (all four of them) had crowded about "Hade." They simpered and smiled as he nonchalantly told some sort of story that involved long measured arm swinging, as if he held, in both hands, conductor's batons.

There was a ring of empty desks buffering that group from the rest of the boys (who kept on shooting nervous glances at the quintet) and myself. I officially hated my gender. Why did girls have to pretend to care about "hunky" guys? Feminism really needs to get its bum in gear and burn some more brassieres, because I'm getting tired of all this wishy-washy behaviour.

Whatever. He spotted me and called me over with the same measured motions that accompanied his story, as if he wasn't really motioning me but continuing his tale of mystery and woe. I ignored him. When we were supposed to be correcting homework with partners, he just walked away from his gaggle of girls to sit next to me.

The girls sighed, the boys tried to relocate away from him, and Ms. Fish reprimanded them but not Mr. I'm-so-cool over here. What spell had he cast on this school? Something powerful. That is the only way he could get such a misanthropic old curmudgeon to let his disregard for classroom etiquette slide.

"*Guten Morgen.* I don't think we were formally introduced. I'm Hade." He stuck out the smooth pampered fingers of a favoured child in my personal space with a small grin. I took the slip of notepaper on top of his notebook instead of acknowledging his irritating presence. "You look really nice today. Some special occasion?"

I blinked and glanced down at my apparel. Oh. Yes. I was wearing a dress. Darn.

"No occasion, just all-purpose stupidity." I generally practice the tactic of self-deprecation. It has saved me from having to spend my life doing other people's homework. No matter what grade I earned on a test, I always announced that it was "simply atrocious," making other help-hungry students leave me be. Let them think I am an awful test taker. It is their loss if they don't wish to be my friend because they actually *like* me. Forgive the particularly dark scribbling there. I'm just bitter distracted.

Anyway, he laughed and said, "Really? You seem so smart I can't imagine you doing anything stupid."

"Yet, you know nothing about me." It was scandalising really, how familiar he was being. I may be old-fashioned, but really, such action is unbecoming even in this modern day and age. He touched his temples and closed his eyes melodramatically.

"Your name is...Inanna, like banana..." He said it in a ridiculous English accent. "You are a senior at...just a moment, it's becoming clearer. Jackson Academy of the Sciences in 'Music City', and you *are* a devoted student. I have never seen such dedication in any of my other clients, my dear. I wonder if you would be so dedicated in all parts of your life... Hmm, What else do I see?... You shall, in the near future, see the latest last-of-the-summer blockbusters with a handsome stranger. Looks very nice, if my inner eye isn't on the fritz."

He leaned forward and held out his hand for me to shake. It was kind of sweet, to put on such an elaborate act to enlist my affection instead of relying on the legion behind him. For such an ingenious line as that, he really wasted it on a girl like me.

"Your inner eye isn't on the fritz. It's completely obfuscated, I'm afraid." I am completely unimpressed. He even seemed surprised I wasn't on my knees begging for the honour to lick his polished Italian leather derbys.

Why, I don't know; if he really knew anything about me, he would know I have no interest in romantic inclinations of any sort. Mostly since they don't interest me, but that's also how you keep out of trouble in high school; shun attachment like Buddha in a glue factory (Isn't that mental image fantastic?).

"Really?" he asked.

"I don't even know you," I pointed out.

He shrugged and answered, "I'm an actor, well-liked by most everyone around. You know, I bet you do this to all the new boys. Scare them away so they won't bother you. I don't scare, though." He smiled flirtatiously, retracting his hand oh so surreptitiously.

I saw red, and then I tamped it down to a smoulder. It wasn't his fault that I already knew him to be most likely just another bully roaming the halls.

"Really, I'm so glad that you know my mind so well. Otherwise, I would think you an insufferable, hebetudinous blowhard."

Really, the more I talked with him, the more I disliked him. The feeling is not reciprocated, unfortunately. I would have much preferred it if he would have gone after me to bully me instead of this mock-flirting. Then I could fight back. Even if I could just hide away in the crowd, that would be fine.

"I wonder why you use such multisyllabic sentences in your everyday life. Are you just pretending to defend a literature thesis every time you open your mouth?" he asked as he handed back my proofed homework.

Why he was insulting me so, I had no clue. Maybe because I was being cruel, but I didn't think so at the time. So I just ignored him, like my mother always says. "Ignore, ignore, ignore, Inanna." The words bounced in my head as Ms. Fish began her lesson on simple probability, and that prick slipped a note on top of my book. I never read it (for it went straight into the trash the moment class was over), but he was wearing on my nerves.

Fifth period was torture. I listened to everyone caterwauling their lines like toms in heat. It made me want to cry. Why did they twist their pitch and tone so when they read Shakespeare? Was it that hard to just read it like real language instead of some impenetrable foreign tongue? I pleaded sickness and fled at lunchtime. I would have gladly stuck my fingers down my throat if it meant getting out of the incompetence...and away from him, of course.

Yes, he made it all the worse. Every ten minutes or so, I would have to move because he followed me over to my seat, asked me questions, and badgered me incessantly. Why did he have to invade my sacred personal space? Why couldn't he just pick a normal pretty girl to fuss over? I'm not even pretty, I'll readily admit to that. I'm obscenely short. My jaw is too strong and my eyes too "piercingly judgemental". I'll pick you apart before I even speak to you. That's what an old friend had said. My hair is never fashionable; it's too long for that. I'm an old schoolmarm in form and affectation, and I like it that way. No one expects me to be anything else, and I don't want them to.

But him. And it makes me want to heave.

I returned from hiding for sixth period, but not because I wanted to. My already stellar attendance would not be blighted by an annoyance of little consequence.

At home, I collapsed into bed for what felt like a few hours. Waking up with the golden afternoon sun on your face just does wonders for your disposition. I pulled out my computer and checked my mail. Just as promised, two fat files waited for me attached to a friendly generic greeting in German. I busied myself with translating the prologue until bed.

I dragged my feet going to school the next morning. Why wasn't everything going like normal? Normal was classes, learning, and leaving to do better things with my time; there is no skipping of classes or sniping conversations in front of teachers in "*normal.*" Just because Ms. Fish was busy being human at another student does not make my behaviour in any way acceptable. Ugh. Again my morning was peaceful, allowing me to prepare for that idiot by fourth period.

"Can I borrow your notes from yesterday? I left mine at home." A likely story from you-know-who.

"What about your friends over there? Don't they have acceptable notes?" I looked down on him, regardless of the fact that he was taller than me even while seated. I made it work after years of long practice.

"I'm afraid I'm in a bit of a jam. Seems the girls get angry here if you leave them without a goodbye." He shrugged, and I sighed in a put-upon fashion.

"Be my guest." I handed over my notebook. It was filled with numbers and shorthand, not really user-friendly. He frowned at my notes for a long moment.

"Ahh, yeah, I know this code. I use it too." Was that supposed to impress me? I used the simplest shorthand possible; a *monkey* could write in that style.

"Grand, now scoot. I have to do my work, and I can't unless I have my book..." I sent him an imperious look, but he took no heed. With care and grace, he took the book to his desk beside mine (The girls were now evenly distributed). He carefully copied out a few lines on a borrowed sheet of notebook paper, and then handed it back to me.

"Thanks."

"Whatever," I replied cautiously. No need to make him think you like him in any sense of the word. Yep, so I sent him a mild glare for good measure. "You should have brought your own notes."

He just smiled, satisfied, then turned back to his nearest friend. I rolled my eyes, glad he had finally gotten over vying for my attention.

But drama was dramatic, to say the least. The list was posted outside the door of the theatre. I was up there somewhere, probably Viola, but maybe Tucker decided to "gender bend" again, who knew? Yup, near the bottom, in alphabetical order is "Viola" connected ever so delicately to my name. So excited, so surprised, I'm just jumping, hopping in place in joy and enthusiasm. Couldn't you tell?

Now that you have survived that sarcasm overdose, I looked for my love interest. The count was to be played by the student who was Lysander last year. Good. He's the first to learn his lines in any performance. I slipped inside to tell Tucker about the musical rights and costs and the like. Leitmotif demanded I pay in euros, which I was happy to accept. The euro had fallen sharply in the last few years down to the now defunct deutschmark levels (about 2:1) but was heading to the old franc levels (nearing 7:1) if I were to guess... Now that I have overburdened you with extraneous facts, I'll go on. Tucker surprised me by speaking before spoken to.

"You go well with Sebastian," he informed me.

"I didn't see who took Sebastian."

"Fresh Meat." He called everyone that the first month he knew them. There was only one new boy, though... Shit. No, please don't pair us up in a mad attempt to make me more "passionate" or some such rot. I do not need more chemistry with my costars.

"Antagonism doesn't equal chemistry. He's utterly full of himself and insufferable."

"And you aren't?"

I was kind of outraged by that. When had I made trouble for Coach Tucker?

"You know what I mean. It's like you threw a brick wall between you and everyone else. We only talk through a crack—"

The reference made me beam, surprised. I hadn't even realised he read Catullus. Then I remembered that Pyramus and Thisbe are also in *Midsummer Night's Dream*. Smart, In, so, so sparklingly intelligent, you leave all others spinning, nauseous in your wake.

"—but the rest are left to the wayside. Opening up will make you a much better actor." He eyeballed me significantly.

"I'll take that under advisement, sir," and I scurried to my seat. Its neighbour was occupied by the very subject of the previous conversation. *Great, more ignoramuses trying to impress something upon me.* I must have had a put-upon expression on my face because he straightened under my gaze.

"Hey, is it okay if I sit here, sis?" His attempt at levity fell flat.

"Whatever you want." I sat with a bit more force than intended. Maybe I was sulking, maybe I was making a point, I'm not sure I remember. Looking back, I'm doubly surprised he's still chasing my attention after such a cold and rude reception. If he had left then, looking hurt and chastened, I would have felt guilty, at least, and maybe attempted to offer reparations.

No, he just stretched out as if he owned the place and granted me a smile. "Good. Do you want to work on lines after school?"

I rolled my eyes. "We don't have the scripts yet, nor do we have more than the finale together. I see no need to do so."

He pouted at me like I'd taken away his favourite toy. "Come on, I think Shakespeare's a bit ornery. Maybe you can help me?" He smiled cheerily at me, hoping to infect me with good-natured feelings through long-term exposure.

"You seemed to be fine on Monday," I pointed out.

"Well, that was Monday. I hadn't been totally distracted by how interesting you people are compared to this dull old story."

I ignored him and his utter disrespect for good literature.

Tucker was handing the copied scripts out to everyone and barking out orders about how he would skin alive anyone who lost their script and then turn the tanned-leather-them into a stylish hat. Nice imagery, Tucker, I have to say. Especially when we had several suspect leather hats in our costume room. That day was just a read-through, along with Thursday. After that, the fun of drama began. Practice.

He *insisted* on sitting next to me on Thursday too. Friday, as well. What was he getting at, following me like this? Trying to distract me from my books and class work. Obviously, he failed rather spectacularly. I'd burned through ten chapters of my fun book, finished an exegesis of Kierkegaard, and evaded finishing any of my homework at home. That week, however, was just a primer for the next stage of his neuroses.

I'll explain what happened the next week tomorrow, after I've finished my biography of Goethe.

Maybe I should just add a bit of space above the paragraphs and clean up my scribbles so they are at least legible...or write on a computer. Whichever I think to do first.

9/2 SUNDAY
*(Typed, saved under Folder: Marshall)*

*Ich bin so müde jetzt. Sie würde nicht glauben...*Sorry about that. Too much translating late into the night. In any case, back to what happened to make me so very angry yesterday. I don't think, now that I've had a moment to cool down, I'll really abandon my education over some silly boy. That would be too cliché, even for me...

But, on with the recounting. On Tuesday, I was reading before class in first period when someone meandered in. I assumed it to be the poor girl who liked to be away from home as much as I, and thus, didn't look up until my light was blocked by some person.

"Funny meeting you here. Are all your classes AP?" Hellfire and damnation.

"Don't tell me you switched classes just to bother me." I didn't look up from my book.

"No, just found Bio 2 way too boring for me."

Frick, it was too early to deal with him. I needed at least two hours of mellow class time before I could brave his self-amorous shenanigans. Would you believe he already had every girl sizing him up in first period? Oh, the gossip. You wouldn't believe the gossip you hear, regardless of whether you want to or not.

In any case, I replied, "So you chose AP Physics C instead? Isn't that a bit of a leap?"

"Maybe for you, but for me, it was the logical next step—"

I continued to read instead of listening to his self-congratulation. He was cut off by the teacher, Mr. Carwhile, thank god. He may be the blandest person I have met in a long while (since the last time I saw my great-uncle Karl, who slept through the Second World War), but by god if he was not able to disrupt every private conversation ever attempted in his class. It was a talent he must have honed after years of arduous training.

"Now, we have a new student today in class...Miss Drew, do you know our new student?" He was also adept at stating the obvious, the boy was nearly sitting in my lap he was so close to me.

"Unfortunately."

He smiled (thinking I was being humorous) and, amid a chorus of disgruntled sighs, assigned me to "catch him up." Damnation and hellfire twice over, add Hades and Helheim in there, too, for good measure. During class, the fool next to me just stared intently at my notebook as if it held the very secrets of eternal life and salvation (Which it did not. That is in my Latin folder). After class said insufferable creature asked me thus...

"So, when is the first study date?"

I put away my things in lieu of responding.

"Tonight? Great," he answered for me.

I sighed heavily.

"My house or yours?"

Now, I was growing impatient for silence.

"Mine? Well, fan—"

"I will meet with you in the library after school. It should only take you a few minutes to catch up if you are so talented." I did not run away. I can swear to you that I only...picked up the pace and lost myself in the grateful anonymity of a crowd, no matter how small.

Second and third were monumentally unexciting. Very happy about that indeed was I. He actually stayed away during fourth, gladly relishing the lavish laudations from part (only a small part, mind) of his burgeoning cult. Drama was also quiet, for drama at least. This silence was beginning to bother me, as if he were biding his time, saving up his stupid, blind lasciviousness for after school. I was on edge the entirety of the day.

I do not want to talk about what happened next. At all. But I feel I must so that you may know just how terrible a child this brute is. I knew there was no way this was going to be easy, or end well for that matter, but at least the library has a soothing atmosphere. It was the old personal library of the Chief of Medicine and looked the part with its stained glass, cherry panelling, and secret reading rooms once used for private consultations. I had my notes from the last week in my hands and ready when I sat down, and wouldn't you know it, he just pops up as I settle into the chair.

"Hope I haven't kept you waiting... Well, don't look too excited to get started." He slinked to his seat and spread himself as far out as possible, brushing my leg in the process.

You know, as an aside, I hear that animals like to make themselves as big as possible in order to ward off predators. Did he see me as a potential threat? God, I hope so because I'm probably much more dangerous than most give me credit for. I said nothing about it, in any case, shoving the papers under his nose.

"You know I was kidding in class, about the whole my-place-or yours-thing. I was just trying to get a laugh out of you." Which hasn't happened yet. Has he even seen me laugh? Has anyone in this school outside of the stage seen me so much as crack an honest smile? He looked a little contrite. I didn't fall for it.

"Well, you failed," I said shortly. "These are the notes and homework assignments from the past five days and today's. I trust you can still decipher my handwriting?" I may have been a little harsh, but he deserved it, you'll see.

"As well as my own." The bastard.

"O-kay. Read them and then return them to me in class tomorrow. I'll need them for exam revisions."

"Don't you need them for homework tonight?" he asked lightly, as if it was actually difficult to finish a single page worksheet during class.

"No, I'm done," I said, checking the zippers and buttons of my pack, a classic signal that I was intent to leave.

"Do you ever do your homework at like, you know, home?" he asked with a raised eyebrow. Hah, like I brought home busy work in the last five years.

"Unnecessary for me, but maybe for you it still is. It was the logical next step for my academic advancement." It was snide and petty to throw his words back at him (even if they were a bit garbled in translation), but I couldn't repress a feeling of triumph at his disappointed face.

"Really, can't we at least be friends? Just a little?" He straightened just to look at me soulfully, and it made him look like a cow. I stared him down for a good minute before he admitted defeat, looking away to examine the many posters plastering the walls demanding that everyone *READ!* in the most imperious and obnoxious way possible.

"I'm not in the market for new friends, but thank you for the offer," I said politely.

"But you don't have any friends at all. I've never seen you hang out with *anyone*," he pointed out rudely.

"Do you dog my every move?" I snapped. "Is everyone so eager to be your hangers-on that they report my every conversation to your waiting ear?"

"I see what I see," he said stubbornly, crossing his arms and frowning. "All you do is read. Frankly, I don't think you'd know how to have *real* fun if it came up and bit you in the [bum]."

I was scandalised. How dare he presume to think that I couldn't enjoy myself? "I have plenty of fun. I also know when to do more than charm my teachers and attract a cult following," I huffed.

"Hey, I have *friends*, not followers. Just because you don't know what friends *are*—"

"Shut up," I hissed. The librarian was staring at us, and I was not eager to get in trouble in the least because of some stuck-up brat who continually insulted me. "Why are you even here still? You have what you need, and I suspect that you may not be the kind to tarry overlong in libraries."

"Are you...insulting my intelligence?" he asked incredulously. "I'm on the headmaster's list. I have a f[ri]cking 4.0, and I'm going to one of the best universities in the *world* next year."

"Well. So. Am. I." I got up, unwilling to listen to him prattle more about how amazing he was at life and how terrible I was at being a human being. I seemed to be the only sane one left with the way all my classmates swooned and fawned over him for being a fresh face.

He pulled me away from the seat I had so firmly and resolutely exited from and crashed into me a bit clumsily. "Hey, we're not done. You don't get to just piss me off and walk away."

"Oh, why does my opinion matter to your massive ego?" I sneered at him. "I'm only the friendless wretch, the unloved Ophelia. Why should I matter to you, oh Balder the Bright?"

"Because you're not an idiot," he said strongly, not letting me go. "And we're gonna be working with each other all year in drama. I'm not making enemies the first month of school, da[rn] it."

"Not if you keep this up, *Sebastian*," I hissed, twisting out of his grip easily, but he was persistently grabbing my arm again and again. "We don't appreciate overinflated heads in our society."

"Really? Are you threatening to *tell* on me now? How mature."

"About as mature as grabbing a girl because you fail to grasp that you can't make friends with everyone. Now let me go."

"Why are you so snide?" He shook his head as if he couldn't begin to understand my methods. "Or...or do you enjoy it? Does it make you feel important to look down on *everyone*?"

"I don't 'look down' on everyone. I think you forget who is on what end of the social food chain in this situation. If anyone is looking down, it would be you looking down on me for being happily ensconced in my solitude."

"No one is *happy* being alone. It's evolutionarily contradictory. You're just torturing yourself. Why don't you just change it? You're not ugly, and you're smart. That's enough to get you anywhere. Why do you have to be such a bitch?"

"I'm not a bitch," I nearly shouted shrilly, completely out of my head I was so angry. "Don't you dare insult me like that, you little—"

"All right, that's enough," said the librarian. "Get out. You're banned for the next week, the both of you."

I looked at her in absolute horror. "What?"

"You heard me, Inanna. Now get out now, or I'll make it a month."

I'm not ashamed to say that I teared up a bit at the pronouncement. The library was where I spent my afternoons between work and school: a quiet place to write essays when I had them and read in blissful solitude when I had not. I shot Hadrian, the life-ruiner, a poisonous glare and stalked out of my secret sanctuary.

Can you see now why he's so insufferable? He forced me out of the library and insulted me most gravely to add insult to injury. Without care or consideration for my feelings, he riled me to the point of lashing out, and I was punished for it. Sure, he probably thought it inconsequential, but he understands nothing about my life, my choices, or my feelings on the matter.

What's important to me is obviously on an entirely different level to his priorities, and him trying to push his ideas on how I should act is just insulting and horrifying. I'm not a damn project for someone to happen by and idly fix on their way from one plot point to the next. I'm not some empty, lifeless shell to be filled with the ideals and inspirations of someone else. He...he...he can go fuck himself, all right?

I've given up on censoring myself. It never ends well.

The next morning, he wisely sat away from me but didn't hand back my notes, the terrible cad. Fuck him. I tried not to steam and stew over this new resentment, instead burying myself in my tale of intrigue and veiled motivations over the next several hours. It was only during drama that he dared approach me. I was hiding in the back stage during our break, drinking in the mystery of who the main antagonist *really* was.

"What are you reading?" Of course, he was behind me. How he wriggled his way behind the ropes was anyone's guess.

"Don't you know it is intensely rude to talk to someone without first announcing your presence so as not to startle your intended conversationalist?" God, I get really wordy when I become upset, don't I?

"So sorry. I'll try to remember next time. What's the book about?"

I turned the Bible-thin page, not looking at him towering over me. Not allowing him the power dynamic with him so high above and me brought so very low.

"It's a novel." Did I really want to tell him that I was in the middle of a really intense mind manipulation scene that was horrifying yet strangely affecting at the same time? Answer: No. Did I want him anywhere near me at the best of times? Answer: Also no.

"Why is it in Russian?" Maybe because it only came in Russian, you silly little thing. Does he have a working brain beneath all that hair?

"They write the best tragedies." I only have a one great tragedy a month tolerance before I become inconsolably weepy and silly with a bit of sullenness for good measure. *Now go away, before you become irreparably enmeshed with this mind-bendingly good scene.* I didn't want to see his face when I thought back on this or any part of what is fast becoming my favourite horror story, ever.

"So you like tragedies?" No such luck, but his purely enquiring tone surprised me. Where was the sarcasm, the hidden cruelty? I thought he viewed my love of literature with nothing but barely restrained scorn and antipathy?

I had to make up something fast. Maybe if I sounded exceptionally depressive, he would abandon talking to me entirely? Surely people don't like hanging around depressing people. That's why no one sits with the sad uncle who stands by the fire with his brandy, looking for meaning in the flames. And everyone has that uncle, I'm quite sure. I have one, and every family scene seems to sneak one in that I've had the pleasure to peruse.

"They...are truer reflections of real life, more than other fantasies." My aimless bullshit was quiet, but he still heard me.

"Maybe you haven't read the right fantasies." Was his tone *nice*? He put a hand on my shoulder, and I shrugged it off.

"Leave me alone. Everyone else does." I did *not* mean that in an oh-pity-me! kind of way, but in a "You are an anathema to the norm by taking any vested interest in my various enigmatic foibles, and it causes me to hate you. I do not appreciate it in the least" way. Of course, he would take it like the former instead of the latter.

"So, no one understands you except books?" Oh god, please stop for the love of all that's holy.

"Look, I'm not asking for your dramatic intervention, *Hadrian*." I said it mockingly because I could. "Unlike some people, I actually like being who I am." I...walked briskly to talk to Tucker about...something. He stared down at me inscrutably. Say something, In. Think on your feet.

"I don't like the new boy." Why couldn't it be about something safer?

"I know."

I blinked up at the busy director. Then a second passed. "So, what are we doing today, because I don't feel like working."

He let me go, and I read in the seats for nearly an hour as he tortured the boys with fencing choreography. I escaped school after classes and went about my duties before going to bed. It was quite nice watching the hapless teens get smacked about by their fellows in the spirit of learning over the top of my volume. Unfortunately, I also caught Hadrian's eye at one such moment, and he ruined it.

Much more relaxed than the day previous, I burned through my class work with the ease born of an overachiever. Fourth period, however, was "*nicht so gut*," if you catch my drift. When I entered the classroom, everyone was...bunched in a corner. Seriously, they were all seated in close quarters as far from the teacher's desk as possible. *He* was staring down Ms. Fish.

His charmingness, apparently, had an expiration date.

"I *lost* it. You can't fail me for the day because I lost *one* fricking page."

"Yes, I can, and I will." Ms. Fish snapped, nearly shaking with rage and voice gone intolerably shrill out of frustration. "I don't tolerate this sort of behaviour, not even from my best students."

I slid into a seat directly beside the door as quietly as possible. No need to get caught in the crossfire, after all.

"What makes you so *special*, Mr. Marshall?" Her voice cracked and jumped up at the word special, old grievances and pain rising to the surface. "Why do you *deserve* an exception to the rule?"

I secretly suspect that Ms. Fish was terribly bullied in school, a loner and miserable throughout all of her education, and now takes those years of resentment out of her heart and into the minds of her students. It doesn't change that she is a masterful educator and a fair grader, but it means that crossing her or acting in any way, shape, or form like an entitled brat will earn you eternal scorn and verbal evisceration.

Which is why most everyone fears her, even those who'd never stepped into her domain.

"Because it wasn't *my fault*," he seemed to repeat. Both of them looked strung tight, exhausted from arguing well before class began. "It fell out of my bag. I could do it for you right now on the board if you don't believe me. It was easy. Why would I try to get out of something easy?"

She stiffened at the accusation, as if being easy at the beginning of the school year was a crime. "Then go ahead." She plucked the papers out of his hand. "Write out the questions and answer them on the board for everyone else to check with their own work."

With a stubborn tilt to his jaw, he quickly and neatly wrote each question, then answered them just as neatly beneath. He made a mistake, if skipping a step could be considered a mistake, but I chose not to point it out, and no one else said a word.

"You'll get half credit," she sniffed. "Be grateful I'm in a *giving* mood today."

He stomped over to his bag as Ms. Fish busily erased his work and started up her PowerPoint lecture. Ah, he'd meant to sit where I was now stationed, judging by his harried expression. He collapsed next to me, and I, tentatively, gave his arm a bit of a touch of solidarity. Ms. Fish didn't like me, either.

He let out a loud huff of frustration and turned to roll his eyes in the direction of the teacher. I leaned away and pulled out my notebook.

Looking back, Hadrian wasn't as crass as I thought. Maybe we really did just get off on the wrong foot as he said. I still dislike him for his egotism. It was my gut reaction, and those are rarely wrong, especially concerning personalities. I just don't understand his universal appeal. Some of the guys mildly dislike him, no doubt, but why is everyone chasing after him? He's barely any different from the rest of the boys at this school, even if we rarely have any new attendants after freshman year.

Also, why focus on the girl that is indifferent when he has so many potential playmates? Maybe if I pretend to fangirl over him, he'll ignore me in turn? If so, there will be plenty of girls playing so hard to get now that they would practically throw themselves out of his path if that's what garners his attention.

9/3 MONDAY
*(Typed under Folder: Marshall)*

Update: No. Bad Idea. I don't even want to talk about how bad at the moment. He also tried to join the *mathletes* today but failed. Also, don't translate in school. Hack job done when distracted.


9/5 WEDNESDAY
*(Written in a worn notebook)*

Okay, now I may now speak without candour. Here is how everything "went down"... I saw him before first period, about to enter the library, which was on the way to our classroom.

I asked wryly, "Are you trying again? Bad form to tempt a horse that already bucked you so thoroughly the first time." *Was that friendly enough*? Apparently so, because he smiled brighter than a lighthouse lamp on a foggy New England night.

"Of course. I believe the turn of phrase is: If at first you don't succeed, try, try again."

I rolled my eyes at his grandiose arm movements. Was he trying to impress me by quoting Frederick Marryat? Whoops. I was trying to be nice. I smiled instead of glared. First mistake.

"My first smile, I must be doing something right today," he said with strangely self-deprecating enthusiasm.

"Maybe I just don't want any enemies the last year of high school." I shrugged carefully.

"Hey, are you busy tonight?"

*What the flip?* went my brain.

"Yes." I clammed up and inched to the doorway behind him.

"That's too bad. There's this concert tonight that some of us in Music Theory are crashing. I thought you might like a bit of the local string quartet. It's 'Songs of the Italian Renaissance' tonight." Why he was asking me to go with him is anyone's guess, but still…a string quartet. Oh, that sounds tempting, even now. I am such a sucker for good music.

"Well, that is what you would expect out of Nashville, would you not?" I turned him down like a good little girl and walked to the classroom.

"You look nice when you smile, you know?" he called out behind me, and I just *had* to answer him. No matter that he was trying to win me over with flattery so he could waste more of my time.

"And you're still speaking, why?" It was a more honest question than I intended, but ah, well. I was sitting at my desk by then, and he looked quite foolish outside of the classroom, peeking intently in, but not crossing the threshold like some sort of blunderbuss of a vampire. He just couldn't convince anyone to let him in. So sad.

"Because you need to hear that more?" He shrugged as if he meant it in an offhand, honest way. Liar.

"Somehow, I don't believe you." I pulled out my book (*The Rubaiyat of Omar Khayyam*) and found my page. He did not falter from his perch, regardless of the ever-decreasing time slot between now and morning bell. Did he even realise that Mr. Carwhile was just as forgiving of tarrying at the door as Ms. Fish was of egos?

In any case, the adage seems true. Give them an inch, and they will take a mile. He came inside and sat beside me, then looked at the other students scattered throughout the spacious room. He was trying very hard to weasel his way into my affections by taking liberties with my personal space, and, even worse, inviting others to do so as well.

"Really, don't you guys *do* social in the South?" he complained, getting up again. He was so gregarious I apparently couldn't entertain him alone, so he dragged others to do his bidding. It was a tiny bit endearing to see him bodily move students I'd known for years next to me so that I may socialise "properly," if I were honest with you. But also so, so annoying.

I could get not an iota of peace that day. The only difference to physics was that everyone was suddenly in a cluster rather than spread economically throughout the room like gas molecules. My classmates had solidified by virtue of the strange catalyst I call "a royal pain in my ass." Fourth period was a tense affair of students versus teacher, with all the girls clustered around the centre of the group with the other boys circling the wagons around them.

He was too deluged in set building to make a fuss in drama, thankfully, but even people in my sixth and seventh period were entreating me to socialise, a bewildering phenomenon, which has never happened before, I can assure you. This news must have travelled past light-speed at the idiotically nicknamed Hickory High, bypassing the normal gossip by a large margin.

Tuesday was equally overwhelming and paranoia-inducing. I'd been marked out as a lost cause by every clique imaginable (and some not so much) by Christmas break of freshman year, especially by those that went to Franklin Middle (which was most of them). Suddenly, everyone seems to know everything I have ever done at school. Every little thing of interest I did or said was parroted back to me by my own personal armada of lapdogs, hopping about for a treat. I am thoroughly disillusioned by Hadrian Marshall once again. He stole away my only comfort to be had in this school, and he will pay. No more Mr. Nice Guy. The warrior goddess was coming out to play.

He was casually leaning against my seat at fourth period.

"Go away." Danger, danger, danger, I shouted beneath those icy words.

"Why?" He frowned slightly, as if not really confused at all but playing along for my sake.

"I've no mind to hear more empty platitudes today."

"Really? You're *mad* because people *talked* to you yesterday?" He sounded painfully incredulous, crossing his arms and watching me wryly. "Really? I thought you'd appreciate some company."

"There's no one here I'd like to talk *to*. Everyone is spoiled and horrifically ignorant, and I couldn't *breathe*. Being constantly hounded is not necessarily my favourite activity, unlike some people." I took a seat at the leftmost edge of the classroom and a few rows up, but the classrooms are so small, it only put a few desks between us.

"Like, three people asked you how the play was going and another asked about your family. How is that being hounded?" He placed his hands on his hips like an overworked housewife. All that was missing were the wide skirts and white gloves to complete the picture.

"You underestimate." I waved him off, but he wouldn't be moved.

"And you exaggerate. I'm just trying to be nice."

"Well, this is not how you project niceness as a rule. Being nice usually precludes forcing the prospective recipient into awkward social situations for your own amusement."

"I wasn't—" He breathed harshly through his nose like an angry bull. "Fine. You know. You want to be alone. I'll leave you to it."

"That's all I ask," I said with an expansive hand movement.

"I thought you *wanted* to be friends." He nearly sneered, as if it seemed impossible to him that anyone could enjoy being on their own.

"I never said that." I was getting worked up, all vitriol and Greek fire. "I just want some peace and quiet in school. I just want to be left alone." An emphatic motion. "Solitary contemplation, that's all I want out of high school."

Maybe I should go into the nunnery instead of academia. No more interfering social butterflies to worry about there. Or not. Academics aren't exactly known for their extroverted tendencies as a rule. Excepting conferences.

He cornered me some time later and tried to say something that would painfully offend me by virtue of coming from his mouth, but I beat him to the punch.

"No, I do not want to talk to you. I do not want to see you, touch you, smell you, hear you, taste you, or even become aware of your presence through some esoteric sixth sense. Go away."

"Look, let me at least *say* something before you jump all over—"

I gave him a long look because hadn't he just decided to ignore my existence not an hour before?

"Don't give me that look."

"How I arrange my expression is not dependent on your preferences. Allow me to utilise my multisyllabic sentence structure to tell you just how invasive and painfully impetuous you are."

"Impetuous?"

"Just. I want you to cease and desist from following, chasing, pursuing, tailing, shadowing, or otherwise bothering me. Is that so difficult for you?"

"Swallowing a dictionary must've been pretty hard. How'd you do it?"

I almost fell for it. I almost got really angry and screamed at him for insulting me. Swallow a dictionary, obviously my main method of word research was a *thesaurus*.

"Don't try it. I won't have you ruining another day with your ungracious interference into my life. Maybe I should just label you a troll and block you out instead of attempting any form of discourse."

I may have evaded serious confrontation on Wednesday (or maybe I just bruised his ego somehow), but I have a feeling today is going to be monstrous.

UPDATE:

"So, I know we weren't all that...um. Nice. About your mom but—" It wasn't even Hadrian that set me off but one of his puppets, one of his moppets that had no sense of self-preservation.

"I don't care what you have to say." I interrupted her, because no good ever came of anyone mentioning my mother at this school. It was either Mr. Collins, eager for family gossip, or old acquaintances I wished to forget, eager for blood. Because teenagers and tragedy were a match made in hell.

"Why so touchy? I was just trying to be nice," the girl called from across the room for all the world, as if I were some deadly viper ready to attack her unsuspecting brood from below.

"Well, don't try. You haven't tried to be nice to me for six years, Sara Jane Wells."

It's a bit of a surprise to them that I even know her name, the most popular senior girl at Jackson Academy of the Sciences. I'm not gormlessly wandering through life like they think I am, my goodness. I'm just violently antisocial. Well, I only became so visibly vitriolic this year. Before, Sara Jane was probably mostly unaware of my existence, no matter how many classes I took with her or how many play dates we had as small children.

I mulled over the tragedy that had become my life during the next few classes. Why did she have to bring that up? What motivated her to be so intentionally spiteful? I had been almost-friends with her once upon a time. I used to be happy and well-adjusted amongst my peers. Really, I promise. Compared to the present, I was an angel of normalcy. Now they suddenly decided to once again mock me with my past inability to keep my emotions and thoughts from running away from me, from my heart to my sleeve to past my lips before you could blink?

"I heard you told off SJ in Health. What's up with that?" The magister of spitefulness, the disrupter of life himself, deigned thus to ask me such a plebeian question to ascertain the effectiveness of his poisoned puppets.

"You're not my confidant, nor even a friend. So, I think no."

He sighed resignedly. "Really, maybe if you just took your head out of your...books, you could actually learn to be a fully functional human being. Humans are social animals if you remember your biology." He did not just say that.

I shot back, quite scandalised. "I know my biology backwards and forwards, and nothing I do contradicts the physiognomy of my species. I also like the way I am, regardless of your assumptions. I prefer to stand ahead of the race and watch the rest of you struggle to the finish line instead of slowing my pace for your sake."

He was unimpressed. "Somehow, I don't believe you, Ina."

I glared hotly at his retreating back (Back to his assigned seat? Will wonders never cease?) and went back to my work. I really should never have given him so much attention, regardless of the emotions behind it. Teenagers are programmed to seek attention, and adoration or abjuration work in much the same way.

Couldn't he just leave me be? I don't want anyone prying into my business, pretending to be nice just to dig up some dirty laundry. I know how this shit ends, without fail. I just want the popular guy to quit pretending he likes the quiet, unobtrusive, awkward smart girl for whatever twisted reason he came up with. And there better not be a bet involved, or I am sure I will have an existential crisis, realising that I am, in fact, a living after-school special.

He obviously wants something. He wouldn't try so hard to befriend me, even if his attempts at flattery sent him in the negatives when it comes to my good standing. Everyone seems to be out to make an ass of me, to fright me, if they could (Poor Bottom out of *A Midsummer Night's Dream*, pulled to and fro on the whims of crazy omnipotent Fae). I won't be, though. From now on, everything will be different. All the things they say shall roll off my back as if I were a particularly hydrophobic duck. They won't be able to stir a teaspoon of the rage I keep tamped down. I shall simply rise above it.

A new day, a new me.

# October

10/1 MONDAY
*(Typed under Folder: Marshall)*

It's been a month or so since I started writing about these...confrontations between my present quasi-friend and myself. I'm honestly surprised at just how angry I was. Well, that has changed. Circumstances changed. Things happened that made me forget about this little project of mine, but the record will recommence, mostly because it's pleasant. And I'd like to add some more pleasant things back into my life.

Nothing too terrible on the Western Front (Ha-ha, referencing school as a battlefield from the Great War. Hear my bitter laughter ring across the barren wastelands of battles long forgotten outside my very door); my college applications are sent, the first act of *Dreams* is done (and done well), my book collection is nearly read through (just Gaddis and the *Quran* left, really), and Hadrian Marshall left me be.

Well, not really.

After my resolution, nothing changed in the immediate sense. It took time, as do all things. At least the rest of the school returned me to my status quo of invisible loner. Hadrian has continued *talking* to me, but the grating irritation it inspires has since dulled to practically nothing. And we are paddling through *Twelfth Night* swimmingly.

I think he's growing on me, though I'm loath to admit it. He's not insisting that I feel a certain way or pushing me to act the way he wants me to act, which is certainly a hell of a plus. I think I won the battle for my own personality.


## 10/3 WEDNESDAY
*(Typed in the Folder: Marshall)*

And just like that, he bullocks it up. I thought he was genuinely nice, just clingy and attention-seeking. No. He's an awful, insensitive idiot-child just like everyone else. He invited me to another concert (Hadrian had invited me to a lovely symphony on the 9th of last month with his musical fellows; I cried and cried), and I exploded.

"Please, darlin'. You'd have fun, I promise. Maybe you can finally get off the crazy train you've been riding."

"Don't call me 'darling' because I'm not."

He rolled his eyes. I knew it even if my eyes never left the rather riveting paragraph of text I was gorging on. I swear, ever since the 7th, he's been one big mother hen instead of some incompetent Don Juan who picked me as his comic relief sidekick. Granted a mildly sophisticated, existential hen, but I wouldn't know the philosophies of any given barnyard fowl.

"You didn't answer my question, Ina."

"It's a school night." I turned the page.

"Like that matters," he said contemptuously. "It's not like you do any work after school." I didn't bother correcting him, because I was not dying on this hill. "Why stay cooped up at home with that..."

I sent him a scornful look over my newest acquisition. "My *father* isn't that bad. You needn't trail off so significantly. Besides, he needs me."

"That's what you said last week. I swear…he's taken over your entire life. I thought you were the independent one, here."

I continued to read my book. Not on this hill.

"Ina," he said, asking for eye contact without saying.

"You wouldn't understand."

"Try me."

I didn't want to try him, but I didn't want to go. I was tired of *feeling* things, which music must do by design. "Family obligations are more important than concerts." Sitting in the study with my father, staring at nothing, was obviously better than going *outside* with *people*.

"Are 'family obligations' going to run your life forever or just until the end of time?" How fucking awful for him, right? His life must be so fucking terrible. This must be the straw that broke the proverbial camel's back, my not wanting to waste my time listening to major and minor chords until my chest bursts with the strain.

"Yes," I said because my family *was* going to run my life for the rest of my life.

"You know you don't have to front with me." He gently took my arm and turned me to his direction, looking into my eyes and trying to convince me with his earnest glance alone…then I went off on him.

"What are you saying, then? That I have no idea what's best for me? That I'm incompetent? Feckless? Bumbling? Should I just hand the reins of my life over to you instead of my father because you so obviously know best?" I was tense and uncomfortable and angry. Anger won out in that war of emotional dominance. "You have no idea what I want, what I plan to do, nor what I'm going through—"

"You're hoping a goddamn pirate ship will come and sail you away!" he rebutted, ripping *Daphnis and Chloe* out of my grip and letting it skitter across the floor.

"Pick that up." My tone was heavy with foreboding, but he ignored it with practised ease.

"No. Whatever happened fucked you up, and you need help, not these fucking fairy tales!" He was working himself up, pointing at my poor third-century Greek literature accusingly.

"Don't desecrate my books!" I wondered briefly how I got to be standing on the table, but rage makes you do strange things. I took a breath to really begin my diatribe.

"Get down from there! What, do you wanna launch at me WWE style? Come on, you could hurt yourself."

Tears tracked down my cheeks for whatever reason. "Stop interrupting me. Stop putting words in my mouth when you mock me for having too many there in the first place. Stop telling me what to do!"

"Okay, okay. I promise. I'll shut up, okay? Just get down, and we can fight or talk about it like civilised people. Whatever you like." His hands were outstretched to placate or wrestle me down. Either way, it was *not* helping. In fact, it was making everything much, much worse.

"Fuck you, you vacuous cretin." I *flew* from the picnic table we'd been working from and into his arms, screaming and crying. He fended me off easily, but I would not be heeled. "Fight me!" I screamed. And, just to prove that no man is truly saintly under fire, he pushed me off him with a single, easy motion. I stumbled back, completely unbalanced.

Really, in my defence, he should *not* have used a wrestling analogy on an obviously mad person flailing about on a table. He's lucky I didn't have a thematically appropriate folding chair to hurl at him as well.

"All right, crazy-bitch-time is over. Come here. I'm putting you in time fucking out."

I screamed at him, cursed him till I was blue in the face as he tossed me over his shoulder in a fireman carry and dumped me into his car. I was locked in until I was calm enough to politely ask to be released. Which took more than a little while, I'm ashamed to say.

The school, it seems, was used to these after-school outbursts whenever I chose to study with Hadrian and Hadrian said something twerpish. Maybe it was because it was the first time it happened or because it was outside and between sports practice and drama practice. Maybe people weren't so much tolerant as ignorant of the situation. Or perhaps I've begun thinking of the school itself, the building and the grounds, as a living entity that approves or reviles the actions of its students and wields some sort of karmic power over us all. And I have been petting the walls quite affectionately as of late...but I digress.

I've resolved never to speak to him again. I'll close up this stupid journal and forget this whole mess ever occurred. Yes, forgetting seems to be for the best at the moment.


## 10/5 FRIDAY
*(Written in a worn notebook)*

All this pretending nothing is wrong is wearing on my nerves. How is it I can read about women and men who live their entire lives like this, yet act like nothing is wrong, like nothing happened? It's like wham, bam , thank you, ma'am, and then forget about it. Is it only a device for heightening dramatic tensions and engaging sympathy that the author just forgets about once the love interest gives them an empty speech about love and living and why they should submit to living like normal people do?

Normal people must live utterly callous lives, and I am a bleeding heart because I cannot imagine what the next twenty, hell the next two years are going to be like. It all happened in one fell swoop. It still kills me to think about it, yet it never leaves my mind. Is it masochism or mourning or possibly cauterisation?

Well, I'm no fairy-tale protagonist. I don't have some insurmountable challenge to pull me away from my sorrows. I just have time, and it creeps [...] excruciatingly slowly [...]


UPDATE:

Sorry for the drowning in sorrows back there...I thought about cutting it, but I can't bring myself to blacken out an entire two and a half pages of crazy. I cut out the first page, though. You did not want to hear about that. What has gotten me into such a mood, you might ask? Hadrian gave me a *dream journal* today. He thought I could use something to "write my thoughts in." If only he knew I was compiling his every wrong move in this very, though admittedly motley, revealing transcription. Ha. I'll throw the trash away once I pass by a recycle bin. Bad dreams or no.


10/10 WEDNESDAY
*(Typed, under Folder: Dreams Translation)*

He's taken to stalking me again. He watches like some daunting bird of prey, lurching through the crowd to catch me before I can escape to the relative safety of class and enforced, yet inefficient, teaching techniques. I have cut him out of my life as easily as a table saw cuts through a fingertip (if you'll forgive the bloody simile).

Why is he still insistent on uncovering the reason behind my, admittedly, somewhat touchy disposition? He should know. It's all over school, whispered in the corners and shouted from the rooftops. The school itself knows the particulars of my most intimate secrets. I won't tell you because this is not a vessel for recording my every petty emotion, but to give record to the injustices put upon me by a cruel and malignant figure that haunts my very dreams at times.

Between September and October, several instances and incidents occurred that temporarily changed my opinion of one Hadrian Marshall. One: there was an incident with the family. Two: he noticed my subtle distress and reacted kindly instead of awfully. Three: he acted like a friend, an honest to God friend to me, and that made a world of difference. He even gave me a gift when I mentioned once that I was having nasty night terrors.

Now it just hurts with a kind of inarticulate ache in my chest. I just feel lost, like he was the last little filament of normality in my life. Now that I am actively ignoring him, I just have no reason to go to school. Why should I even bother? With everything going on, I should be allowed to take a break. A break would be so nice. Away from my family, my school, my convoluted hang-ups.

I would really go for a bit of R&R, really. Maybe if I ran to the ends of the earth and just wandered for a while, I could get my head on straight. Yeah, that sounds like a grand idea. As soon as I can, I'll just...pick up and walk away. Once my father calms down, and once I can get Hadrian to stop sending his minions to check up on me constantly.

I'll update you, I promise.

10/11 THURSDAY
*(Dream Journal)*


10/11-None of this is getting out of my room. I don't care what Mr. Wilde may say about a young girl's musing in *The Importance of Being Earnest*. These are entirely my own, and I intend to keep them like that. I am loath to admit it, but I think if I write them down every night, it will help. The first one isn't horrible, just weird.

I was eating a sandwich filled with bell peppers. Someone behind me asked for a bite of the sandwich, and it sounded like Hadrian so I said no. I turned around, and it was a giant blood-thirsty penguin that tried to eat me instead. I ran for the ice fields and hid away in Ross Island's anti-seal compound. Then everything turned green and flew away until it was just me and the penguin. It called me a killer of his kind and smooshed me under a single truck-sized webbed foot.


*(Written in a worn notebook)*


I thought about overdosing on sleeping pills during final dress. Is that not lovely and not an all-together stupid, mad dash to senseless oblivion? Hadrian, that steady thorn in my side, promised it would be all right, even if Olivia still didn't know all of her lines. Yes, of course, like he has any idea what I was stressed about. His pretension dis-endears him to me by the earful.

NB: Alucinor is best at repelling dreams, fuck the side effects.

## 10/13 SATURDAY
*(Dream Journal)*

Glad I didn't sit backstage much, I would have fallen asleep during a quick change if the crew weren't there to truss me up. Had no sleep Thursday. At all. I'd doze, dream of men on horseback and seas of black blood, wake, doze, dream of women tearing at their hair and gouging out their eyes, wake, doze, dream of Hadrian glaring down at me contemptuously, telling me I am less than human and unworthy of anything less than Hell, wake up crying. I'm going to watch *Winnie the Pooh* until I fall asleep tonight. Hope that helps.

## 10/14 SUNDAY
*(Typed, under Folder: User Interface)*

I don't know if I trust my father anymore. He's been acting more and more erratic since September. Sensible, but still, I always thought he would be more Russian about this sort of thing. He may even be rifling through my computer. If he isn't, I'll be relieved, but he keeps on asking about any boys from school I might be interested in. He keeps on insinuating that I should date and be social while at the same time spending every available second of every day with him.

He seems to want me to have a double life, some duplicitous affair, just so he can act like always and critique me, punish me. ??? He hasn't killed my credit card yet, so I don't think he's reading all of my files, just the ones in the intriguingly titled folders. I'm suddenly glad I saved my last few entries in the wrong directory.

In fact, all the men in my life are acting erratically. Mr. Collins cries every time he sees me in the hallways and during assemblies (I give updates on the mathletes' progress, being the most erudite and least socially awkward—Wow, I know—of the misfits in that particular group). My teachers, regardless of sex, are giving me tremendous liberties. I still turn my homework in on time and perfect, but they insist that I don't even have to come to class if I don't feel like it. It's very disconcerting.

And last of all is Hadrian. I saw him pumping Ms. Fish for information before class one day, almost demanding to know "what's happened." She saw me along with the rest of the class on my heels and froze.

"I...I think this conversation is over, Mr. Marshall." With that, she went to grading her papers. I wonder what kind of scandal he's gotten into now. Maybe he's solving some sort of intriguing teen mystery. Like, he's a secret agent for the police or something and out to bust teachers for paedophilia and drugging their students... Oh, my heavens. Look at me.

It's all the novels' fault. I've been reading trashy romance novels to fill the hours. My father and I haven't been to a good bookstore for ages, and I always feel uncomfortable buying good books without his approval.

The only things we don't buy together are "cotton candy for the brain" books: stories without a single shred of edifying elements; stories that somehow still have painful grammar and spelling errors even after multiple edits.

Well, enough of this digression. Let us venture onward to Hadrian, the anthropomorphic city of madness and uncertainty. He sent me all these significant looks, as if trying to tell me something without saying it, trying to prompt me to interact with him. No way. I ignored him like a champion of discretion.

He would try to find me in the mad throng of teenage bodies, but I was too quick for him. He was always waylaid by admirers and courtiers ingratiating themselves with His Nibs, the ruler of all petty childhood vices. He lost me time and again because of his own popularity.

He was trying to get to me, to question me and find out the reason for my rather strange outburst at the start of the month, just as we were beginning to lower our arms and link our hands in friendship. I admit now, reading back, that I was quite frazzled indeed. I'll tell you later, since that story is becoming more and more entwined with this whole affair.

If he can weasel it out of me, I'll tell you… Look at me now; I'm starting to treat you like an actual audience instead of a private account. If that's not dreadfully sad, I don't know what is. You're turning into a diary. Soon enough, I'll be regaling you with stories of every little detail of my life. How fucking trite.


10/15 MONDAY
*(Typed, under Folder: Dreams Translation)*


I am so glad the play is over, even if we got our parts for *Phantom of the Opera* today. We auditioned earlier, but I neglected to mention it for all its banality. Guess who is the Phantom? Not me. The only part I could sing in the damn play, and I get chorus. I think Tucker is punishing me. Well, that means I'll just not try at all in this play. Hadrian is Erik, and I refuse to be jealous of his rising fame. He will realise how daunting it is to get that kind of part at this school soon enough.

**10/16 TUESDAY**
*(Typed, under Folder: Marshall)*

Hadrian has really changed. We're getting married as Tennessee's age of consent may be eighteen, but you may marry without parental consent at sixteen. What a stroke of luck.

*(Written in a worn notebook)*

Ha. I think my father has had a conniption. Hadrian is still being strangely nice and irritating simultaneously, and I am still studiously avoiding him and his flock of friends. I really need to figure him out once I get a handle on my own problems. He's sort of in the way at the moment, isn't he?

**10/17 WEDNESDAY**
*(Dream Journal)*

Hadrian burned witches for a living, and I was the village crone imparting herbs and lore for the locals. He set me free to live in the woods because he didn't think I was actually a witch, just a poor old lady. I was turned into a girl by the gods as recompense for my trouble, and he burned me to dust.

**10/20 SATURDAY**
*(Dream Journal)*

He broke my arm in a rage. We were finishing homework and I corrected his spelling. He started screaming at me and pulled me up. He punched me and twisted my arm, screaming incoherently, until the limb snapped with a horrifying pop. I fell to the floor screaming, and he laughed. I tried to run, but he grabbed me by the hair, pulling me back. I have never felt so helpless against a man. He told me I deserved it. Everything is my fault.

**10/23 TUESDAY**
*(Dream Journal)*

We just sat in a coffee house and discussed the apocalypse in garbled Russian. Hadrian told me he never wanted to eat fish again. ??? The rest is a blur of pain and red.

**10/26 FRIDAY**
*(Dream Journal)*

I dreamt of counting dropping heads during the French Revolution. His head rolled to my feet and asked me why I didn't save him. I woke up terrified.

10/27 SATURDAY
*(Typed, under Folder: Pictures)*

Some simpleton gave Hadrian my cell phone number. Probably Sara Jane. How they found it themselves, I have no idea. Now, he won't stop texting me. It alternates between touching kindness and sweetness to rather ruthless bad-cop-style interrogation. I really should learn how to block him, but my grasp on the inner workings of this complicated behemoth of a machine is mostly just poor. As an example:

Hadrian: *Are you busy tonight?*
*Yes.*

He never really listened when I said that, because sometimes he's able to convince me regardless, the conniver.

Hadrian: *Have time for a little stitch n bitch?*

He was still trying to involve me in some sort of social activity, even if we weren't really talking.

*No*
Hadrian: *PLZ*
*No*
Hadrian: *Then tell me what's up*
*Que*
Hadrian: *Anything you want to talk about, of course?*
*Stop texting me*
Hadrian: *No pressure, but I think you'd feel better if you actually, you know, talk about stuff.*
Hadrian: *With me*
Hadrian: *Or someone*
Hadrian: *Anyone*
Hadrian: *I promise*
Hadrian: *No judgements*

I turned my phone off. I couldn't leave it off whenever I left the house because my father would sometimes get it in his head to obsessively call me for an hour or more. If he couldn't reach me, he would call the police and report me missing. Believe me, it actually happened the first time Hadrian began running up my phone bill. The paperwork alone was exhausting, not to mention the money...


10/31 WEDNESDAY
*(Typed, under Folder: Marshall)*


Happy birthday to me. Hadrian gave me a gift. Actually, several people gave me gifts, my first ones since I started refusing them on the grounds that gifts celebrating anniversaries were useless as representations of love because you were required to give them, not because you wanted to give them. I think I was seven.

Yeah, it was my seventh birthday, and I told off my parents because they looked so harangued by the hoopla. I just harrumphed and herded my classmates away to cake so I could have a "discourse" with good old Mom and Dad. Ah, memories of my younger days of precocious liberality. I was quite the little socialist. I think it's because my mother was denouncing the horrible literature Hitler created in *Mein Kampf*. So I just started reading Karl Marx because that was the "total opposite" in my mind....

I digress once again. He gave me a little package before first period. I didn't even know he knew my birthday. I didn't open it. He sat beside me at the start of drama, before rehearsals began proper. It was a sort of proto study hall sometimes. Such dictates depended on our workload and Tucker's mood.

"Open it." Why couldn't he just stop being so nice and pushy and annoying all at once?

"If I do, will you leave me alone?"

"Depends on how much you like it," he shot back, stretching in his seat and exposing a bit of a six-pack. I couldn't help noticing. His shirt must have been too short. Anyway, I undid the little bow and popped open the lid. Inside was a card. It was a pass. I nearly screamed with delight. It was a pass to private tours of the best mansions and historical sites in and around Nashville.

I could wander wherever I wanted, stick my nose in anything with this pass. Oh. My. God. I bounced madly in my seat. If only Mother could see this, she would go just as crazy. We both would try to escape the carefully monitored tourists' groups to actually explore the buildings when we visited them. Now...my mood immediately crashed and burned like a zeppelin caught in the London blitz.

"Are you okay? Did you not like it, or..." He was immediately closer, touching my hand. I pulled back and closed the box carefully, lest I bend the laminated card.

"No, no. Thank you for the kind gift. I have...never been so excited in my life." I didn't mean to deadpan it, but it sort of came out that way.

He remained unconvinced. "What's wrong?"

"I said thank you. I love it. Don't ruin your shining moment of positive attention."

He was treading on thin ice now.

"No, something else did that for me."

I got up and went to talk to Tucker.

"Act 2 is almost done," I said with studied casualness, not looking at him.

He acted just as strangely as the rest of the staff. "In, if there's anything I can do for you, you know you jus' have to ask, right?" He said it in a rush, as if forcing himself to say it.

"I'm fine. It's almost been two months. I'm fine."

He closed his eyes and pinched the bridge of his nose. "Two months ain't long enough to—"

"Would you like the draft or not?" I felt a bit bad for interrupting him, but goodness. Must he bring up such subjects in public? It is most unseemly. He held out his hand reluctantly. I ran back to my seat, pulled out the sheaf of papers while ignoring a curious pair of blue eyes, and placed the packet onto his outstretched palm. "It's wonderful, you'll see."

"In, I think you're pushing yourself too hard. All these APs, drama, all those other after-school things ya do, and… It's just too much. You've got to slow down." He placed a heavy hand on my shoulder, and I shrugged it off. What was it with people placing their hands on my arm? I only just move or push them away. Why are they all so insistent on physical contact?

Besides, why was he bringing drama in as a stressor? It has always been a steam valve for my life's long parade of inconveniences, not an additional constraint on my peace of mind. His pushing me back into complete obscurity has only made my mood worse instead of alleviating my stress levels.

"I like being busy. If anything, being bored is the last thing I want to do at this point in my life." I left him at that, grabbing my bag out of Hadrian's grasp with a sharp nod. I ran. I am unabashed in saying that. I ran to the back of the theatre, among the comforting sounds and smells of the backstage. I read by the light of one of those little book bulbs until lunch was over and rehearsal shuddered into life behind me.

I confess, though, that my reading speed was quite altered. Usually I can speed through a text like the TJV; now I was a stubbornly dilapidated tugboat, chugging along only to stop and start again at uneven intervals.

# November

**11/1 THURSDAY**
*(Dream Journal)*

I was wandering through the halls of Winchester Mansion, getting dropped down trap doors and slamming into bricked-up doorways. "Let me out!" I finally shouted. Hadrian walked up to me through a door that led to the sheer wall outside. He told me that I was dead and trapped here because I couldn't pass on. If I could find my way outside, I could be free. I searched and searched to no avail. As night fell, black started oozing out of the walls, leading me in a new direction. Then I found the front parlour. There was a coffin, the wood stained with blood, then waxed to make the black monstrosity shine. I fell to the ground and begged for the coffin to let its captive go. There was silence.

**11/5 MONDAY**

I am dreading *Phantom*'s opening. It's a total mess, and we are just flying by the seat of our pants. Exciting, but very much hideously nerve-racking. Do. Not. Like. I swear I'll start sleeping in class just to get through the day. Class work is getting more and more boring as my father obsessively sends me larger stacks of advanced essays and tests to grade from his students and others from every department imaginable. Work is just work; like always. The Alucinor is starting to fuck me up more than it's helping, so I have to stop. Maybe I'll start Melinol next. Anything to get a good night's sleep.

Hadrian keeps giving me treats during drama. Mostly I just bat it away with a dismissive word, but those Snickers are looking mighty nice during my prolonged middle-of-the-day slump. I can't eat in the cafeteria, too many people for my tastes. And I don't have time to make a lunch in my mornings. He must be mad to keep on talking to me. I don't understand it. I'm not too mean anymore; I just don't have the energy for that, but still!

Why is he such a doggedly nice guy most of the time? He's still a little Casanova and too inquisitive for his own good, but goodness. He can really make up for all the stupid shit he does by just acting like himself instead of like he thinks I want him to act. It's hilarious to see the difference between his actions now and two months ago.

Two months ago, he would smile and lean just so and say something inconceivably corny if I sat next to him. Yesterday, he just scooted over and handed me half a sandwich. I think we really are friends now, more so than in October. Before, I was just feeding off of his attention in a desperate attempt at finding equilibrium, and, today, I enjoy his company when he's not being clingy or accusatory.

At least one thing in my life isn't blowing up in my face, and I am grateful for it.

**11/9 FRIDAY**
*(Typed, Encrypted)*

I want to drop out of school right now (I know! *Again, In?* I ask myself), it is so uninteresting and uninspiring. Why should I even attend class when I'm guaranteed a spot in Vanderbilt with either GED or diploma? I've received the early decision from Vandy. They said yes and plopped a scholarship in my lap. I guess I know what I'm doing this time next year, but what to do in the intervening months? Hadrian is all in a huff over the incident. I don't care. He's going to Chicago, it looks like, and he doesn't want to leave me alone, I suppose. Fears for me for some reason.

Am I a sad little puppy he found on the side of the road that he dotes on and cares for? Really. It's as though I have no idea what I want in life, and he has to guide me on the right path like a willing dolt out of some simpering Edwardian novel. I'm the heroine of a feminist, bombastic manifesto compared to that kind of mess. He doesn't have a clue and, no matter how sweet and kind he can be, will never have one.


**11/11 SUNDAY**
*(Dream Journal)*

He murdered me last night. It's too horrible to describe. He ate my soul, consumed it, and left me empty and hollow. I sat there in nothingness for an eternity. Then he threw the final, careless blow. What did it matter if the body survived? My spirit was viciously stolen. I was nothing, and he took everything of interest in me.

*(Written in a worn notebook)*

I went to a military cemetery today and Hadrian tagged along somehow. How he insinuated himself into this expedition, I have no clue. I was getting ready to go, putting some flowers in my hair, when the doorbell rang. He was wearing a black button-down and black jeans to match my dress. *What are you doing here*, I asked myself.

"Of all the homes on West End, you had to walk into mine." I gave him a look to prompt a response.

He did not disappoint. "Now, I like *Casablanca* as much as the next guy, but why don't we talk about *Joyeux Noël*?" He held out a small bouquet of poppies.

"How did you—"

"You're a history buff and particularly morbid lately. I just hoped I'd catch you at home." He smiled radiantly when I took the flowers.

"Do you really want to watch *Joyeux Noël*? Because I always cry near the end when the soldiers are broken up." I had hoped, a little, that that would fend him off like every other male relative I know. He was not deterred.

"I hope you have ice cream and tissues to share."

"You are incorrigible," I gave him a slight punch in the arm. "I'm going to visit the war memorial and a cemetery first."

"We'll take my car." We walked together to his obviously better-loved car. I directed him to the World War I statue beside (or maybe in) Centennial Park. I left a few poppies.

The survivors and martyrs of the Great War are the men that I most admire and exalt. It's almost a forgotten war with the way that WWII is so beloved by Americans today. It seems the growing pains of democracy and anti-aristocracy are of no interest to most men of this day and age. Hmph.

Since I have no idea where any Great War cemeteries are situated in the US, we went to a little Confederate cemetery instead. Losers need a little love too. I will never agree with the whole institution of slavery. It makes no sense to me, but most of those dead boys were poor white-trash farmers with no chance of ever having slaves or real rights themselves. They were too poorly educated to know that they were fighting for rights they never possessed in the first place, nor would ever have. Hadrian was unimpressed with my explanation.

"Inanna, I know none of your family even fought in the Civil War. Why are we really here?" I told you he could never leave well enough alone.

"Because we are Americans. And I get to wear my hoop outside of work if we go to the Franklin cemetery." We were sitting in the park parking lot and arguing, like always.

"You own a hoop?" He sounded incredulous.

"I live in the South and I like history. Where do you think I work?" I shot him a dubious look.

"I didn't even know you worked after school," he said defensively.

"Every other day I give tours at Carnton Plantation, and of course I have a job. It builds character."

"We won't spend an hour talking to a statue there, will we?"

I swear, he has no respect for anything at all.

"No," I said with my fingers crossed. We drove to the little cemetery but stopped by the plantation to change. I came out in a lavender shawl, straw hat, and hoop. I always loved dressing up, regardless of what my parents wanted me to do with my precious time.

"Wow, what happened to your waist?" He poked my corseted torso, my pinned bodice, and I scowled.

"I ate it." Said as tartly as possible.

"That sounds a bit counterproductive," he mused aloud, opening the car door for me. "Are you going to fit in that thing?" To prove that I could, I carefully folded myself into the passenger's seat and shut the door. "Well, colour me impressed."

"Are you finished mocking me for today?"

He chuckled at me, the horrible cretin. "Cool it, babe. Just trying to lighten things up some. You are taking this whole thing a bit far," he pointed out rightly, but I wouldn't give him that in a million years.

"At least I have some respect for the dead," I snipped, leaning as far out of reach in the confined space of the vehicle as possible, glad indeed that he hadn't fixed a muscle car instead of this lovely, old monster.

"I thought you didn't believe in an afterlife. Why are you even doing this?"

I fiddled with my gloves a moment before taking up my fan. I snapped it open to cover part of my face. "Because we need to remember our pasts and the pasts of others. Otherwise, there's just no point in living."

He snorted and started the car.

I made an abbreviated commemoration, leaving my flowers for the soldiers and twining the remaining poppies into my braids. It is always soothing to do this kind of thing. The action of letting the dead know you have not forgotten their sacrifice or their lives is very nice.

I hope that the sanctimonious ass that ruined my life is spit upon in life and death, then forgotten in a shallow grave. Excuse the outburst, I'm still not entirely happy and content with any consistency, yet. All of the day's pleasantness has worn off by now. We went back to my house, and I sent him into the den to put in the movie. Of course, my father would be down there working on his Sudoku's.

"And who the hell are you?" I could hear his voice ring in the otherwise silent house.

"Nice to meet you, sir. I'm Hade, a friend of Inanna."

"Really?" Oh, hell.

"Daddy!" I called down the stairs. "I didn't know you were home." Then, from below, Russian ripped through my eardrums. I will not translate it here, but let us say that he intimated that I brought boys back home when he was out and he would not have it in this house. I may have covered my mouth to keep from having a panic attack, but no one was there to see me before I descended the stairs. I looked at my father a bit despairingly and waited for him to stop.

His face was tinted ever so subtly red as he finished. "I'll ask him to leave, Daddy. I love you," I replied in Russian.

He took a breath and put his fallen glasses back on his long nose. "See that you do," he sniffed and sat back down on his armchair, content. I motioned to Hadrian, who obediently followed me up.

"Do you need a place to stay? Did he kick you out or something? I know Regina owes me a favour, and she lives near here. You could crash there until—" Wow. That had been some torrent of quick planning on his part. I was very nearly impressed.

"I'm all right; he's just upset that I didn't tell him about bringing anyone home. I'm afraid we'll have to rain-check the movie." I also wasn't sleeping on the couch of one of his amicably separated ex-girlfriends.

He was staring hard into my face. "What did he really say? That can't have been all."

I stared straight ahead, internally cursing that he had to be so damn tall and take up so much space. "Just get out."

"He called you a whore, didn't he?" It wasn't a question. "I picked up a few words from you, when you curse."

I hit him. I didn't think, I just threw a punch at his chest. He blocked it easily. Damned depression making me lose weight and muscle mass, damn you to one of the mouths of Dante's devil.

"No. We're not doing that. Why would he even say something like that? You're the most chaste girl ever to walk the planet."

"It's 'chastest,' Hadrian." I was opening the door, not looking at him.

"Fuck's sake, Ina! There's something screwy going on with your dad. Having a *friend* over shouldn't be a punishable offence. He's crushing you under his boot. Just tell me what's going on and I can help." He was on the verge of shaking me he was so frothing with righteous indignation.

"Let go of me," I said steadily. "You can't help me because nothing's wrong. This is what real life is like. Parents are unbearable until we learn that they really weren't as bad as we thought when we get older—"

"Only because you've forgotten how horrible they really were. Honey, you're confusing maturity with repression."

I had managed to herd him from the front hall to the threshold by moving as slowly as possible while still being grappled with. "Don't do this to me, please. You're not helping," I tried, looking back towards the den, but Hadrian jerked me back to glare weakly into his face.

"Because you won't tell me what's wrong!"

With a perfunctory twist to free myself, I shut the door and locked it. I suspect I shall get the cold shoulder tomorrow, but I can't help it. I won't be bullied into telling him what he already knows.

11/12 MONDAY
*(Written in a worn notebook)*

Quite the opposite, in fact. He's hounded me. He's left me notes. He's texted me. He's threatened to burn down my house with my father in it. He's acting like a lunatic, like some moonstruck fool trying to impress someone, to make a statement. Why can't he just let it go? Why does having friends have to come with this sort of price tag? Whatever happened to disposable, fair-weather friends?

I'll turn him down, cast him away, and hope he comes to his senses. He'll just have to get on the rest of the year without my sorry self to create more drag on his beautifully sailing ship of dreams. I'm not dealing with this right now. It's simply too much.

*(Dream Journal)*

He ripped up my essays and made me clean it up. I was on the ground, frantically picking up the infinitesimally small pieces of paper. He bent down to my face, lip twisted in hatred and spite, and took a breath to chew me out. Suddenly, Hadrian was pulling me up off the ground and punched him in the face. I was tossed to the ground and watched as Hadrian strangled him. I begged him not to. He did not listen.

11/17 SATURDAY
*(Dream Journal)*

Hadrian and I were rival rulers fighting for Lorraine. I was Germany. He was France. He threw baguettes at me, and I tossed blood sausage back. He squealed like a girl and ran away. I laughed, a lot. I was still chuckling when I woke up. First *nice* dream in forever.


11/19 MONDAY
*(Typed, Encrypted)*

We received our next parts today (Before the play is even close to done! It's obvious he wants this finished as much as I do). Last week was all severe reprimanding and intensive rehearsal procedure. I'm Lucy, and Hadrian is Van Helsing. I wonder why I was plucked out of the crowd to play the air-headed damsel in distress rather than the modern heroine Mina... At least Dracula is Lucas Winters, who played Malvolio and Raoul.

He's become rather competent during the course of the year. I'm slightly perturbed that I have to let him stand so close to me, though. He doesn't exactly smell like roses, more like AXE lathered on much too thickly. Hadrian was very disappointed in his casting and took pains to tell me so.

Surely he comprehends that Tucker dislikes him, yet cannot kick him to the curb because he is disgustingly talented. Or is he that dense?

At least he's been mollified slightly with regards to my family life. I told him a rather elaborate fib I constructed to explain my father's previous and subsequent behaviour. He now thinks that my father was denouncing not me but

Hadrian. I then told him (my father) that it upset me greatly to hear my friend spoken to in such a manner, and he promised never to upset me such again. Thank heavens that boy believes me guileless when I cast my eyes to the ground and fiddle with a pen or something.

11/20 TUESDAY
*(Dream Journal)*

Hadrian promised to perform necromancy to bring my father back from the dead. I only had to sell my soul to him. No hesitation. I did it and was caged in pure gold as my father wrenched himself back to the land of the living. He cried that I didn't have to do it, that he was fine being dead. I told him I wasn't. He deserved to live for all I did for him. All the suffering I endured to make his life comfortable would not be in vain. No one would ever die again.

I asked to visit my mother a few days later. Hadrian graciously stepped me out of my cage and walked me to a little stone cottage. "Long time no see, Inanna doll," my mother called. I ran into her rooms and cried. She held me and smoothed my hair and told me that everything is all right. All was well. "Your sacrifice was well met, lovely. Good job." I didn't want to wake up.

11/21 WEDNESDAY
*(Dream Journal)*

It was straight out of the story of Medea in *Metamorphoses*. Hadrian gave me a fur coat and swung it about my shoulders and fastened it. It strangled me, crying out for its lost flesh.

11/22 THURSDAY
*(Typed, Encrypted)*

He's too much of a handful (though, you won't hear me telling him that). I talked to Ms. Fish and she graciously allowed me to attend class only when I chose to attend class. She knows I know more mathematics than her and is giving me slack in recompense for not giving Hadrian grief for his outrageous behaviour. In drama, it's easy enough to evade him. He's constantly practising his songs, and I am doing nothing at all. It works out well enough.

# December

12/1 SATURDAY
*(Typed, Encrypted)*

*Phantom of the Opera* finished to lukewarm reviews. Christine's voice cracked in "Think of Me" and I nearly cried. For a high school play, I wouldn't judge it too harshly. For a performance of any merit, the artist in me cries for the incomprehensible dullness and ineptitude inherent in the actors' interpretations of the characters. I just want to take a nap that lasts thirty years and wake up a professor studying abroad on sabbatical. I just want to skip all this crazy and get to the nice stable part of my life. Yes, a nice nap without dreaming sounds delicious.

I also need a new book. Perhaps Swift can alleviate my weariness with wonderful satire?


12/5 WEDNESDAY
*(Typed, Encrypted)*

I bullied my teacher into giving my exams in advance. I just don't want to deal with them anymore. I don't want to go to school anymore. It's sort of sad that my last bastion of safety and security is now just another bane in my life. They were so easy too. I almost fell asleep. Thus I am allowed to skip an entire exam week. Joy.

Hadrian was asking me why he spied me in the halls after school when there was no play to prepare for. I was taking an exam, and he was on his way to swim practice (When did he even get on that team? Did I just completely miss that?). I told him to mind his own affairs and leave me to my wandering. He thought it was funny. I was trying to be serious.



12/7 FRIDAY
*(Typed, On Flash Drive "201")*


I actually did it. I ran away. I have to take a moment to catch my breath, but I really did run away. And was it exhilarating, let me tell you. I didn't go quite as far as I was intending. Flying to Siberia is surprisingly expensive and requires too many extended stops for my tastes. Also visas. I hadn't regaled you with the various foibles and difficulties and adventures in setting this up, because it had nothing to do with anything important. It's only time spent, nothing more.

I am, at this very moment, sitting in the Frankfurt Airport waiting for one of my many cousins to pick me up. I just finished an email to my father telling him I had to take a break and that I hoped he didn't mind that I left so sudden-like... Yes. I can feel the tension drain out of me in increments as I sit in my homeland.

I never told you I was foreign, did I? I was born here, as was my mother and her mother and so on before me. My father is a Russian mathematician (Don't even ask about his story, it's a nightmare of mistranslation and mafia shenanigans) who escaped from East Germany in the late 1980s and sought refuge in my Oma's/Grandmother's farmhouse for the night.... And the rest is history.

Enough with the backstory. This is about the newest chapter of my life! Hadrian has no clue. I take vicious pleasure in that fact. He still thinks he can call me and I'll be within arm's reach. No, siree, not me; not anymore. I will be incommunicado for the rest of eternity (If you'll forgive the hyperbole). I figured out how to block him before I left. A smile of pure unadulterated malevolence adorns my face right now. It could frighten children.

I am just so tired of his constant henpecking and intrusion into my affairs. Maybe this will teach him not to be so obsessive and silly. I'm still smarting over the vitriolic things he said about my father in the intervening days between their confrontation and my fabrication. It was intolerable to hear the poor man spoken of in that way.

In any case, I am punishing my father in my own way by leaving, even if I am only gone a little while. I suppose I just really hate taking care of people. Time apart is always good for fixing that sort of thing, as my mother would say.

And I'm digressing again. I have decided to remain isolationist for the entirety of the trip, which includes writing in you. So, I didn't include my computer in my packing list (this is an airport computer). I'll tell you about it when I get back.

# January

1/5 SATURDAY
*(Typed, Encrypted)*

Dad chewed me out but has no power over me anymore. I'll take care of him, yes, but he is *not* my overlord. It just took a little distance to figure it out. Phone is now officially on and Hadrian has left...eighteen voicemails! What the hell, and he must have called at least three times a day! They've clogged up my memory with all these messages, him and my father. Father at least stopped calling after a few days, content to let me blow off steam (He probably forgot I was even gone), but this boy is persistent! Well, I can deal with him now. Yes, I can.

It has been amazing abroad. I saw libraries and churches and some of the most beautiful scenery in the world. I hope to go back again. Hopefully there will be more nice fishermen and fewer men in riot gear next time. I gave myself a full-on detoxification; no books, no music, no computer. It was just myself and my little backpack against the world, and it was thrilling, exhilarating, invigorating! I feel like a new woman, and probably act like one too. No more moping about and acting like a fool. My assertive, opinionated self is back and won't take no for an answer. Fuck loss. Fuck bad dreams. Fuck the people who try to tear me down. I will take them on, each and every one.

1/7 MONDAY
*(Typed, Encrypted)*

Hadrian looked tired today. That's the first thing I noticed this morning. Not shadow-eyed, desperate-for-sleep tired, but...worn down. So I sidled up to him in the few minutes before class began.

"Are you okay?"

He jumped from the wall and stood, slouching and staring at me in unabashed surprise.

"You've gained weight" was the first thing to pop out of his mouth.

"Well, hello to you too, Hadrian," I murmured amusedly, not angry in the least. I had gained weight on my trip, but it was the reassuring weight that covered ribs and softened sharp edges. I refuse to have typical teenage image problems along with everything else.

"No, no. That's not what I meant. You look great. When you didn't answer my texts or my calls, I thought...I don't know," he said in a rush, reaching forward and pulling me into a tight embrace.

"Why were you so worried? I was only gone a few weeks," I asked quizzically, disentangling myself from his grasping fingers.

"Do you do this often?" He was rather desperate for a negative answer, so I obliged him, despite his mildly exasperating behaviour.

"No, but why are you so upset?"

"Because I'm your friend, and you didn't even call me." Was he chastising me? "Please don't do that again." Hmm, what was he worried I did? Murder someone and flee the country?

"You thought I killed myself or something, didn't you?" That would explain this unique brand of weirdness today, fear. Death has a way of frazzling people, and uncertainty would certainly make it worse.

"Shut up," he said gruffly. "I'm just glad to see you looking so good. Where—"

I glanced at the clock and cut him off. "Mr. Carwhile gives candy to the first person who returns from winter break. I'll talk later." I went into physics feeling like my namesake for the first time in ages. I didn't need anyone to make my decisions for me. I was fine.

Drama was certainly formidable. Tucker just watched me, looking for those latent signs of cracking only to find smooth, polished marble in its place. I had the ultimate okay from the writer/producer; the boss's agreement was in the bag.

"I met with Leitmotif, and he green-lit the production." I grinned at him while the class split into groups to practice lines.

"I hope you know what you're doin', In" was all he would say on the matter.

Hadrian pumped me for information during lunch. I told him I took a nice vacation, sparing him the boring details, same as you. He kept on commenting on how nice I looked and how healthy I seemed to be. Was I really that frail before? I really hadn't noticed. I'd so many other things on my mind that my appearance fell off the face of the earth.

It was a little weird to be so heavily complimented, though. Maybe I should have let him know that everything was going swimmingly, but how could I have known he would react so strongly?

Pfft! I should have guessed. He's a little like my father in wanting to know the whole world's gossip. Probably has a thriving Facebook he checks throughout the day on his phone. He was horrified to learn I did not, in fact, use that outdated bit of software to connect with people I know. I just call them.

I'll have to do something nice to him. He's too much of a worrier.


## 1/8 TUESDAY
*(Typed, Encrypted)*

"Where'd you go? Was it fun?"

"I went home," I said absently, turning another page. I was once again devouring my old Russian tragedy, *The Serf Anna*. "Wandered north."

"Home? I thought you were born here."

"I was born near Frankfurt, Germany. Didn't I say?"

"Nope." He grinned. "And here I thought you were an American."

I bristled. "I am a naturalised citizen, excuse you."

"So, you were spending Christmas with family?"

"For a while, why?"

Hadrian shrugged, looking back at his homework. "Did you have fun?"

*Did weeping into potatoes constitute fun*, I wondered before lying. "Of course. There was snow." We were quiet a beat before I realised he wanted *me* to question *him*. "Did you have a good holiday?"

"Was all right," he said. "Why'd you ignore me? Did you read my texts?"

"I couldn't—" But I didn't finish.

"Who said you couldn't?"

"Leave it alone," I said in irritation. "It doesn't matter."

"Why doesn't it matter? Do you even care how I *felt*?"

"I needed to be alone." It came in a loud burst, unexpected as a clap of thunder in a clear sky. "I just needed to be. By myself."

"You could have told me that, Jesus."

"Why does it matter? You have a family of your own, don't you? Aren't they more diverting than me?"

"Well, I couldn't focus on them when I was wondering where the fuck you'd gone." There was only one thing to do when faced with such a forbidding countenance.

"I'm sorry." It seemed like the best course of action. There wasn't any need to stand my ground regarding what was, in truth, a hasty decision on my part. "I wasn't thinking about anyone but myself."

"And that was fucking mean-spirited." He ran his fingers through his hair, and I smoothed out the frizz reflexively before responding.

"I should have told you, but I'm not going to be shamed for thinking about myself."

He sighed, and side-eyed me. "Jesus, that's selfish."

"If we weren't selfish on occasion, we'd go mad. Aren't you taking AP Psychology?"

My life is a tangled cat's cradle, pulled taut until the knots are obvious and irrevocable.

I didn't even look up from my book as he huffed once more and returned to his frustrating homework. He would scribble something, continue on, return, scratch it out angrily, and start the cycle again.

"What are you working on?" I asked, mildly annoyed with the noise.

"I don't understand this piece of shit. I've been stuck for twenty minutes and I still can't figure it out." He growled a little and erased his marks particularly fiercely to punctuate his aggravation.

"Let me see it." I pulled the paper from his hands to find an AP Chemistry problem before my eyes. "And just how many APs are *you* taking, sir?" I examined the word problem for a few minutes as he explained his difficulty over my head. "You forgot to carry the two here, and the symbol here should be a triangle." I marked it in pencil, handed it back to him, and grabbed my book. I was nearly to the halfway mark.

"Are you a genius, seriously? How did you even notice that?"

"Father is a mathematician. You don't need a chemistry major to solve a basic math irregularity." I also took the class myself sophomore year. I read a sentence before he interrupted the silence again.

"Is that why you do your homework at school? So you can go over it with your father at home?"

I rolled my eyes, sure that I wouldn't be finishing this page any time soon. I placed my bookmark in the appropriate spot, put the book carefully down, and looked at him.

"No." I smiled. If I brought home any homework, I would be slaughtered by my father. He would rip it apart, correct it, and send me off to rewrite it regardless of subject. He took pains to explain to me just how little I knew. He is my ultimate harbinger of humiliation, and he is very accomplished.

"I thought you'd be 'more candid' with me?" he asked pointedly.

"I thought you were done asking impertinent questions."

"Oh, so I hit a nerve then. Don't tell me he punishes you for not finishing it on time." He was joking. Thank Shakespeare for that.

"Nothing like that. I just like to finish things promptly, is all. I have an after-school itinerary too busy to clutter with homework."

We returned to our work until the bell rang for class to begin.


## 1/9 WEDNESDAY
*(Dream Journal)*

I was a librarian to some mysterious man. I was sorting ancient books into his strange index system (Everything was in Greek with Arabic characters) when I heard noises downstairs. I stopped, listened, and stood to investigate. I walked through a maze of doors and corridors carpeted in blood and guts. I went to the mysterious man's bedroom and found Hadrian about to kill him.

"Stop," I shouted.

"Only if you give me what I want." He looked thunderous in his black armour. He walked up to me and ripped out my heart. He ate it before my eyes.

His eyes flashed violet and his hair turned blindingly white for a moment before light filled the room. My heart regrew in its place and monsters were encroaching into the massive room. I stole the old man's sword and ran one through as he screamed at me that it was his turn to defeat the monsters.

*(Typed, Encrypted)*

Not sure what to do about everything. Father is sulking so much, it's a joy to do any sort of classroom activity, and that's saying something. I feel so nice and light, though. He can't bring me down, no matter how much he restricts my driving privileges. After all, he can only curtail that activity by cutting out my gas money. I only have to dip into my own savings to compensate.

I promised Hadrian I would go with him to the Nashville Symphony; they would be playing a selection from Wagner's *Der Ring des Nibelungen* or *The Ring Cycle*. Regardless of the man's rampant anti-Semitism, he could still compose beautifully and bombastically.

I'm quite excited to go, but sometimes I wonder how Hadrian possibly possesses the money to even take me (and the entire Music Theory class every other time) to the symphony. Sure, his parents may have season tickets as he said, but that still bespeaks of having more money than the average layman to casually allow others to use such a valuable (to me and others, no doubt) status symbol. We couldn't afford to make little gifts of such tickets or insane passes to my favourite places on earth, that's for sure. I only received the opportunity to pick up and run because that money was reparation for gross acts of despicable incompetence.

The remainder shall go into a long-term savings account, not to be touched for a few decades without penalty. I go to private school out of scholarships and a little out-of-pocket expense. He must obviously then be a trust-fund baby. I've known many of them in my tenure at Jackson Academy of the Sciences. Sometimes I wonder what sort of family he came from in order to mould such a personality as his: unabashedly attention-grabbing, smooth, and manipulative. Maybe I'll ask him on the way tonight.


UPDATE-11:39 PM

I just got back from the symphony, which is why I'm inserting the time. Before I go to bed, I want to write down exactly what has transpired in the intervening hours before I get distracted and forget great swaths of important dialogue.

I dressed up for the symphony because that has always been what I guessed to be the dress code for such functions. I told my father I had a dinner meeting with my drama teacher about the upcoming play. He bought it because he never looks too closely at what I'm wearing. Otherwise, that would have been a very interesting conversation.

I plugged the directions Hadrian gave me into my dinky little GPS (as I always seem to get lost the first time I go anywhere) and drove away from town to Belle Meade, where the rich people make their beds with gilded four-posters and antique, hand-dyed silk coverlets.

His house was huge, even for Belle Meade. Well, no wonder he's so incredibly popular.

I just sort of stared at it agape before remembering I was on a schedule, damn it. With the car parked in the expansive car park (I wouldn't dare call it a driveway) I marched in my pitifully worn dress (two years old) and scuffed heels. If you can't tell, I was quite intimidated, regardless of the fact that I thought I looked quite polished before I left. His house just made me feel as poor as a church mouse. Hell, I hoped to never see the inside of it, I was sure that would send me into the throes of an intense inferiority complex. Clutching my second-hand purse with my dirty, unpolished fingernails, I tentatively rang the doorbell.

A stranger opened the door. "Ah, you must be Inanna. I'm Hade's brother." He stuck out his broad hand for me to shake, and I took it. Goodness, he must be in his thirties. He took up the entire doorframe, so wide were his shoulders. He just sort of loomed pleasantly, smiling, and led me inside despite my pathetic protests, which stalled the moment I was inside proper.

Oh my goodness, if the walls were gilded and the floors carpeted in marble, I would not have been surprised, considering the outside outlandishness, but instead it was clean white-washed plaster and exotic hardwoods. Of course, the walls were not unadorned. The hall was quite Victorian in the sheer accumulation of stuff. Tables lined the walls, laden with eclectic conversation pieces: ivory chess pieces, delicate clocks, and faux Fabergé eggs (I hope. For those valuables to be displayed as such, unguarded as if they were mere baubles, would have sent me into conniptions). I gawked unashamedly as "Hade's brother" led me into what could only be described as a smoking room.

"I hope you don't mind coming with the whole family. The romance of it may be spoiled." I hadn't realised the brother was still beside me, I was so distracted by the shiny.

"What? What romance?" I asked stupidly, dumbstruck by the Louis XIV furnishings (Oh, Sun King! Your reign may have been long, but damn if you hadn't fucked up France for your descendants).

"Oh, I thought you were dating the way he goes on and on and on. Or is he just imagining things again?" He smiled cheerfully as he motioned me to sit in one of the beautiful antique chairs. I did so very, very carefully. I have had more than one antique collapse upon itself for me to act otherwise.

"Oh, no. We're just friends. I think he does have a girlfriend, or several. I never really asked."

He raised an eyebrow. "Several? Hade's more of a lady killer than I thought... How's he liking school? It must have been hard to move before his last year, but it couldn't be helped." He shrugged, still watching me intently.

"He's doing swimmingly as the most sought-after boy in school." I laughed softly. "I know I caused him some grief, but other than me, he's had no trouble making friends."

"Yeah, he mentioned that. I don't always know if he's being truthful or play acting. Anyway, he should be down soon with Mum and Dad, and we can start dinner." He fingered a cigar box as he spoke thoughtlessly.

"I have no objection if you wish to indulge. My father can smoke like a chimney when the mood strikes him."

He thanked me, plucking one unlucky Cuban out from its fellows and reached for the cigar cutter.

"Where are we eating?" I wondered what sort of high-class restaurant they were going to drop me into. I was still slightly mortified that my clothes weren't impressive enough to match the setting.

"We'll be eating here. It's family tradition to always eat dinner in if we have the chance." He brought the cigar to his lips and pulled out a box of matches from Tootsie's Orchid Lounge to light it.

"What a nice tradition. My father and I rarely get to eat together as of late. He moved his office hours to torture his students again." I added a little joke at the end, and he laughed gregariously, if a bit indulgently. I couldn't help liking him. He seemed a bit of a dominating presence, though. Is that why Hadrian always seeks out the spotlight wherever he goes?

"Oh, yeah, little brother told me that you're the daughter of old Sticks and Stones. How was it growing up with him as a father?" He leaned back and luxuriated in his chosen vice, puffing contentedly.

"I'm guessing you had some classes with him?"

His eyes were closed in bliss as he responded. "He was my advisor for a month, before I went into business. A hard-ass if ever I saw one. Not that he was a bad guy, you know. He's just—"

"Exacting? No nonsense?" I prompted.

He shrugged. "Strict."

"He's like that at home too, but he's a good man beneath the surliness," I said assuredly.

"I'm sure he is."

We continued on this vein for a little while, making idle chatter about Vandy, then musicians and composers until the rest of the family came down. And come down they did. I almost expected a herald to announce them as they walked with stately elegance down the steps of the massive staircase facing the parlour's open double doors. *My goodness, his mother must really be a queen,* I thought as the silver-haired lady glided down the steps clasping both her husband and youngest son's arms.

"Mother, this is Inanna Drew. Her father taught Carson at Vanderbilt."

"Yes, I remember. He nearly failed Carson for an error in his margins." Oh, that was a poor introduction.

I was standing by this point and reached out my hand. "I'm afraid his moodiness is legendary when it comes to small oversights, Mrs. Marshall, but it is a pleasure to meet you. Hadrian talks about his family all the time."

I was laying it on a little thick (and lying flat-out), but she brightened marginally and offered her delicate, gloved hand in return. We shook in that particular weak-wristed way of the past while staring each other dead in the face.

She smiled. "Only good things, I should hope." She nodded to her husband, who made the introductions.

"I am Gregory Marshall and this is Julianne. Our daughter Rebecca is unable to join us, unfortunately. Business."

I nodded, wondering if this "business" was related to the mafia. They do seem so suspiciously wealthy. Of course, they didn't look Italian/Russian/Romanian in the slightest (Yes, there are innumerable other crime organisations out there in the world, but I have a feeling the dame wouldn't dirty herself with such activities in any case). They were probably English transplants who carted their wealth across the pond to make even more of their profit margins.

But I digress, as I do time and time again. I shook hands with the family as Julianne gently reprimanded her eldest for smoking inside and nodded to Hadrian, who seemed incandescently pleased that the realms of family and friend were not clashing too badly.

"I'm dreadfully excited to meet you. School seems to take up so much time; we don't get *too* much of a chance to talk about our families."

His father surprised me with a booming laugh. "And I should hope so. With all the money I'm throwing at his education, it should be taking over his attention completely." Gregory Marshall's visage struck me in that moment. He looked exactly like an older version of Tsar Nicholas II. He had the same slight frame, brown eyes, moustache style... I wonder if he liked chopping his own firewood and darning his own uniforms.

"And it is, Dad," Hadrian added darkly. He was not as pleased with his grades as I was, I knew from the sheer number of times he'd harped on it.

"Were you ever in the military, Mr. Marshall?" I wondered aloud.

"I was Fleet Admiral in Her Majesty's Royal Navy once upon a time. Why do you ask, child?" He peered down at me curiously, but I couldn't let myself become nervous around such obviously illustrious people. I have an image to maintain, after all.

"You have the bearing of a military man. I was just wondering what branch you ascribed to." Damn, then he was more like King George V than Nicholas II. At least I was close.

He quirked an eyebrow and cocked his head. "Is that so? Do you think I should sign Hadrian here up for the navy as well?"

I wondered what that even meant. I know, I shouldn't have answered if I had no clue what he was driving at, but I couldn't just stand there awkwardly. "If he doesn't want to sign up, I would be at arms. But if he had a burning desire to eat hard tack and stare out at miles of open water for months on end..."

He laughed as he led the group towards the dining room. Carson slunk behind, snubbing out his cigar and shedding his jacket.

"Then I wouldn't object. He just seems a bit too...insubordinate to flourish in the military, I think."

Gregory nodded even as Julianne sighed heavily.

"Enough of trying to push my baby into harm's way, darling. Now, Inanna, what do you plan to do after school has ended?" She stared down her nose at me as we passed by some of the most beautiful recreations and original art pieces I had ever seen. This hall was exceptionally long, you see. We still hadn't reached the end of it that adjoined to the dining room.

"I'll be assisting my father in the summer. He wants me to work in the library when I have the time to better acclimate myself to Vanderbilt's *unique* inhabitants." As if that were at all necessary.

Hadrian cut in. "Like she even needs it, she's been running around there since she could walk. All the professors adore her."

I smiled as he mirrored my thoughts exactly. Good boy, it seems I had trained him well. Unintentionally, but still. The congratulations go to me.

"Yes, I demanded an honorary degree from every department head at least once in my life. While I was very young, though. I don't think I understood the mechanics of degrees at that point." I smiled as we took our seats in the cosy little room. Light wood and stone floors were lit by a crystal chandelier. There were neatly labelled little name tags on each seat. I counted four different forks on my plate alone. *Oh my. I am in hell*, I thought to myself.

"I suppose you're quite smart then, to gain the respect of so many professors." Was the woman needling me or trying to make conversation?

"Oh no, they just found me adorable. I was chunky cheeked, and my mother made me these precious little dresses.... All the tenured professors still pinch my cheeks. I'm taking pains to keep *them* out of my schedule as much as possible in the future."

They smiled all around, but Carson was staring down at me thoughtfully.

"How old are you?"

I frowned. "Eighteen. Why?"

"I think I remember you from when I was an undergrad. I used to see you toddling about hand in hand with one of the staff. You couldn't have been more than five years old." He peered at me intently, but I refused to squirm.

"Probably, I was always about at the end of father's lectures. Sometimes I even sat through them when I was patient enough."

"Well, what a life you must have lived. Any reason you decided to stay in town?" Julianne asked pointedly. "I gathered from Hadrian that you intended to 'get as far away from here as possible.'"

I bit my lip and then stopped. It was an uncouth gesture of nervousness. "I'm afraid things happened, and my father wants me to stay nearby. I'll probably transfer to another school next year," I fibbed, embarrassed. Was all of his family so nosy?

"Things?" she prompted.

"I'd rather not talk about it." I wanted to curl up and die under their intense gaze. The first course was eaten in silence. The second course arrived, and I steeled myself.

"I'm sorry if I ruined the flow of conversation." I took a steadying breath. "I'm just not very good at being sociable. My mother would be mortified by my behaviour...Have any of you been to Iceland?" I ventured nervously.

"No. I suppose you have?" Carson came to my rescue.

"It's beautiful to be sure. I was blessed enough to do a bit of travelling recently, and that was my last stop. I had never seen their old sagas and epics from the last millennium until I wandered into a library. They were breathtaking: laconic and heavy with..."

The parents were continuing to just stare at me.

Okay, change subject quickly. Something to engage the father. "I also travelled on an icebreaker near the Arctic circle."

"Did you really?" Gregory leaned forward over his lobster and asparagus. "Where were you? What sort of vessel did you ride? Did you help work the machinery at all?"

Thank Jules Verne for navy men. They are all distracted by the same things: sex and ships, and I was all out of sex stories.

I managed to garner Gregory's goodwill just like that. We talked a little more on vessel types and proper strengthening techniques before I steered the conversation from ships to wines (don't ask; European parents).

Because I had some idea of the difference between a Chardonnay and Chianti, I gained a bit more respect in the eyes of Carson. Mrs. Marshall was a harder nut to crack. We finished dinner with limited fuss and made our way to the luxurious BMW with plenty of room for all five of them. I looked at my poor beat-up Honda and ruthlessly beat down my burgeoning inferiority complex with an imaginary hammer.

The trip was filled with pleasant family talk, which I observed with interest. No matter how stuffy the parents appeared to be, they definitely were devoted—to their children and each other. Julianne would trace her fingers lightly on Gregory's forearm as she fussed over Viviane, Carson's wife, from afar (She was ill and unable to come as well).

I sat between Julianne and Hadrian at the symphony. The seats were amazing, let me tell you. I cried a little at the particularly beautiful song the strings created (my heart nearly burst at the beauty of it). I looked over to see Julianne's tears carefully blotted away with a handkerchief near the end. I think I like his family now, and I think they all like me to an extent. At least the ones I've met thus far.

Father was asleep by the time I got back, and I immediately went to the computer to tell you what happened. Things are looking bright, finally.

1/10 THURSDAY
*(Dream Journal)*

I was sailing through the Aegean Sea, the most terrifying and awesome pirate if there ever was one in Bronze Age Greece. I captured Hadrian, who was clutching this waifish blonde for all he was worth. He agreed to join my crew for his love's safety and the girl, Arachne, taught me how to weave on board.

Then we somehow got into a fight with Poseidon, invaded Troy, and stole an infant Nero from the space-time continuum.


*(Typed, Encrypted)*

I'm rather baffled, to be honest. I watched the sunrise this morning just before 7. Maybe that made me incredibly sentimental. My parents and I used to get up before the sun and visit Radnor Lake. I really miss those days. We had our problems, of course, but those seem so small compared to how fucked up everything has twisted itself to become. It makes me feel tired and old. I went to classes tired and mildly sullen. Hadrian asked me, later, how I liked his parents.

"But I wonder what you've told your brother about me."

"What did he tell you?"

"He thinks we're dating. Wouldn't your fan club be displeased?" I smiled distractedly. I was having trouble decoding a rather obscure reference to...something unpleasant. Was it the Spanish Inquisition or the *Malleus Maleficarum*?

"Oh, heartbroken, I'm sure," he responded after a pause.

"I like your parents very well, but why would they come here?" I gave up on the damnable paragraph and focused solely on him.

He shrugged. "My father has cancer."

My heart clenched for him. Of course. Vanderbilt Medical has one of the best oncology departments in the US.

"Carson and Viv lived down here already. It was a good move for them and for me. I'm much more popular here than in New York."

"Did you live in the city or the state?" I artfully avoided the elephant in the room named Things That Happened.

"Upstate, near the border really. It was nice, but cold." He stretched. "I like the warm much more."

"I'm sure it gives you a greater ability to show off," I said idly.

"And what does that mean, Ina?" He cocked his head the same way as his father did, eyebrow raised.

"I'm sure when summer rolls around, you'll have to be wrangled into a proper shirt by your mother every morning."

He laughed. "Sorry about Mum, though. She never approves of anyone 'of inconspicuous birth,'" he said with great aplomb and accent.

"I'm sure she'd love to hear about my family history—lots of illegal activities, border crossing, and idiot aristocrats... Did you know my mother used to go on about how her brother broke into a national bank to put food on the table before she left?"

"Wow, really?" He leaned forward, interested. I told him about my history, my favourite family stories. My mother's funny childhood stories, my father's centuries-lost aristocracy, the plight of serfs carried through the generations. It was nice to reminisce, especially when I was so introspective. It made me miss home, not my house but the feeling of being at home. I haven't felt that in nearly... Truss up Aristotle in crinolines. It's been five years, hasn't it?

In any case, I blathered for a good while longer than I intended, midway through a delightful recounting of heroism and unintentional hedonism from a paternal uncle when Hadrian poked me to awareness. Oh my. People were starting to stream through the doors and into the auditorium. Evening drama practice was about to begin.

I don't think I have ever been so narrow-minded as to completely ignore a plethora of noisy teenagers.


1/15 TUESDAY
(*Typed, Encrypted*)


I think I need to read *Jane Eyre* again or something written solely to send its readers spiralling into a severe depression just to remember how well off I am in comparison to probably 90 per cent of the world population. I am feeling much too privileged at the moment. Hadrian kept checking up on me this weekend.

He's just making a mountain of a molehill that really needs not be disturbed. My life is extraordinarily blessed given the circumstances. I could have been sold into sexual slavery or outright died of a lamentably preventable ailment had I been born in an impoverished country. I could have been strangled at birth with my own umbilical cord had I been in a more patriarchal country. I would have probably died of some easily cured communicable disease had I been born before the age of penicillin. It's a miracle that I still live and breathe at this very moment. It's selfishness to want a life overflowing in happiness. I would instead like to inspire happiness or at least a dearth of discomfort in others.

Moving on with my maudlin, *Eugene Onegin*-flavoured thoughts, Hadrian has invited me to another dinner with his family, including his sisters in blood and law. Sometimes, I just don't get the boy. Why is he always inviting me to things I have no business attending? I told him to show off his newest girlfriend, what's-her-face (I'm afraid I don't pay attention to his pontificating sometimes. I was sure he had informed me several times when I was paying him no mind), instead of a silly friend of his.

He told me, rather coldly, that he was not dating at the moment, nor had he since winter break. I won't print the exact language, because it was a bit crasser than I would like. It was a bit of a surprise to hear the announcement.

I may have responded with disbelief, and he may have intimated I thought him a whore, and I may have called him not a "whore" so much as a "rogue," and he may have reacted unpropitiously once again.

"You know, being wanted isn't the same as being loved," he said severely, staring out the far window. "Maybe I want more than girls hanging off me because I'm rich."

"Well, at least you have one and not neither," I said blithely. "And most of us are not blessed with your many and varied privileges, my friend."

"Those privileges don't make my life any easier, Ina," he argued.

I stared at him. "Of course it hasn't," I said venomously. "You're good looks, wealth, education, *good health.* All of that simply made your life harder, didn't it? It must be so terrible to be catered to in every walk of life because you have the money and the family that everyone dreams of."

"My family is just as fucked up as yours!" he shouted.

"Then you are lucky!" I shouted right back, picking up my things and running off.

Ah, well. I'll just have to take on more hours at Carnton to avoid this.


1/30 WEDNESDAY
*(Typed, Encrypted)*


I haven't updated because Hadrian and mine's relationship has cooled considerably since last I wrote. Apparently, thinking him a bit of a Casanova is an *incredible* sin (right above reticence). Last August, I would have been ecstatic with his cold shoulder, but now it's a bit disheartening. I suppose the thought that no matter how horrid I was to him, he would always return with a strangely pertinent kind comment had an expiration date.

It has become routine, and to break that...it's confusing and hurts a little. I like having my precious free time once more. I have been able to dig into *The Romance of the Three Kingdoms. Serf Anna* has been put on hold once again, much too depressing for the moment. I definitely don't need any more distressing stories of powerlessness and fear and pain to clutter my subconscious.

In fact...*Serf Anna* has been with me since before all this unpleasantness began, hasn't it? Maybe if I finish it, all this will dissipate into dreamy evanescence, never real to begin with. 'Tis a pleasant thought indeed.

I still dislike being Lucy in *Dracula*, she is so...flippant and careless. I am much more like Mina, except for the whole added bit where she falls in love with Dracula for one reason or another. Not canon, ladies and gents.

Ah, well.

In any case, Hadrian and I are no longer talking outside of necessary drama talk and the like. Tucker suggested that we had a lover's spat, and I nearly slapped him on principle. The idiocy of the man, as if one could not have a meaningful relationship with someone without romance somehow getting involved. He's just as bad as everyone on the internet.

Whatever is wrong with us definitely has nothing to do with sex, except that apparently he is not getting any, and I didn't realise he was a bit of a prude. Well, maybe prudishness is a bit too far, but definitely a sense of chastity I hadn't picked up on.

All the same, I may miss him. He broke up the daily grind with his attention and presence. Now everything is dull and monotonous outside of my growing pile of reading material. Books have never let me down like people have, I'm sad to say.

Speaking of people letting me down, I argued, once again, with Coach Tucker about trimming *Dreams*, which I refuse to do. We've been having spectacular rows about it too. The other students nearly noticed one time when I threw my shoe at him for suggesting that the heart-rending moment when Franz Joseph is forced to face his own impending overarching loneliness and let his wife go via a symbolic drug-induced hallucination was *padding*. *Padding*?!

Argh, maybe I'm too close to the thing. I can't bear to part with a single note if I can help it.

# February

**2/2 SATURDAY**
*(Dream Journal)*

I was canoeing placidly through a heavily green rainforest. I saw many of my classmates sitting on floating desks and writing in notebooks. Leather-bound grumbling monstrosities, they were. There were little eddies and currents that led into ponds regularly spaced along the river's straight path. Then I passed a heavily rusted snack machine. It seemed that my entire school had been eaten and then spat out by Swamp Thing with a penchant for dramatic colour combinations.

As I continued on, the colours of the flowers—lilies, roses, lotus blossoms, jasmine, saffron—became all the more weird and unbelievable. It was beautiful and lovely.

Hadrian was slogging through the turbulent water ahead, the staircase/riptide. I closed a door to interrupt the current, and he told me he didn't need my help and would I please open that door again, he was having fun! I was rather abashed and continued on after acquiescing.

I forded a few rapids before finding myself faced with frightful features captured in a fractured mirror. What fairy tale was this, I wondered? I felt normal but was actually made of plants. I looked at my arm; it was a gleaming, waxy green with bright colourful moss at the joints. Was I creating this? Was this my vision of a perfect school? Am I really this into nature? I woke up contemplative.

2/15 FRIDAY
*(Dream Journal)*

I was underwater, neither a mermaid nor drowning, just breathing placidly. The sea was clear and full of life as I looked above and to the sides, everywhere. It was soothing and warm and home. A hand reached down from above, disrupting the wildlife, and pulled me out of the water. I saw a man in scrubs, face obscured with a surgical mask, and felt a blast of terrible bone-shattering cold before I woke up.

*(Typed, Encrypted)*

Hadrian did something exceedingly queer yesterday. He gave me a box and some strange cross between a despairing, exasperated look and a glare. I haven't had a chance to open it for all the fanfare regarding *Dracula*, which looks to be the best of all of our plays thus far despite my sadly lacklustre performance.

I have had that entertainment and my books to keep me company just fine in the intervening month or more since my friendship cooled nearly solid beneath our feet. In fact, I shan't open the present at all. No need to accept gifts from non-friends when I refuse them from family. Indeed, I shall give it back to him tonight before we open.

UPDATE–12:54 A.M.

"It's a Valentine's Day gift," he had admitted mulishly as his grey hair paint was carefully applied to his skull by Mina. "Keep it."

"I'm not taking peace offerings. Either take it back, or I throw it out." I held it out to him imperiously, waiting for a response.

"What if it's a book? Would you really risk throwing out one of my father's naval monographs just to get back at me?" He had me there, but I shot a dubious look at the object in question.

"It's too small and light for that sort of volume, and you know it. I don't want anything from you, Hadrian. The only reason I didn't give it back then and there was because I was reading when you slipped it on my desk!" I shook the box a bit to punctuate my point.

He winced. "Why can't you make anything easy?" he asked tiredly.

"I do make things easy. You leave me alone; I leave you alone. You give me gifts; I give them back. Especially when they are unwarranted."

"It's a *Valentine's* Day gift." Must his tone be so pointed? I knew what it was.

"All right, so you picked a holiday to torture me with unwanted material goods, congratulations. You won the solid gold Kewpie doll."

As he covered his face with his hands and made an exasperated noise, I dropped the gift in his lap and walked out.

"Is she really?" the girl asked him.

"Yep." Argh, that boy was a menace.

The play went swimmingly, even if Dracula was a bit too close for comfort during the death scenes and such, but that is a given when the play dictates exaggerated neck gnawing action. And now, I'm going to bed.

2/18 MONDAY
*(Typed, Encrypted)*

Prepare for a long entry because this may take a while to backtrack and explain. I have been leaving you out of the loop of all things not Hadrian-centric and that has not amounted to much recently. Let's have at it, yes?

During class on Friday, the drama students learned what their final play was. Tucker glared down at us, clutching his clipboard like a shield against we heathens. "I hope you remember your lines tonight, if y'all fuck it up, it'll be your heads, not mine. Remember that!" he barked by way of a preamble.

"The last musical this year is called *Dreams*. It has three leads, twelve female roles, and five male roles, which suits us nearly perfect." He stared down the disproportionate female population surrounding a still slightly sullen you-know-who (Unfortunately not Tom Riddle. That would be too interesting). "I'd show y'all a performance, but this'll be the first time it's produced in English, so I won't confuse you."

There were little snatches of whispered conversation floating around me. People were wondering what a foreign play would be like, whether it would suck like *The Phantom* or not, the usual noises erupting from the rabble. "On Monday, singing auditions start, so don't skip. I don't care how tired y'all get. Sunday is a matinee for a reason!"

They were silenced and chastened before they had a chance to really protest. This happened in some form or another at the end of every play. Tucker would threaten and then cajole us with sweets at the end of the first audition. I was finishing reading *Aucassin and Nicolette* during the entire exchange. He handed out the sheets of music I organised and instructed them not to fuck up/lose the CDs I burned for them.

"There're no extras," he warned ominously.

Thus was Friday. That night was a success, as was Saturday and Sunday. Hadrian had the cast party at his house, but I never attended those so it didn't really matter. I ran out of there still covered in grease paint to cover a coworker's five o'clock shift, anyway.

On Monday, I listened to all my fellow "thespians" scramble with lost sheets of music, trying to cram in at least one perusal of the music we would use that day. I glanced down again at the song choices: Male solo: tenor. Female solo: alto. Male solo: baritone. Female solo: soprano. I knew them all back to front by now. If I didn't, I would have shot myself long ago out of sheer shame.

Maybe one of the reasons I loved this story was the accessibility of the music (to me, that is). I couldn't pull the highest notes of the soprano's part without slipping into a wispy nigh-silent falsetto no matter how hard I tried; I'm more of a contralto/mezzo-soprano kind of girl. I belt dramatically, not warble delicately. Really, nothing about me is delicate.

We picked numbers out of a hat, and I took note of my seven. Magic number and all that rot, you know. I paid no mind to my competition; I wasn't hell-bent for any real part in this debacle. I am quite content now with chorus and the third title line of the playbill. I was startled out of my reverie (not daydream, mind) when Tucker called my name. I rose, and he continued.

"I want to hear Sissi's part from you."

I shrugged. "Yes, sir." I got up, music in hand out of habit, and waited for the music to start. This was the first song of the play, a desperate plea for success in a fruitless, pointless war against whom we never even find out. Actually, I never explained any actual part of the play to you, have I? This will only take a moment, I promise:

Elisabeth/Sissi (the female lead) is caught in a dystopian future, fighting for her life and freedom. She is mortally wounded in a guerrilla shootout among the rebels, and Death (an anthropomorphic representation akin to Diskworld's death, also the male lead) arrives to send her off. He is struck by her courage and strength. She had taken at least half a dozen extras down with her within the first five minutes of stage time. He offers to leave her be, to let her live. She begs him to only let her dream once more before she dies, because there is nothing left in life to give anyone joy anymore.

Magnanimously, he sends her "back in time" into the age of Empress Elisabeth of Austria (1837-1889) to live her life, tinkering with it to greater and worse effect. She genuinely believes that she is the lady in question until her "death", as is the way with dreams. After being stabbed rather viciously by an anarchist, she returns to the battlefield, bedecked in the same extravagant white dress, shoots one more insurgent trying to raid her corpse with her futuristic multichambered assault rifle, and truly dies. She enters the ether (in the same blood-splattered dress) where Death, who has been watching and meddling all this time as well (because he can), offers to lead her past the twilight. He has grown fond of her and wants to keep her nearby to amuse him (the hints of which are littered liberally throughout the score, his "love theme" taking centre-stage, musically, by act three). They kiss, and it ends.

I may have cut it a bit thin, but that is the play's plot in a nutshell. I sang my bit and made to sit down.

Tucker reprimanded me. "No, I want you to actually sing this, not bleat like a dying sheep. Don't think I won't send you to the back of the chorus."

My right eye actually twitched in ruthlessly suppressed rage. I pointed to the woman at the piano (our music player had been confiscated by the band), and said, "Excuse me."

Regardless of the fact that she was our chorus teacher and had every right to reprimand me, she fled to Coach Tucker. I rearranged my skirts as I sat, straightened my back, and played the basic melody. I'm no great shakes at the piano, but playing all those notes over and over again to keep the words in the strange and winding tempo Leitmotif created made this score easy under my fingers.

I started it softly, whispering fervently, a sudden crescendo, a cry, a mournful turn. That was how the song was supposed to go.

I finished to silence, got up, and went back to my book. Hadrian was some time later but not last (The last girl was truly horrendous, couldn't keep in tune and forgot half of the words). I looked up long enough to know that the little ingénue would nab the part of Death or Franz Joseph (Emperor of Austria) easily.

The rest of the class was consumed with study hall, while Tucker called me to his office. I had no clue why at the time.

"What was that back there? This is your baby, In." He took a deep breath and ran his hand over his steely buzz cut. "Fuck if I don't know you can teach everyone this play with how you're obsessed with it. I wouldna given you another chance if I didn't know you. You could do so much better if you *tried*. Don't sell yourself short because you think you don't need to try, damn it!" He looked ready to shake me physically to match the ferocity of his statement.

"All right?" It was a mix of agreement and entreaty to keep it together.

"In, I'm torn. I can give you the part because you deserve it, and it's your last year, or I can send you to chorus for your sake." What?

"I'd like a part, but if you think 'my sake' is so important, do what you think is best." I was already too wrapped up in the story to distance myself from it. Whether I was given a lead or not, I would still be content with the work I put into this musical tour de force.

"This ain't like you, In. Last year, you would have screamed in my face for suggesting chorus. Your performance in *Phantom* was fuck-awful, and your Lucy was flat. I don't want you ruining your own baby by your shitty acting."

"I am not a shit actor!" I shouted, suddenly incensed. "I'm fucking exhausted! Do you know what I have to put up with at home? No! You have no clue what it's like to live like this." I took a breath and glared at him. "Give me the part, and I'll show you what a skilled actor I am. Drop me in chorus, and I'll watch you try to rearrange the deck chairs of the Titanic from the sidelines. You won't be able to carry this without me."

He smiled grimly. "And that's the In I know. Now keep up the energy and I'll see you on Broadway next year." It was a blatant lie, of course, but it was nice of him to say. I nodded shortly and exited the room without another word.

I ruminated on his words, sitting in the back of the auditorium. Had I really become that uninspiring and bland? I had felt so at peace last month, but that seems to have dissipated like so much fog on the horizon, leaving me to bake under the heat of my own aggravation and overt masochistic suffering. I should be better. I have accepted my pain. I shouldn't be dissolving into a lacklustre doppelganger without the energy to do something great, damn it—

But I digress. Hadrian sat next to me after a dozen or so minutes, catching me in an extremely volatile mood. "What was that about?" he asked.

"Why? Have you decided I'm suddenly worth bothering with because I might have gossip?" I already had a book in front of me. I did not need human companionship at the moment.

He ignored me with an ease born of practice. "Look, I know we haven't been talking, but if something is going on...you can always come to me. I'll listen."

I rolled my eyes at his pronouncement. "A touching sentiment, Casanova. Try it on someone more susceptible and I'm sure it will work wonders."

He frowned and narrowed his eyes, obviously displeased. "Why do you keep bringing that up? When have I *ever* acted like a man-whore?"

"It doesn't matter. I'm reading." Of course, my mind was far from the page, but I wouldn't tell him that.

"No, I don't understand why you keep on saying that. You don't actually believe that, do you?"

I did once, I wanted to add. I only thought we had a "don't ask, don't tell" policy regarding our love lives. It's pretty easy to realise in hindsight just how many times he would choose to spend time with me rather than a hypothetical girlfriend or six these last months. I suppose I really am losing my touch.

"Just leave me be, Hadrian. I am in no mood to argue with you or anyone else." I gave him one contemptuous look before returning to *They Fought like Demons: Women Soldiers in the American Civil War*, which was much more interesting than fighting with the overindulged rich boy next to me (even if I usually read histories for edification only). He wouldn't leave well enough alone, of course. You would think I'd remember that from last semester. Alas, my evasive abilities must have dulled from disuse.

"Ina—"

"Please, stop calling me that." I snapped.

He stayed silent for a moment. "Fine, if you want to be alone for the rest of your life. I'll leave you to it, *Miss*."

He stalked to his group and unabashedly relished in their unadulterated love and praise. I fumed for a moment before returning to my book. What right had he to intimate that I would be alone if I was unfriendly to *him*? He is not the only person of merit in the world, no matter what he may think.

My mind travelled, as it was wont, from the book in my hand to the other books I had yet to finish. I have at least five past the midpoint and another six waiting in the wings. *Serf Anna* was the closest to completion, relatively speaking. I still had several hundred pages to go, but I was nearly three-fourths of the way to the finish line.

I was really interested to see what would become of the quite terrifying couple, the Count and poor Anna. She had gone from strong-willed, clever, and able to demure, to witless, and frail in the course of a hundred thousand words. The count was like a vampire the way he drained her of vitality and replaced it with blind devotion. I hated him even as I marvelled at his manipulative skills. An awful, awful, beastly creature is he.

And my digressions just get longer and longer as I write, do they not? Tonight, Hadrian actually had the gall to call me. I was at the grocery store and answered without checking the ID.

"I'm almost done; I'll be home in a bit." Of course, I would assume it was my father. No one else calls my phone after six.

"Well, that's great, Ina, but I'm waiting for an apology not a foursquare update." That was snippy, I must say.

"Why should I have anything to say to you? You told me I would die alone today. I don't see why I shouldn't just hang up right now."

"Because you messed this up, and I'm calling so we can fix this and go on like before."

"Which before? The before where I loathed you, the before where I tolerated you, or the before where I ignored you? We aren't terribly adept at acting the part of bosom companions, Hadrian. Maybe staying out of each other's way is a good thing."

"But you're interesting," he insisted, a twinge of a whine tainting his tone. "You're the only interesting thing at school, and I want at least one *friend* when I go to college."

"Don't tell me you were some unloved nerd up north, because I won't believe you in the slightest," I responded flatly, picking up a gallon of milk as I spoke. "And intimating that without my companionship you are bereft at Jackson is patently ridiculous."

"Maybe I was exaggerating, but...I don't want to be the one to apologise. That was a fucking mean thing to say."

"Then I apologise if I made you uncomfortable." I actually said this sincerely, to boot. "Goodbye." I hung up without another word and wound my way to the register. He'll be angry again tomorrow, but I will not give a care, none whatsoever.

I am really getting tired of the drama he's stirring up, and I don't know how many times I have said that anymore when it comes to Hadrian. Next thing you know, he'll be back to his old tricks, pestering me about the things I won't tell him until I am forced to sew his lips shut just to achieve some semblance of peace around here.

I need a nap; that was a bit too violent, even for me.


2/21 THURSDAY
*(Typed, Encrypted)*

And guess what he's doing now? Even though we are *not* cordial, he is still asking me about why exactly I went overseas and why I must be so maudlin on a constant basis. Do wonders never cease? He can still be clingy and attention-seeking even without finding my companionship pleasing.

We received our parts yesterday; I am Sissi (Yes, yes, I know. Duh) and guess who Death is? Of course, it would be the true-to-life Death of Me instead of our previous go-to leading man, Araz. I actually liked him, after a fashion. I shall be forced into close quarters and singing in both of their faces for the duration of drama practice in any case. At least I can muster up enough dislike to simulate passion. Had this play taken place four months previous, I'm sure I wouldn't have been able to do even that.

Enough of my self-commiseration. We read through lines, and I only glanced at my script every so often (when someone fucked up a line *they were reading off of a page*). It was a bit anticlimactic to finally be practising the play that has taken over my life for so long. I almost expected everyone to suddenly know the thing as well as myself just to get the annoying line flubs and misunderstandings out of the way.

Hadrian sat next to me with Franz Joseph (real name Araz Chelki, one of the few non-WASP children to rove Jackson Academy of the Sciences) on the other. Araz was perfectly cordial; we had a lovely working relationship. He would learn his lines, and I would go out of my way to work well with him. Hadrian kept on nudging me with his elbow and trying to entreat conversation during breaks and lulls.

I stayed seated in my chair after the lunch bell, unreasonably exhausted. I finally got up, picking up my book (*Hypnerotomachia Poliphili*) hidden under my seat, and went to one of my many hiding places scattered throughout the theatre. Hadrian had gotten there first, so I made to leave.

He noticed me even if he did not turn around to look me in the eyes. "Is it really so hard for you to apologise? Do you just *not care* about anyone but yourself?"

I looked down to compose myself, my fingers were white as they dug into the hardback hanging suspended before my legs. I wanted to just walk away, forget I ever heard his name and go on in my life.

"Don't even say that. You can insult me all you want, but do not dare insinuate that I don't *care* about other people."

"You only care about your father. That's the only other real person you talk about. Your own mother doesn't even matter unless she's in a funny story to pass the time."

I wanted very much to have a temper tantrum. I wanted to throw my book at him, scream, and try to hit him. To beat him within an inch of his life and ask him how he liked that because that is how I feel *all the time*. It was making me dizzy; I wanted to hurt him so much. I swayed, indecisive and faint.

"What, did I hit a nerve? What is it with your mom? Do you hate her so much that you block her out completely?"

I ran away, or at least I wanted to. I stumbled past him, tripped, and grabbed blindly at the rigging.

"Ina?"

Footsteps behind me. "In, are you all right?" Large, rough hands pulled me upright, but my legs were still gelatinous. "Come on, In. Stand up for me. That's a girl." Light spotted back into my vision, "You've been skipping meals, haven't you? You'll be all right, just sit down and catch your breath, In."

"I'm all right. Tired is all." I rubbed my eyes absently with my sleeve. I was feeling a bit better, just tired as hell.

"Kid, what happened?" Tucker barked, letting go of me to stalk over Hadrian. He was still sitting, wide-eyed and horrified, staring at me.

"I-I. We were just talking and—"

Tucker sighed. "Let me get you a power bar from the office. I'll be back. You." He pointed at Hadrian. "Beat it." He stomped away, aggravated and disturbed. He kept a cabinet filled with candy and energy bars for his players as a result of his brief stint as wrestling coach. Those boys would drop left and right, trying to lose much too much weight to be healthy for their matches.

"Ina, I—"

"Don't talk to me," I spat, rubbing my temples.

"Was it something I said, or have you been starving yourself?"

I growled, eyes closed and head throbbing. "Stay away from me. All you do is hurt me." It wasn't even all that venomous, just wearied.

"It's not like I *try* to, dammit. But you just never tell me anything. Is it what I said about your mom? I can't see how she could be any worse than your dad, to be honest."

I wanted to cry at his ignorantly callous words, but my head... "My mother's a fucking saint," I bleated into my folded arms, leaning against the cold cement blocks of the backstage wall.

"What's going on in that head of yours?" he asked, gently pushing the hair out of my eyes. That scant physical kindness broke the dam, regardless of pain. I cried, shying away from his hands and curling into myself.

"What— In. What did you do?" More steps. An argument I didn't pay mind to. Steps away. A hand on my shoulders. "I have a Snickers and Cliff bar. Which one would you like? Or would ya like to sit in my office for a bit?"

I stifled my cries to a sniffle with no small effort and looked up at Coach Tucker, who looked unexpectedly soft and approachable. It was strange and unbelievable to see, to say the least.

"I'll take the Snickers."

He half smiled and handed over the candy.

"Give me a minute. It's a...*feminine* issue," I admitted (A blatant lie, but ever so useful against nosing males). He stepped back a bit but nodded and left me be. I sat in the dark and ate the fuck out of that damn Snickers.

I stayed there, sequestered away in curtained darkness until lunch ended. By that time, my constitution had mostly rectified itself. I droned through the rest of class, switching seats with Araz. Hadrian left me a voicemail after school, which I did not listen to.

Today was droll. Hadrian pulled a sandwich out of his ridiculous lunch pail at fourth period and demanded I actually have *food* for lunch ("What a marvellous idea, Hadrian! I never knew you could *eat* during school. *What an unexpected windfall in the quest for proper nourishment!*"). Tucker left another Snickers bar on my seat as well. Does everyone have chronic feeding-people syndrome now (already afflicting millions of mothers everywhere, and now the men are consumed as well)? I didn't know I was that helpless. You nearly faint once and all of a sudden *everyone* wants to take care of you.

I'm not having any of it, though. I'm not helpless, and I can learn from my own damn mistakes. No one needs to hold my hand. I'm just thankful no one reported this to my father or I'm sure I'd never hear the end of it. He would harp on continually, watching over my diet and exercise, demanding I work less and stay at home "for your own safety and my peace of mind." What a load of crock.

## 2/27 WEDNESDAY
*(Dream Journal)*

He slayed a dragon last night. A dragon that wore a pince-nez and waistcoat. I was sitting, surrounded by gold and swords, on a throne made of the skulls of men who thought they were heroes. It was as if I had power, if only on the vermin that infested the cave. He fought the dragon and won, slitting it down "from the nave to the chops" à la *Macbeth*. I cried for the fallen beast. It had been my only companion since I could remember. He had been dreadfully funny.

He didn't come to me, though, didn't bother with anything but the treasure trove piled up to the ceiling. I threw books at him until he left me be, carrying a comically large sack of gold behind him.

# March

3/2 SATURDAY
*(Typed, Encrypted)*

If I can't at least update this thing every few days, the least I can do is give an update at the beginning of the month. I think, in all seriousness, that Hadrian has decided to become my caretaker rather than my on-again off-again friend. And you know just how much I enjoy being taken care of, don't you? It makes my fucking skin crawl, and it erodes my language into crassness beyond what polite conversation permits.

He makes me lunch at least every other day. He seems to think he's priming a pump of conscientiousness rather than playing with my metabolism. If he hadn't enraged me past anything, I wouldn't have acted like I came straight out of Dickens's *The Pickwick Papers*.

And the way he natters would be almost amusing if they weren't erroneous commentaries on my home life that result in these kinds of exchanges:

"Hadrian?" I interrupted his meandering offer to take me to see the latest art house film he thought would interest me. He was always asking if I wanted food or transportation or entertainment. Always offering to pay for everything and making someone make lunch for me during the school day. I had to ask.

"Yes, ma'am?"

"You think I'm poor, don't you?"

"Hey, you never bring lunch. I'm just being nice," he defended himself feebly.

I sighed. I had always thought his insistence on feeding or otherwise taking care of me were merely castoffs from a bygone era. Unfortunately, I am apparently a charity case in his eyes. I rolled my eyes emphatically.

"For Heaven's sake, my father is a *tenured professor*. You know that. My family is firmly ensconced in the middle class, though that may seem like poverty from where you're standing." I handed him back his lunch pail to keep from losing my temper. "Do you even know what poverty looks like?"

"I—well. You're my best friend. Friends take care of each other." There was that pleading tone unique to Hadrian. The perfect mixture of contrition and stubbornness.

I sighed heavily. "You can be so arduous at times. Please stop trying to help me, I beg you."

He grumbled but retook possession of his meal.

Now even my classmates have noticed this strangeness. They avoid me as if I have the plague, especially the girls. Honestly, that confuses me; one would think that having someone dote on you consistently would be a dream come true for each and every girl's heart of hearts. Maybe they think I'm actually going to die and wish to distance themselves from the inevitable end result. I shrug it off. If they leave me be, I won't complain, but I confronted him again regarding his mothering moods today.

"Stop trying to feed me. I'm sick of it." I batted away the sandwich threatening the view of my new literary criticism focused on famous novels of the 20th century. The plastic could have broken and left me with a page completely unreadable! "Why do you get in these spells? I'm perfectly capable of caring for myself."

"Yeah right. If that were true, you wouldn't need my help all the time," he responded without guile.

I sighed, slightly exasperated. "You just like taking care of something. Why don't you get a pet to dote on instead? Or maybe a plant. You'd suffer through less backtalk to start with—"

"Unfortunately for me, you're more interesting than a pet, Ina. Humour me, please," he cajoled.

"Please, Hadrian." I imparted a soulful look to further encourage the guilt blooming behind his eyes.

His self-righteousness stalled for a moment. "If I make you pay for the movie, can you drop this?"

I sighed a little, then leaned towards him.

"I'll take that as a yes."

I nodded absently from behind my book. "I can buy my own candies, all right?"

He laughed, and we were basically patched up. Which was a really spectacular improvement to my acting ability in class, I'm a little ashamed to say. It's just very comforting that when we begin practising Act One, he won't "accidentally" drop me off stage out of spite. That would be painful and embarrassing.


**3/6 WEDNESDAY**
*(Dream Journal)*


We were the original Bonnie and Clyde, zipping through ancient Sumer without a care in the world and raiding temples for the thrill of it on Hittite chariots. Hadrian nearly got caught in Ur grabbing a few trinkets in the temple of the sun god, An. We *outran* the god of sunlight. It was dreadfully fun.

Then there was a murder mystery with Sara Jane and Regina as sassy girl detectives, Hadrian as the femme fatale, and myself as the overworked police chief in *Maltese Falcon*-era New York. Hadrian apparently wears bright pink garters under his designer slacks when he's out seducing overworked gumshoes.

3/7 THURSDAY
*(Typed, Encrypted)*

We have started afternoon rehearsals again. It's been rather nice to belt frustrations in stirring songs of independence and encouraging steampunk...awesome-sauce (I really couldn't think of an actual word to describe the moxie that particular song inspires in me. Thus, portmanteaus must come to my rescue).

Hadrian and I are spending even more time with each other, which is all right and unsurprising as we are friends once more. Of course, we still have something between us, unresolved tension waiting below the surface for our weakest moment. It's a little scary to think that, though we act as close as in January, we are really still in October when October was so very bad, indeed.

I may be a little sorry that we have to continue with superficial kindness and deep discontent (Because it *is* my fault. If I hadn't blacked out, we would still be honest with one another), but I don't want to lose even an artificial good thing right now. It's all I have to look forward to, outside of my play...

Now, doesn't that sound pathetic? "The only thing I have to live for is my best friend. Everything else is meaningless!" Next thing you know, I'll be spouting pathetic love sonnets and begging him to take me away from this awful place. I am incredibly unimpressed with my self-sufficiency right now. I am not going down the road of the old heroines, who appear badass only to crumple at the first sign of difficulty. I'm not that thin-skinned, am I?

*(Typed, Encrypted)*

There are too many people. Instead of there being a whole brood of people that you know and understand, we are given fleeting glimpses of more people than I can count. I couldn't keep track of all the people I see on a daily basis. I don't have the mental acuity to notice little parts of them and note when they are nursing a secret sorrow or particularly ecstatic secret. They all appear the same in the halls, all with dour expressions and low-slung backpacks.

I don't understand how Hadrian could do something like that. He seems, to me, to be the most empathic human being on the planet. He told me, after class, that he was going to comfort Samantha Grange because her boyfriend just dumped her in second period. I have second period with her and her boyfriend, Jonah, and I had no clue this even went on. I can understand Hadrian, my family, the other people I interact with on a daily basis, but how he can keep up with the sheer magnitude of his posse without breaking a sweat boggles the mind.

3/9 SATURDAY
*(Typed, Encrypted)*

I met Hadrian's sister-in-law today. She stopped by to give him dinner because he was revising with me all through our meagre break between classes and drama practice. Whenever we do this, which is quite often as of late, his parents or brother usually drop by with food of some sort. They are just as kindly as I remembered them to be. From afar, I couldn't tell if she was an early bloomer or an exceptionally short adult. It was the latter of course. I'm sure she's still carded at bars even though she's past thirty.

"Ah, there you are, Hade. How's the play going?"

He beamed incandescently. "Great, Viv. Has Car been giving you grief or was it Mother?"

She laughed, and I wondered how Hadrian could have such good relations with every single one of relatives. Maybe that is why he couldn't comprehend my family at all. We always *did* have one too many blood feuds for my taste.

"I just wanted to see you, and your friend." She turned to me. "Ina, right?"

"Guilty as charged," I smiled and held out a hand for her to shake.

"Viviane Harding-Marshall, you may know my niece."

"Rachel Harding? Of course, I can really see the family resemblance." The freshman in question was also fantastically vertically challenged. "I always seem to see her. She is very gregarious amongst the upperclassmen."

She smiled gamely. "I may have asked her to watch out for her little cousin here."

I laughed as she pointed out a mildly mortified Hadrian.

"I'm sure he wouldn't be as popular if it weren't for her. Rachel's always crowing about what a good job she did 'priming the pump,' if you will." She was quite affable, even bringing a second dinner for me, some sort of unidentifiable noodle dish with seafood, which was delectable.

Hadrian was still a bit miffed by the time his sister-in-law bade us good night, but I just gave him a pat on the shoulder. He glared petulantly, but I didn't mind it at all. It was nice to know he wasn't completely responsible for his own popularity.


3/12 TUESDAY
*(Typed, Encrypted)*


"I wish I was her sometimes. Don't you?" I asked, gesturing with my book. It was an adorable little fable mixing Christian mythology and a taste for the macabre, a relatively new author. Apparently, it was the wrong thing to ask at the wrong time.

"Do you only care about characters?" he complained petulantly.

"No, of course not. I care about a lot of things other than my books." I frowned at his sudden attack. "What's got you in a tizzy?"

"You just don't care about anything anymore. Before, you at least made a token effort. Now I only see you by yourself, reading or doodling. I bet you wouldn't notice if I just left half the time!" What in the world?

"Of course I would notice, what would I do without my nosy snack machine?" I tried to joke, but now was not the time for jocularity.

"You don't care, do you? I don't know why I put up with you."

I stood, and he began to pace, keeping me at arm's length. "What in the world? What's brought this on?" I grabbed at his arm but he jerked away.

"*You* brought this on," he snarled, eyes flashing in anger. "All you do is read and talk about reading and nothing with *real life*. For fuck's sake, can you be more boring? And your condescending ivory-tower bullshit? Can't you just get your head out of your ass and see what's really going on? Can you even *see* real people anymore? I didn't sign up for this when I tried to be the better person and hang out with you. Why do I even *try*?"

What in the seven Hells of Dante's inferno? What had I done? I'd done *nothing* differently. I'd changed *none* of my habits. Why would he just suddenly round on me like a wounded animal, gnawing at me until he escaped my clutches?

I was silent a moment, staring at him agog. "Fuck you," I whispered and fled. I don't know what caused him to blow up at me, but it stung something awful. I wasn't intending to go anywhere. I just wanted to put as much space between the two of us as possible.

Sometimes, I love my school. It's just so easy to hide. I'm almost sorry to leave it behind. It's been of such good use to me over the years. I slipped into one of the many "secret passages"—hallways seldom used but still available for possible expansion—and vanished from one side of the school to the other, passing the ancient defunct boiler, too large to exhume, on my way through the dark and dusty corridor. It was far enough from civil (and uncivil) company that I believed I could reason out what the fucking hell had just happened.

I climbed up the service entrance from the old kitchens to the modern (i.e. shiny and covered in gaudy sheet metal) science wing. I was now on the opposite side of campus, but I could still feel him, glaring down on me like some malevolent, churlish god. I wouldn't leave campus; if I did, I would certainly miss practice. I just needed some time to clear my head and knock some understanding into that offending organ, my brain. What had I done wrong? Was this just something that had been churning beneath the surface that a foul day tossed into relief?

*Müde, müde, müde.* I am so tired of people right now.

I climbed out of the wing onto the fire escape and sat on the roof to watch the sun go down. It must have been something I'd done to set him off. Those kinds of thoughts don't just come from nowhere... *Let us see*, I thought to myself, *he believes I do not pay him enough mind and blames my bibliophilic tendencies for my inattention.* Clearly.

Why now? We weren't even conversing properly. I *just* mentioned my admiration for a character while he was working on a take-at-home test, and he jumped at the chance to attack me. I didn't know what to do. I couldn't think of a rational train of thought to explain his behaviour. I just sat there, watching westward, until the start of evening rehearsal. As I picked my way back to the music room, I paused, then cursed energetically. We were beginning our choreography in earnest today. I turned around and took another hallway below the school...

All right, I admit it, most people don't know about this because most don't realise that our *beloved* academy used to be the only sanatorium in Davidson County. Well, it's their loss that they didn't realise that our spectacular architecture obviously predates the school's 1946 inception date. I suppose the children of Nashville's rich and famous have no need to crack open a local history book.

"And where were you?" Tucker glared from across the room when I entered, breathless and five minutes late.

"Disposing of a body, sir."

He rolled his eyes. "Is that why Death is late too?"

I boggled, trying to catch my breath and think critically at the same time. Man, I am out of shape. I'll need to start running again if I end up winded after such a mild sprint.

"I left him where he laid, sir. I—"

Of course he would run in from the other door at that propitious moment.

"Coach! I—" He caught sight of me and paused. I kept my eyes on Tucker, no need to grant the boy any more attention than the peripheral.

"Good, now if you prima donnas are done, we got a show to do."

I looked down, chastened.

"Sissi, go down stage right; Death, centre; Joseph, next to Sissi."

I followed his direction, but I was intensely uncomfortable with the scene we were to work on. It was near the end of act one.

I was vocally ruminating on whether anything I had experienced was real. Very existential, almost painfully so. I was sedately waltzing with Araz while Death watched from a raised dais. The final chorus was a duet, with Death telling an obviously distracted Sissi that the only thing real in this world is death and life. None of the details merited much notice for him, I suppose.

I was in a good mood for this sort of song, self-searching and lost, but the subtly lovelorn tone Death used would be difficult to attain if the actor hated me.

Araz and I waltzed at half time as I crooned softly. There was no need to overexert myself this early in the game, Tucker knew I could sing this song, after all. We wound a circular path, making loops and such but ultimately circumnavigating Death as if he were the sun and we, a reticent planet and moon.

When we finally reached the next verse (I was fouling up the dancing by leading Araz about like an idiot), I was surprised to hear the emotion in Hadrian's voice, as if it were already damned yet still trying for freedom. I looked up, choreography be damned, and he had his hand out, reaching for me. *I'm sorry, I had a bad day,* his eyes told me. I forgave him because I am an idiot. Well, forgive but not forget. I am not a total imbecile, after all.

3/15 FRIDAY
*(Typed, Encrypted)*

I've really too many feelings floating about my encephalon. This is the only place I can just express myself, no matter how desperately sad that sounds. I don't *have* to be a genius-level, fanatical scientist, or a madcap positive or surly isolationist, I can just say what I mean and mean what I say. This is also ridiculously sentimental bullshit. No wonder my earlier entries are so strange and incoherent. I'm trying to impress what essentially boils down to a diary recounting my interactions with a single person. What a fool am I...

Well, I certainly know how to pick them, that's all I have to say. Hadrian and I are at a bit of war. I won't give up my books, and he won't explain his outburst (which reminds me of how alike we can be when the mood strikes). If he would only tell me what he meant, I would be more amiable to doing as he pleads, but he is not building a very convincing argument. I'm perfectly all right with him keeping secrets, but if he wants me to do something, he should at least try to convince me instead of stubbornly telling me it's for my own good. That is simply bad rhetorical practice!

And the Ides of March is not a good time to try to convince me not to read *Julius Caesar*.

"But it's tradition. I always read Shakespeare today." Lend me your ears because Hadrian was having none of it.

"Tradition or not, you promised to cut down on the uptake, and that's gotta be the fourteenth book you've started this week." I gave his stubbornness a mulish look. So what if I had finished four books thus far, started another five, and bought another two for the future? That is only nine, including *Julius*, which I'll finish before the day is out!

"I made no such promise, and you know it." I crossed my arms and prepared to stare him down, confident I would win.

He gave me the most pathetic look you ever did see. "Please? I'll let you take me to that remake you were talking about." His lower lip even trembled ever so slightly. How could I say no and still claim to have a beating heart, working brain, and pubescent hormones?

So, I pouted a little to press home that I was capitulating under duress. "All right, I'll stop reading during *every* class, just the boring ones." Which was all of them excepting drama.

He gave me a pointed look.

"And sometimes even abstain in those. I would think you *live* to ruin my entertainment and leave me expired from tedium."

He desisted from his emotional attack and gave me a hug. I'm growing into such a sap. I swear I'll be baking cookies for my graduating class if this keeps up.

"Obviously," he smiled gamely. "Because we're watching *2012* tonight."

"*Oh, my Goethe,*" I moaned dramatically. "What about the reimagining of *Clarissa* with *aliens*?"

"Friday," he promised. "And I'll buy the popcorn."

My phone is ringing. Apparently, Hadrian wants to talk to me. I'll inform you if anything comes of it.


## NEAR MIDNIGHT
*(Written in a worn notebook)*

I'm about to be sick. I really am. My stomach is leading a massive revolt against the rest of my organs.

All right, I've thrown up, and I feel a touch better. The call was from Hadrian all right. He called to tell me that his father was still in the hospital and needed to talk to *someone* about it or he would explode. Apparently, poor Gregory went into surgery on Tuesday and still hasn't left the hospital, days later. Though his biopsy had confirmed it a benign tumour, it was monstrous in size and difficult to cut out. Age, as well, was a factor in his poor healing.

He nearly bled out on the operating table. Only a bit of quick thinking from one of the nurses saved his life. He's being kept under observation for a week, just in case. I demanded that I visit the first chance I could, and Hadrian said he was already at the hospital, that he would ask if his father was up to it.

I was already running to the Vanderbilt Medical Centre by the time I got the okay (Another excellent reason to always dress so that you can look presentable and still run a half marathon at the drop of a hat). I hung up on him as I entered the automatic doors to the waiting room. Not missing a step, I waved to the orderlies I knew and raced for the elevator, which I later regretted.

I needed to move and the run had only been a mile, maybe less. I fidgeted, watching the numbers slowly inch ahead. I speedwalked out of the elevator and down one hall, then another, looking for the damnable room number Hadrian had directed me to. He was waiting outside, fiddling with his phone. He looked up at me, slightly haunted, and tried to crack a smile.

"You still block my texts?"

"I forgot how to unblock it," I huffed, hands on my hips to open up my airways, allowing more oxygen making its way to my extremities.

He held out his hand. "I'll fix it."

I handed him the phone, looking at the closed door. "Is it all right that I go in? Should I have changed? Is he in pain?" It came out in a torrent.

He smiled grimly. "No, he'll be glad to see someone that's not a nurse or family. Go on in."

He looked so frail in that hospital bed, propped up and attired in a horribly pink-and-blue-chequered hospital gown. I froze when he turned to look at me.

He cocked his head. "Is that the little girl that went to the symphony with us, Carson?"

I wondered how he could fail to remember our subsequent meetings and why he was assuming a shadowed portion of the room housed his son. Ah, the other brother was sitting on the opposite side of the room, reading a book. I am *not* the paradigm of logistical thinking when I panic.

"Yeah, Dad, that's Hade's friend, Ina." He didn't even look up from his topsy-turvy (read: upside down) edition of *The Catcher and the Rye.*

"The icebreaker girl," he smiled, a little drugged up. "You've come to visit me?"

"I wanted to make sure you were well, Admiral." I tarried about the door, unsure.

"Oh, none of that, child," he waved dismissively. "I'm just glad you're not another nurse come to pester me."

"Just tell me their names, and I shall have a stern talking to them about staff/patient relations."

That got a smile out of him. "I'll have them down the moment I have a pen and paper with which to write."

I took a step closer to him, to better examine his face. "Fucking incompetent doctors," I breathed.

He looked even more delicate up close, as if he had aged millennia over the course of a week. "Doctors are not immune to error, but I appreciate the sentiment, my dear. Now come closer and tell me some more delightful stories of your fisherman friends. The family can be so dreary at times like this."

I came close enough to squeeze his hand before launching into a funny retelling of one Dover sailor telling ghost stories in a café overlooking the windswept sea.

He laughed uproariously despite himself. "I wish I could have met him, my dear. We would have got on smashingly! Hmm, you seem to have a talent for attracting old sea dogs like myself, I suppose?" His voice was feeble and uneven despite his efforts at an unconcerned drawl.

Only because I'm so lovely to talk to, I wanted to say, but that sounded too impertinent. I asked instead, "What was it like in the Navy? How did you come to that particular vocation?"

He favoured me with a grin that was practically brimming with mischief. "Oh, I liked the Navy very well, suited me perfectly. I was a second son, you see, so some sort of military occupation was a given for me. That or the rectory." He shuddered theatrically. "Yes, Her Majesty's Navy may not be as bustling as Elizabeth's, but I made my way."

"Where are you from, originally?" I had never asked, assuming he was British. Apparently not.

"The proud land of Denmark, child." He seemed surprised I had to ask, then remembered himself. "Of course, the name would send you astray! Gregory von Der Maase, at your service." He held out his hand, and I shook it, mildly befuddled.

"Why did you change your name, then?" Did you do something *bad*? I wanted to ask.

"You said you knew the nurses." Carson interrupted his father before he could speak. "Is there anyone you don't know in this city?" It was gentle and teasing but determinately steering the conversation away from sensitive topics.

"Carson, get me a water. I'm terribly parched."

The son sighed as if he'd already been asked a hundred times in the last few days, but kindly left without another word.

"There. Now, you would like to know why we changed our name, yes? Dreadful business that. Haven't even told my own children!" His eyes were lit with an unholy fire.

Oh, Robert Louis Stevenson, he *was* involved with organised crime! I knew it! I ruthlessly quashed my glee, unwilling to let a good secret escape for such a paltry reason as my curiosity.

"Sir, you've probably taken quite a bit of pain medicine. You might not want to be telling *me* any family secrets—"

He headed me off with a wave of his hand. "No, no. They don't want to know that my money didn't spring from nothing fully formed, and they don't *have* to know if they wish to remain ignorant. If you want to know, I will tell you. I'm not ashamed of my past." Even if it cost him his home and name? What had he done? "I was a bit of a rascal in the Navy, you see." He winked conspiratorially. "Once I got on the track towards admiralship, I straightened out *a bit*. They only noticed after nearly twenty years of service!"

I was very tempted to prompt him a bit but feared upsetting him in his present condition.

He looked out to the city lights beyond his window and sighed romantically. "Yes, I was stationed outside of Vietnam as a youth, the year Turkey butted into Cyprus, if I recall. It was my first boat, and I was eager to do *something*, you see, so I may have...bullied a few ships out of sheer boredom. Smugglers were pouring out of the country at the time, you understand. We would take the stolen goods, with the intention of returning them, of course, and sink the offending vessel. I say 'intend' of course because you wouldn't believe the money you can rake in using intimidation and scuba gear."

"Scuba gear?" I asked, breathless.

"I paid my way into a lovely little circumnavigation project years later. I spent quite a bit of time sending my sailors down to old wrecks to see if there was anything interesting down there. Wouldn't you?"

I stared at him, impressed and nearly disbelieving. "You're having me on," I breathed, secretly delighted.

"I swear on my life, even if it's not worth much. They found me out, but I had such loyal seamen that Her Majesty didn't bother to exile me. I later bowed out gracefully, for the politicians' sakes, of course." He nodded indulgently, probably imagining the stuffy aristocrats getting all in a tizzy over his activities and devil-may-care attitude.

"I applaud your daring, sir. That must have been quite an adventure; pirating and exploring all at the same time," I gushed.

He motioned for me to sit closer beside him, and I complied.

"It was quite a life, I must say. I shall miss it once I'm gone, of course. I should have wanted to see *all* of my children married, and at least one grandchild, but one can't have everything in this life."

My heart clenched. He couldn't die, I wouldn't let him.

"You're not going to die, sir. It's just hospital. They always gave me the willies."

His accent just cried out for me to intertwine my speech with British vernacular, even if I didn't notice the code-switching at the time.

"No, I'm fairly sure the end is near. I am glad I shall die on land rather than be lost to the sea."

I wanted to cry and hit him simultaneously. "Don't be silly. I don't visit dying people. I only visit people who live to be one hundred and three. Are you going to disappoint me?" I gave him the stern schoolmarm look I learned from my great-grandmother (who could corral fifteen children with that look and taught me well).

He laughed, and it sounded stronger than before, to me at least. "Then I shall just have to live another thirty-seven years. Oh, what a trial that shall be!" he cried bombastically, even adding a touch of careful arm-waving for emphasis.

"Good, glad we got that out of the way." We talked a bit more before both brothers reentered with a water pitcher and glass clinking with ice.

"Took you long enough," Gregory grumbled, taking long draws from the glass. "I was quite parched!"

"Sorry, we couldn't find any ice, Dad. You're looking better, though," Hadrian insisted. I'm not sure if he was telling the truth. As I talked with him, he just seemed to get weaker and weaker, more and more vulnerable.

He sounded honest, though (but he *is* a more accomplished actor than I am). Of course, I was weaving back and forth between convincing myself the man would outlive me and utterly sure he would die in my arms this very second. Panic is not a pleasant state for me to exist in. Not at all.

"I feel better. This girl of yours has a lovely bedside manner."

I felt suddenly sickened by the praise. I didn't feel helpful at all.

"Such a delightful child."

I didn't see anyone else's reaction as I stood slowly, carefully. I couldn't stay any longer. I felt suffocated in the tiny, scrubbed-down box—no, *cage*. "I'm glad I could be of some use, but I'm afraid I have a seven o'clock shift tomorrow at the House. I think I've imposed on you long enough."

We made our goodbyes, but Hadrian must have followed me out. I walked to the staircase; it was closer than the elevator by measures. I stifled a few sniffles on my sleeve. I couldn't break down, not until I was out of the way. That's what I recall thinking.

I opened the door, closed it behind me, and cried as I flew down the steps.

"Inanna!"

I ignored the noise as I tried not to impale myself on something in my frenzied flight. I ran blindly out of the hospital and into the night. I will never again go into another hospital. Never. Not even if my heart literally skips a beat and threatens to stop altogether. I'll die at home where at least everything is familiar and warm and smells right and...

Needless to say, I am a bit of a wreck. I am in need of sleep, enough sleep to blot out the existence of sorrow in the world.


## 3/25 MONDAY
*(Typed, Encrypted)*

Gregory von Der Maase/Marshall is hale and hearty once again, and I can't help but resent him a bit and, through him, Hadrian. He stayed in the hospital for nearly a fortnight and was released on Friday. Hadrian kept me updated on his progress because I patently refused to see him again. I sent him funny little cards to cheer him up through Hadrian, but not much else. I freely admit I am horrified by hospitals and always will be.

Now, it has become difficult to look at Hadrian and not think of his father. If I think of his father, I am just trapped in other cyclical guilt trips and painful hospital memories that stretch back for years. It's simply terrible for my health. So, of course I take to avoiding Hadrian who now thinks that I am dreadfully disgusted with him for...something. Possibly for seeing his father in such a sorry state.

I don't know how I'm going to lookat him and sing so tenderly at the end of Act Two when all I see in his eyes is actual Death staring me in the face.

**3/29 FRIDAY**
*(Dream Journal)*

It was winter. The cold bit and nipped at my bare toes as I struggled with a heavy cart, carrying bodies. The stench was awful, decay and sickness hung in the air as I sent the poor creatures to their final resting place. It was black-and-white. Like an ancient movie, there was no sound. No music played in the background; I couldn't even hear the sound of my feet crunching into the snow.

I could only smell and feel, desperate and hurting. I stumbled, and a hand reached out to grab the cart handle away from me. It was Hadrian's father, gaunt and bruised. He pointed solemnly at the bodies, and I looked, fearful as to what I was carrying. It was—too horrible to describe. I woke up screaming for Mother. Of course, no one came.

# April

4/1 MONDAY
*(Typed, Encrypted)*

Like an idiot, I nearly cried in class today. I have been unsuccessful in straightening out the Hadrian problems as of late, so I'll just describe them as quickly as possible to get them off of my chest.

He honestly thinks I despise him or something equally insane. He gives me all of these sad, pathetic looks, and I can't take it. It makes me sick to think of anything anymore. I thought I was better; *no, I am* better. This is just a minor upset, a blip, a cosmic burp to upset me.

I have been trying desperately to explain it to him, but just looking at him sends me into fits. I've taken to hiding on the roof or in the basement instead of staying in the more trafficked thoroughfares of campus. Really, I've evolved into the Phantom of the Academy in the last week or so.

I'll get over it. I have to. I am confident that if I take in his visage in small, steadily increasing increments, I will be right as rain by the end of the month. If not, I shall simply ignore every instinct I have and continue with the show. I have been able to convince Tucker that I am perfectly fine, just in the midst of another "lover's spat", as he so delicately calls it. No matter that neither of us is romantically interested in the other.

My father has mellowed once again from his most recent breakdown. Apparently, a lull in activity from me causes a loosening of parental paranoia to ensue from him and a higher than average possibility of him completing his work without incident. Felicitations. He hasn't called me to account for any less-than-perfect grades. He has a greater chance of noticing such things the longer I am around him, and I have been steering clear of everyone as of late.

It is refreshing not to fear your own father's actions. He would never hit me, of course, but he has been rather abrasive as of late. Now, he's almost acting like normal, possibly because I'm staying at home and not stirring up trouble...

Oh, I saw Mr. Collins last week and realised that I never noted when he finally stopped going into hysterics when he caught my eye. Really, a crying man is so unattractive when the cause is the mere presence of a teenage girl.

But, yes, enough of digressing. I shall inform you as to my similar act of hysterics during fourth period, which I have still been attending rather sporadically since winter break. We were doing something so simple an infant could do it without a calculator. 'Twas so incredibly boring, I could nap in class. I read *Serf Anna* instead (because I was feeling masochistic), and I had just reached a point of no return for the protagonist.

She could open the door, so to speak, and realise the Count's dirty laundry like the heroine in *Bluebeard*, or she could relapse into "sickness" and refuse to meet with the mysterious conspirator with "frighteningly piercing" green eyes. She started feeling honestly faint during dinner, and I realised her choice had been made for her. The count had drugged her plate or ordered someone to do it for him, more like. He doesn't dirty his own hands for anything.

As you can see, the fall of a particularly intriguing protagonist along with my own rubbed raw emotions led to a quiet round of snuffling and claims of early-onset seasonal allergies. I was not very well put together for drama, and thus didn't inform Hadrian of why I was acting so strangely. Somehow he took, "I don't know. Something in the room must have set me off," to mean "I hate you and never want to see you again." Or at least that is what I could surmise from his facial expression at least.

That boy is just so sensitive. Needless to say, I couldn't take that, especially when he looked like he would keep his lovingly made lunch all to himself. I did not have the strength to go through the day on six o'clock oatmeal and pineapple alone.

I collapsed against him and cried instead of forming a convincing argument. Really any argument pales in comparison to the emotional release created by tears, and, besides, Hadrian is not the most reasonable child I've ever met. The emotional approach is usually the better one when it comes to him, and he is so beautifully manipulated by tears, as well.

Thankfully, we were outside, where no one ever went for any discernible reason. Maybe because I spread a rumour that the ghosts of tortured students still played in that part of campus? It was part of the school's lush array of urban legends now. (Say it with me now; Huzzah for impressionable freshmen!)

In any case, he stood there stiffly as I mussed up his shirt. And I discovered that it was so much easier to talk to him when I didn't have to see his face. *Who would have thought?*

"I don't hate you, damn it. Just-just don't make me look at you, and I'll be—fine," I hiccupped as he closed his arms around me.

"So there's something wrong with my face now?" He sounded hurt, but relief had outweighed it by a ton and a half of emotional baggage.

"Jus-Just let me cry." And we stood in silence for a while until I got a hold of myself. "Sorry, insomnia and compelling narrative."

"What?" It was really interesting to hear his voice through his chest, I noted dully. "Are you crying because of that door-stopper you lug around?"

"Yes?" I took a peek at him and found his visage much more agreeable after such an emotional release. I could deal with him better now. A good cry always helps clear the head of nasty hang-ups.

"God, Ina. Don't scare me like that." Scare him? What does that even mean? He patted me between the shoulder blades, and I pulled away. "You really shouldn't care so much about characters; you always pick horrible stories to get invested in. Why couldn't you just get a nice, fluffy romance instead?"

"I'd die of boredom. It's not my fault I'm gushing blood—"

"Oh God. Please, do *not* finish that sentence. Just for my peace of mind, please."

I smiled privately as we walked back to class. I really had no desire to explain any of my complex neuroses to him at the moment. Vivid imagery always works well as a deterrent. Hurrah for American prudishness.

We only had six minutes until drama began again. He accepted my explanation without further comment and let me go back to drama unscathed. I still can't look at his face for prolonged periods without wanting to bawl or run away, but actually crying has syphoned much of the power behind that urge, rendering it mostly manageable. I shudder to think what it would be like to actually see his father again.

NB: Send another card of encouragement to Gregory. I've only sent three thus far, and that is *not enough*.


## 4/20 SATURDAY
*(Written in a worn notebook)*

I've been extremely busy as of late; Vanderbilt has been asking if my repeated attendance and participation in certain departments merit automatic credit or not. I think they just want a reason to push me through the undergraduate programme and later through their graduate programme so I can work for them full-time for nepotism's sake.

I realise that sometimes I must come off as an insufferable genius who never had to try at being smart, but that's not true. I'm not actually exceptional. My parents just never let me quit or do anything less than spectacularly well in any given area of my life. It's amazing what that sort of insurmountable pressure can foster in a child.

And I honestly am not any more competent than any other student my age. I have just been afforded several opportunities to ingratiate myself with professors before I even knew what the word "ingratiate" actually meant. They do so like the familiar, those instructors of our youth. I'm sure it's the department heads pushing the mountains of paperwork on me as well. I shall have to quit working for money just to keep up under this workload...

Switching gears now. *Dreams* has been going along swimmingly, if at a lightning-fast pace. We have finished choreography and shall start doing run-throughs and ironing out details before the end of the week.

Tech for this show will be painful, I already know, but I will not bend and make it easier on actors or techies. They will make my vision perfect, or I will start defenestrating people right and left, even if there are no windows in the theatre. I will drag them across campus if I have to.

The Hadrian front is still mired in a classic Russian winter; frozen, incomprehensible, and impossible to ford for another six months if not longer. He's no longer afraid that I loathe him utterly and completely, but I have heard him muttering to his posse that "girly problems" shouldn't last this long, should they?

I nearly laughed at his infantile behaviour before chastising myself. I was the one being infantile. I couldn't separate memories from faces from relatives. If that is not the saddest thing, I don't know what is. At least he's stopped asking impertinent questions for the moment. Probably because I must look ready to start wailing pathetically whenever he's about to grill me for answers.

I'm fine. I just wanted to write that down, you see. I am fine. Regardless of what I may say, I am in full control of my faculties and headed toward a bright future in academia. All is well on the damned Western Front, or I'll eat my hat. I am only acting like a teenager.

And I may just be a moody teenager, but I'll be damned if I am not surrounded by teenagers equally moody and not nearly as erudite and eloquent about sharing their feelings as me. My emotional turmoil is being blown out of proportion because that is all you hear about. No one else thinks I'm ready to collapse in on myself—

And, of course, today is the day everyone is supposed to light up a joint and pass around Mary Jane (I only just saw two "Rastafarian" white boys pass by, red-eyed and giggling. Must they be so pitifully obvious, and in the park no less?).

I really truly wish I could do the same sometimes. Maybe then I could relax at school, at home, in my sleep... I need another break, damn it, and I don't know *any* of the drug dealers on campus. Shoot.


4/27 SATURDAY
*(Typed, Encrypted)*

I really hate bad dreams; they have the queerest ability to ruin your entire day before you even wake up. I'm writing in here, not another update regarding Hadrian (because that train wreck has not yet had the decency to clean itself up on its own) but an entreaty to myself.

I looked back, just scanning some of my previous entries, and found that I am a thoroughly warped personality bent on making a villain out of everyone because I don't want to be open with people about the things that rip and tear me to bits. So, I am sorry. I am so sorry that I cannot fix myself like I thought. I cannot free myself from my own demons, and I am afraid I'll always be saddled with them.

So, Self, if you ever look back and think "Wow, I was certainly melodramatic as a teenager. Glad I grew out of that in a hurry." Good on you. If you commiserate or find yourself one-upping my current misery, move to the Australian Outback and disavow modern life altogether, please. Don't wait. Just do it. If you can't be better than this, then there is no point in keeping my memory alive at all.

Burn all of my writings and destroy this computer while you're at it too.

# May

**5/1 WEDNESDAY**
*(Typed, Encrypted)*

Tomorrow is final dress, and I think I have my melodrama behind me. I am no longer a wreck around *anyone*, thank you very much, my singing has much improved with my health, and I am skipping two and a half years of school before I even start. How marvellous!

I think I have trained Hadrian never to ask me anything because he sort of winces whenever he asks me even the most benign of questions. It's a little funny and a touch sad at the same time. I am a terrible person sometimes, aren't I?

Also, Hadrian is going to have to actually kiss me tomorrow, which will be awkward and weird for the both of us. We shall ford through it, though, because we are...thespians (Feel free to insert a dramatic pose and jazz hands in your mind's eye here). Actors can fib and connive their way out of anything if they are talented enough. That seems to be the only thing I am good at.

I can't take on a persona to save my life. I just identify a part of myself with that character to understand their motivation and lie like I got caught out after midnight with a beer in one hand and a baggy of coke ready to be snorted in the other ("Of course I'm not underage, Officer. I know Tennessee law has a curfew for teenagers. Beer? What beer? This is just one of those non-alcoholic beers, see? Look at the label. That on the table? Baking soda, it's a sight gag.").

And I am digressing way too much...even if that baking-soda line is pure gold. Tucker told me I didn't have to make "kissy faces (Immature much?)" with "lover boy," but I told him I was mature enough to fake it like the rest of the world. He just laughed at me, and I sniffed disapprovingly.

Hadrian has yet to comment on this upcoming occurrence at all, which is a little confusing, but hey. We have never honestly discussed our love lives outside of his angry protestations of chastity earlier in the year, so maybe we won't discuss this (Even after the play has closed, we most likely shan't broach the topic). This just screams exciting times at Ridgemont High, doesn't it? No, not at all, but I really love the title of that old movie, don't you?

Again, I stray from the point. I am sure that everything will be fine from now on. I'm not freaking out at the mere sight of unpleasant memories, which is more important to me than the fact that *Dreams* may actually come out smelling of roses, strange as that may sound.

I didn't need another vacation. I just needed a few moments out of the day to stop and think and accept things (and run. Running is good). I thought I hadn't needed them, but I accept that I do. I'm glad it is such an easy thing to achieve moments of meditation in this school. The classes are dull enough to lull you to sleep.


5/3 FRIDAY
*(Typed, Encrypted)*


I was walking backstage before the show started, in my bloody and artfully torn camouflage, inspecting props. It wasn't my job, but as this production is *my* baby, I feel I have a right to inspect whatever I see fit at any time. We finally have all of our fresh, replaceable props set out all nice and neat on top of their glow-tape labels.

False guns, false beards, tea set, marquis hat, ornamental fan, bouquet... I paused to examine the bouquet used in act two and the wedding scene in act one more closely. It seems they followed the stage directions to the letter ("cool colours with a pop of yellow"). I was impressed.

It was pretty to say the least: poppies in a brilliant purple colour, a ragged green plant with shiny black seeds, bluebells perhaps, buttercups, lovely little yellow blossoms, more decorative leaves, and delicate blue morning glories. The carefully wrapped base felt a bit weird, though. I put it back into the vase and continued my perusal. Everything is in order, I am proud to say, and I am now ready for my final first performance.


5/4 SATURDAY
*(Typed, Encrypted)*


Everything went swimmingly, I'm proud to announce. No big mess-ups, no horrible miscommunication with the audience. Life is so good I could walk on air. I may have strayed as of late in the purpose of this writing, but no one is going to read it so it matters not what I put in it. I have no reason to use this as blackmail material or evidence to the police or whatever nonsense I was intending at the start. I was a bit perturbed about the whole kissing thing, but I'll tell you at a later date what that is about. I have to get ready for the next performance tonight. Wish me a torrid flurry of bad luck!

5/5 SUNDAY
*(Typed, Encrypted)*

Still walking on air before I go to the cast party (which *I* am actually hosting out of peer pressure). Yesterday and today were even more luminescent than opening night, and my father arrived today! I found him milling in the throng of people after it was over and sought him out.

"You did well, Myshka. I have a gift." He thrust a bouquet of yellow roses at me, and I accepted them, a little teary-eyed. He can be so sweet when he tries hard enough.

"I love you, Daddy," I murmured, giving him a hug and smearing a bit of grease paint on his cheek in the process. "Use my special soap under the sink. It will come out, I promise." I laughed when he made to touch his cheek, a strange emotion flitting across his face.

"Are you going to run away tonight?" my father asks.

We had already discussed the party, and he only told me he was going out to eat and take "a very long time" to get back, which probably means he will come back at around ten, long after everyone has left and I have cleaned up.

He bid me farewell, and I turned to find all of Hadrian's family staring at me from across the crowded room. Oh boy. I wove through the crowd to find Hadrian getting his head kissed by his mother. He blushed through his makeup, a major achievement because I really packed on that greasepaint to achieve that "alien, sensual Death" look.

"I didn't know you wrote this! It was fabulous," Viviane gushed.

"Wait, you wrote this?" Hadrian was a mite confused.

"I bet you only looked at the playbill long enough to find your name spelled correctly." I smiled, avoiding the admiral's eye and giving Hadrian a friendly nudge.

"Great job up there, but why have we never seen you out here, before? We've been to every performance," Carson queried.

"I usually don't stay, but this one is very special." I shrugged a little. "This is my baby, and I fought tooth and nail to get it on stage. I'm proud of it."

"We could tell, though Hade could have cut the kiss down a bit. Less tongue maybe, little brother?" I rolled my eyes as Hadrian blushed brighter.

"God. Carson—" His mother decided to take pity on him.

"How did you come to pick this particular play?" she asked, looking down her nose at me.

"It's always been a favourite of mine, and I submit recommendations for our director. It was just fortunate that he trusts me enough to translate a musical and take care of the logistics."

"What if you had failed?" she enquired politely.

"We would have been doing *High School Musical* instead."

Even Hadrian shuddered at the ignominy.

I would have continued the conversation had my phone not vibrated against my thigh. "Excuse me." I did a little curtsy automatically and bustled out of the crowd to pull up my dress and free the silly thing from my garter.

Of course it would be Alexzander Leitmotif, himself. "I have the live music. It was...acceptable."

My legs nearly dropped from beneath me. That is *high* praise for a man of his calibre. Very high.

"Do you have a video of it?"

"I'll send it in tonight." I gushed. "What did you think of the last-minute inflection change in the Boer war section? I know it was surprising, but the boy couldn't sing that high and—"

"This is a quick call, chick. Got business."

My mood dampened a bit.

"Anyway, I wanted to know how you wanted to pitch this to the American producers. Would you like to write the synopsis? My English is perfect—"

I had never heard him speak anything but German.

"—but I thought you would like to." He had obviously reached his business.

I could hear loud music pounding in the background and voices greeting him seductively. "I'd love to, just—"

Leitmotif growled out suddenly "Come here, lover" and hung up. Well, at least he had a good reason to cut the call short. Sex is a good reason for discourteousness, right?

(Answer: No)

I am about to leave for my party, which should at least be a little smashing with all the inflated heads congregated in one enclosed space. Shall inform more fully on the activities' termination.


5:27

*(Written in a worn notebook)*


It seems being so close to an actual college campus has its uses. By the time everyone had arrived at my house and attempted valiantly to eat me out of house and home, no one wanted to watch our last play or reminisce about plays long past. Instead, they hemmed and hawed about how much fun it would be to crash a *college party.* Eager to get the ungrateful whelps out of my abode, I directed them to one of the dorms famous for its excess (even on a Sunday). They escaped in droves until it was just Hadrian and me.

"Why haven't you left?" I was rearranging the artful little embroidered pillows that had been disrupted in the hubbub. Sometimes, I think our sitting room would better decorate a doll's house than a true human residence. There's too much lace and doilies in here for my tastes, even if father refuses to redecorate.

"I can party next year. Wanna watch a movie?"

I shrugged and pointed at our meagre movie collection.

"How about...are all these movies period documentaries?"

"Maybe." I drew out the word and studiously avoided his gaze. He laughed at my faux reticence. "We have that movie-renting thing, though. We could watch one of those." He pulled out the remote and fiddled with it until the cheerful renting programme exploded onto the TV screen. All the recommendations were, of course, documentaries. Hadrian ribbed me endlessly as he picked an old Sherlock Holmes movie starring Basil Rathbone.

We're watching it right now, and it's a little funny in a dated sort of way. The most recent conversation, however, was not so funny.

"Are you glad it's over? No more stressing over lines, no more dance lessons, no more kissing in front of hundreds of people..."

I was in the kitchen making popcorn and glad of it, or I'm sure I would have done more than drop an empty bowl in surprise.

"You all right?" he enquired.

"I'm sure there weren't *hundreds* of people, Hadrian. Your hyperbole is not appreciated," I sniffed, gathering the shards of stoneware as I spoke. "But I am glad school is almost over. I only have AP Physics C and Economics left."

"Lucky you. No exams to take at school. You just get to kick back and relax until college starts." Thank Petrarch he wasn't going to dwell on the utter discomfiture that was our onstage kissing (I'll tell you later, I swear). I brought out the popcorn and sat beside him.

Then he ruined it. "Hey, why don't you date?"

"Why don't you?" I shot back, uncomfortable.

"I'm hung up on someone who sorta hates me," he replied easily.

That poor girl, wherever she is. I wondered if she was from his last school, where he was admittedly less popular. I would have at least noticed if he were mooning over a girl here. He wouldn't have much time to moon, though; they would be upon him so quickly, quite like ravenous beasts upon an abandoned carcass.

"Well, that's a shame."

"And you?"

"Oh, I don't like it."

"Dating?"

"Yes. I don't see the point, especially in high school. I mean, I don't see any allure in courtship or romance outside of traditionalism and presenting proof of suitability as a mate. Sex is probably lovely, though."

"Oh my god."

"I'm being serious. Now, I kissed you for the last few days and that was nice enough. Masturbating is *great*—"

"Oh *god*."

I forged through his embarrassment by increasing my volume as I returned to the den. Everyone masturbates. That shouldn't be a taboo topic.

"So combining the two, *should* be lovely. Am I right?"

He avoided my attention in favour of shoving popcorn into his mouth.

"I can wait you out easily, you know," I pointed out.

"Yeah," he said through the popcorn. "Yeah, it's great."

"Exactly. But romantic relationships are messy, inefficient, and a nexus of misunderstandings and resentments."

"What about going on dates? Holding hands? Knowing they're always on your side?"

"Friends do that? And investing all of my feelings in one person, expecting them to support me completely and agreeing to do the same and more is just begging for disaster."

"Friends and girlfriends aren't the same thing. Like. At all."

"Right, so if we were dating, how would we act differently?" I asked. Well. Demanded.

"Well. I'd kiss you—"

"Outside of sex stuff."

He narrowed his eyes in thought, and I watched him try so very hard. "I'd. Well. I'd—"

"You wouldn't," I crowed. "You wouldn't do anything different outside of fucking me."

"Fuck off," he said crabbily. "I didn't say that."

"You couldn't think of anything."

"Absence of evidence doesn't equal evidence of absence. God."

"You're being obtuse," I said victoriously. "But you're still my *Liebling*."

He pushed me, which led to a shrieking tickle battle that I won handily, and—

And I forgot my knapsack at school. Idiot.


UPDATE:


We are on our way, and even though Hadrian is chastising me for writing instead of figuring out how to break into the school, I am unperturbed. No one is there on Sundays, our school is Christian after all, so it will be easy to enter, capture my quarry, and return.

He doesn't agree, but he doesn't know this school like I do. When I was an incredibly moody freshman, I would sneak into school on the weekends and write angsty poetry, which I have since mostly burned in a blazing Guy Fawkes Day-style celebration.

This will be child's play. Our janitor, bless his heart, is always losing his keys. Thus, he leaves at least one door open, namely the service entrance above the defunct extensive kitchens slowly mouldering away under the students' feet (for they aren't the adventurous sort, I'm afraid). I shall rendezvous through the basement, up into the backstage, pick up my phone and accoutrement cooling its heels in our green room, and return without a fuss.

Why Hadrian insisted he come with me, I cannot fathom. He may think there will be heavy lifting involved so that he may valiantly come to my rescue. Heh, really, Prince Charming, it is much harder to impress ladies in this day and age, especially with the advent of heroines like Nancy Drew. Who needs men anyway?


## 5/5 SUNDAY
*(Written in short-hand on the cover page of a notebook)*

I can see what lies ahead more clearly than anyone. The Chaos. The unbending Fate of us all. The cold fingers are closing about my throat, and my mind may be racing, but my fingers— I write now, before this witch's brew rots my lungs. Fucking disaster, all of this. Fucking world is gonna end late but still end. Goddamn everything, I want my Mütti.

## 5/6 MONDAY
*(Dream Journal)*

There was a girl, with sun-bleached hair and a beaded skirt that chimed in the wind, who was standing on a beach, masses of flowers in her arms as faraway mushroom clouds erupted on the horizon.

"Goodbye, Daddy," she said softly. "Maybe you shouldn't have been a fucking terrorist." Glassy, facsimile human bodies exploded from the sand behind her, and He put His hand on her shoulder.

"In another world, you saved them all." His voice was low but not frightening.

"In another world, they deserved to be saved," she responded and kissed him.

...

I don't even know.


## 5/7 TUESDAY
*(Typed, Encrypted)*

Well, I'm out of the hospital, almost hale and hearty. It was quite an adventure last Sunday, let me tell you. I'd almost call it a setup, if that weren't patently ridiculous.

After leaving Hadrian in the car, I walked across the lawn to the eastern-most edifice, the athletics building. As I knew it would, the little gate beneath the sweeping stone staircase was unlocked. I made my way through the darkness, depending on the little windows near the ceiling for illumination. Into the assembly hall and across the lawn, I scampered, relishing in the thrill that comes of doing something technically unlawful and getting away with it (for

I suppose I can be the little daredevil when the mood strikes me). I went backstage, then to the green room, and then returned backstage only to stop.

The bouquet wasn't where it should have been. It should have either been in the trash like the ones from Friday and Saturday or sitting on the prop table where I dropped it after the performance. Instead, it lay on its side, smack in the middle of my path. I would have crushed it underfoot or at least noted its existence had it been there seconds before.

I picked it up, frowning. Then I heard a noise, the definite sound of footsteps coming straight for me. I turned, my heart pounding. It was a stranger, shrouded in the shadow created by multitudinous draperies and his flashlight pointed in my direction. I shifted my pack slightly, trying to pick out identifying features.

"Who are you?" I recalled the robber at Baker Street and stood taller. I could take him if need be.

"Get out." His voice was gravelly, obviously clumsily disguised.

"Identify yourself, or I'll call the police. I have authority to patrol these halls, do you?" A lie, but if you insert enough bravado into your tone, everything sounds authoritative.

"Drop it and walk away." He raised a gun to punctuate his point, and I panicked.

"You shouldn't have done that. You know how long you'll be incarcerated if you're convicted of a gun crime? Decades! Our congressmen only just extended the minimum sentence last month!" I took a step back, and he matched it.

"I'm not getting caught, though, am I?"

*Holy shit, he is going to shoot me dead and bury me out back in the woods,* I thought. I realised at precisely that moment that prudence was the better part of valour.

I ran, slipped out of the auditorium with him clambering to find my path, light swinging wildly in the darkness. He obviously wasn't a student/alumni, or he would have known the way. Who was he? Left, right, down a flight of steps, losing him steadily as I went, but I had no way out.

None of the doors would open for me, and I had not yet passed a fire alarm to alert the authorities (Damn budget cuts reduced the safety of everyone in the building). He was still too close for comfort as I ran into the "teacher only" district of offices and defunct smoking lounges. I slid into an ancient dumbwaiter in the teacher's lounge and plummeted down a story onto harsh concrete.

(They were probably getting lazy in the later renovations and left it as is; thinking no one would be stupid enough to wrench the painted-over slat up and leap into an industrial-sized laundry chute)

Damned if it hadn't hurt, but I kept going. I had to get to the car, and, in order to do that, I had to escape through the only door in the complex I knew for sure was open. I lengthened my strides to minimise pain, running blindly as twilight set in, lowering visibility *even more*. Damn it.

I took a side door towards the science hall when I heard *something* coming from the main transecting path under the lawn. I was nearly to the athletics department, regardless of my winding path and loping gait. If I could get out of the school, I could sprint to the car. It wasn't far. But he cut me to the chase, somehow. In all probability, he'd abandoned his search for me and was making his way out of the building.

If I were not about as clever as a concussed duck, I would have realised this and stayed hidden until he'd vacated, but alas, he must have noticed my foolish self,

Robbie Burns take me. I saw him pausing with a stitch in his side ahead of me in the half darkness, so I strafed across the way and into the boiler room, knocking about the rusted door in my rush. Smart, In, you are *so good* at being inconspicuous, aren't you?

I paused to control my breathing, taking in my surroundings. *What in the world?* The room was filled with similar flora to the ones clutched in my hand. They were all in a clump beneath the lumbering AC monstrosity jutting from the ceiling. *What is going on?* I wondered, half horrified. I took a deep breath, absorbing the sickly sweet aroma of decaying flowers and harsh coal dust.

He found me as I fumbled for my phone. "Should have left." I turned to see his gun held to my face, and he ordered me, "Move." I fled to the middle of the room, where he had gesticulated with his deadly weapon. "Stay."

The flashlight was stowed in favour of a lighter, and into the pile of flowers the resultant flame went. He slammed the door as smoke billowed up immediately. *Oh no, it might catch the whole school ablaze!*

I dropped everything and pulled off my cardigan to smother the flames. Thankfully, it was no more than a smudge, but the smoke was acrid and burned down my nostrils, entwining with tongue and setting my body to horrible wracks of heaving. Of course, that sent more smoke into my lungs (Thanks, involuntary reactions. I do so love your attempts to end my life as quickly as possible).

My lips numbed frighteningly fast as my eyes watered. I pulled the cardigan to my face and staggered out of the room, into fresher (if mouldy) air. My head spun, and I stumbled along the wall, grabbing blindly for my bag, thankfully. The hall seemed infinitely darker than it was before. I didn't know it at the time, but I had been poisoned, severely. Jubilations.

I looked ahead and lurched onward, determined to exit forthwith. I nearly made it out of the claustrophobic surroundings before the more terrifying symptoms presented themselves. I felt like I was on the moon and Jupiter at once. My head was spinning as the dark shades before me coalesced into bright, malicious spirits. Their grotesque misplaced features looked as if they had been carefully taken apart and reassembled by a particularly malevolent child.

They dared me to try to get past them, that they would add my limbs to their collection without speaking words from any language humans could even *speak*. I wavered, insensible and afraid. I had dropped my security before I killed the fire, I knew. I couldn't turn back, though. When I looked aft, the ground was simply gone. I swayed over the abyss before turning back to the spirits.

They had vanished from my path. Instead, they were behind me, urging me to run, to catch up and have my revenge on the man. "He is the one who did this, after all. Did you not see?" the poison was whispered sibilantly into my ear. The mere thought enraged me past seeing. "He wished to bring us here. And all our ilk. He is our kin."

I staggered drunkenly east, through the dark and into the light, where the fiends abandoned me for their gloomy repose. The building was old, and I'd ripped my arms to shreds breaking open the trap door connecting this building with the rest of the school. It was the morgue outbuilding I found myself in, I realise now. I'd never visited it myself, and now I never shall again.

The peeling paint actually liquefied and travelled back to its original place. Everything reformed into what it was, and I staggered drunkenly passed ghostly patients and sallow nurses. They touched me too. All of the hallucinations seemed very eager to touch me, to pull me away from rotten flooring and unwieldy stairs. They whispered secrets that vanished once I threw myself at the door hard enough to break the rotten wood from its hinges, padlocks be damned.

The sun was setting and great tendrils of light came hurtling down ahead of me, crashing into the building and tearing at masonry. I weaved pathetically through the tumult, yelling for amnesty. It took ages to make my way to the grass beyond the forests, the manicured lawns of precious, damned Jackson Academy of the Sciences.

The late-afternoon sunshine made monsters out of the trees and the path back to school. They tore at my skin most rudely, shouting in some made-up tongue that I was too close. That the veil was too thin. I thought I saw a shining sword and vivid ink on skin.

I don't think I even found the vehicle under my own steam. I remember seeing Hadrian swooping for me and the sensation of flight before things became too blurry to divine articulate meaning.

I must have written that message in the front of my notebook while under the influence. The handwriting is so spiky and unlike my own scrawl. I'd rather think it wasn't from my hand at all. I'm not even sure what I meant by it, I *was* utterly cracked at the time.

I woke up next in the hospital, attached to numerous hideous machines but alive and still hallucinating. It was awful. I sat there and talked...to no one. There was no one there, and yet I saw... I was horrified beyond words when the nurse came in and bodily put me back into the bed. I hadn't even realised I was in motion, but it had said we were in danger, and I... No words can describe how appalling it was. Hospitals invariably make things worse.

The attendants were understandably perturbed that I was still tripping when I had been under observation and mild sedation for several hours. I had to have my stomach pumped, would you believe? They couldn't get a decent answer out of me, so they attempted to treat me as well as they could. They must have believed that I had taken some sort of hallucinogen and ran afoul of a fire. As I came down, I suppose I started making sense, even if my first language had somehow switched to German.

It would have been funny had I not been in rather serious peril. It took me a little while, but I managed to tell them, in broken English, that I had been exposed to the fumes of burning plants. They searched my bag for the offending bouquet and immediately put me out to filter the numerous poisons out of my system. How grand. Father and Hadrian were waiting for news and came to visit me as soon as I was able to take visitors Monday afternoon.

Father gathered me up in his arms and begged me not to do anything like this again or *so help me god, I shall lock you in your room until you learn to take care of yourself.* I was jubilant that he had skipped classes to visit me.

Hadrian came in later and just held my hand, silent and watchful as a gargoyle trying to keep worse demons at bay with his stoic, slightly terrifying expression. Which I appreciated in my own way.

I had already told the staff all that had occurred and thus had policemen waiting in the wings to take my statement and inform me on the situation. Apparently it had been a veritable witch's brew of poisons. Belladonna, Aconite, Henbane, Poppy, and Mandrake along with the several other noxious herbs.

I suppose they gave a sample of the herbs to our prop's manager to incriminate someone in our department (Right, as if any of us were stupid enough to wave evidence in the face of the audience. Excuse me while I laugh). Why someone would want to send everyone into delirium at best or kill us at worst, I could not fathom. I trusted that the police would find the man and deal with him.

I was released today (Thank *Livy*), and I am amazingly not under house arrest. Hadrian also followed me home and parked me onto my own couch as if he were the host.

"So," he said. "That was fucked up."

"Yes."

"I think you should see a therapist," he said all in a rush.

"Excuse me?"

"That was fucked up. You are fucked up—"

"You're insulting me less than ten minutes out of the *hospital*?"

"Sorry, but I'm not wrong."

"So you, what, want to institutionalise me?"

"Look, you're not crazy, but that fucked you up. You can't be *human* and not be fucked up by that."

"People drop acid and don't immediately need psychiatric help."

"People who drop acid don't get chased around by a crazy gunman." He was working himself into a lather. "Look, talk to her once. That's all I'm asking. If you don't need her, then fine. I won't bug you about it. Just please, for both our sakes. I'll sleep better at night knowing you're talking to *someone*, because I know you're not gonna tell me jack shit."

Oh, this was for him, then? Fine. No skin off my nose indulging him.

The fucker.

5/13 MONDAY
*(Written in the margins of a worn notebook)*

Happy Birthday, Mütti.


5/17 FRIDAY
*(Typed, Encrypted)*

I have taken my physics retake this week. Thus, I now have a blissful summer break from school and forty-hour workweeks to occupy my time. Felicitations. Of course, the reason I am writing today is to explicate the events occurring only recently regarding Hadrian, his *sister*, and myself. I'm dragging my feet in the matter because it was embarrassing as all get out. Also, Hadrian's sister is a psychiatrist, because that is my life.

I arrived at Café Coco, which is lovely if one ignores the perpetual noisiness and proliferation of hipsters.

Waiting outside was a stranger I immediately recognised, even if she was much blonder than her brother, the resemblance was unmistakable. Dr. Rebecca Marshall was expensively adorned in silk blouses and designer jeans while everyone else chose a more bohemian style in accordance with their budget and eccentricities. I wanted to dislike her for her quiet, unassuming elegance alone, but I restrained myself.

She looked down from her perch when I approached and smiled. Why did half that family have to tower over me?

"Inanna, yes?"

I nodded, and her smile widened fractionally.

"It only took me three guesses too."

I chuckled more for her sake than my own humour (as thinking of the hypothetical two being harassed by the uncompromising-looking lady at the café door was *not* funny).

I followed her obediently when she turned and entered the coffee shop without another word. She insisted on paying, leaving me with cash in hand and an embarrassed flush.

We sat amongst the throng, and she favoured me with a penetrating look. "You've been nursing some pretty big hurts, haven't you?"

I glared at my hot chocolate. It was as unseasonal as I felt, but it was the sole beverage on the menu without gratuitous amounts of caffeine. I had wanted some idle chitchat before she tried to crack open my psyche, but ah, well. What can you do? I never really get what I want, do I?

"Things happen," I told my chocolate.

"I'm not sure getting chased around in the dark and getting gassed is just another one of those 'things'," she said lightly, sipping her soy chai latte with extra cinnamon delicately.

"Perhaps." I sipped at the scalded milk. "But there's nothing doing, I'm afraid. What's happened, happened, and there's nothing we can do but move forward."

"A very mature way to look at it." That felt like a trap.

"It's practicality." I shrugged, glancing up at the signboard above her head. "And it means that this sort of intervention is half pointless, isn't it?"

"Not necessarily," Rebecca said carefully. "Some people are very good at presenting a front of healthy coping mechanisms." There was the trap.

"What's the difference between a front and honest progress? I suppose there's no faking it until you make it mentality in your book?"

"Faking being fine often does more harm than good."

"For whom?"

"For you."

"I feel fine, though."

"But I'm curious if you're lying to keep up the façade that you're fine."

"Because I should be weeping hysterically? Because I should be loud about it?"

"You could be honest."

I had to close my eyes at that, dig my teeth into my lip because of the *gall* of this woman.

"Honestly?" I began, looking her in the eye. "This has been a really good month for me. I've helped put on a production I love. I've finished high school. I'm *happy*."

"And you nearly died."

"Well, I didn't know that until after I woke up."

She took a long sip of latte. "Does that make it better? That you didn't understand what was happening?"

"No, it means exactly what I said. I'm not trying to read into the situation like you are."

"Inanna. Do you have trouble getting to sleep? Headaches?" Another trap.

"No," I lied.

She looked surprised. "No offence, but you look like you have a migraine right now."

I did, but that wasn't the point. "This is my resting bitch face."

"Hadrian told me you have stress headaches all the time. Though, he thinks they're from reading too much."

"What else has he told you?"

"Too much, I think. I couldn't treat you if I wanted to."

"Because of me or because of him?"

"Him," she answered immediately. "From what I can see, you'd benefit from the talking cure, if you could be convinced to talk."

"And here I thought I talked too much," I said wryly.

"Not about the important stuff, I don't think."

"What else did Hadrian tell you? That I'm constantly suffering? That I desperately need rescuing? Or that I'm hilarious and a delight to be around?"

"I'd say all of the above, but that's not all he's said."

"Oh, really? Has he told you about my tragedy, my story of woe?"

"No, actually. I only know because I googled you. Why are you keeping it a secret?"

I snorted. "Secret? *Please*. Everyone knows. It's on the *internet*."

"Why not talk about it, then? Can you even say it out loud?"

It was a challenge. It was a red flag before the bull, but my throat was stoppered up, my jaw clenched enough to break teeth, my tongue a dead thing in the cavern of my mouth.

"There is nothing wrong with me that sleep and time cannot fix," I said because anything else was too hard to force out.

"Have sleep and time fixed anything recently? Or was it something else?"

My fingers itched to drum on the table top, to scratch at my face, but I restrained the urge valiantly.

"What do you think has healed my wounds?" I accused.

"Letting it out." Of course. From the matter-of-fact tone, one would think she was being *obvious*. "One way or the other, letting it out helps more than waiting for your soul to scab over and scar."

It was a warning I did not heed.

"Forgive me if I disbelieve you," I said.

"Disbelieve all you like, I only have a medical degree, after all. What do I know?"

"If you're done mocking me, I have better things to do than being picked on in a coffee shop."

She finished her drink, contemplative and watching me. Wondering if I would break under the silence no doubt, but the noise of the other denizens more than drowned out any discomfort on my part.

Some girl beside me was bemoaning her chances at getting into MTSU, and, on the other side, two men were arguing heatedly about the merits of using market-oversaturated tropes purposefully to create a meta-narrative within their Nietzschian webcomic/graphic prophecy novel. Really, I could have sat there all day listening to them talk about the use of cliché, the act of beating zombie horses, and the nature of modern media.

Much more interesting than my present battle of wits.

"I'm not going to push you," she decided finally. "You obviously aren't open to any help that I could give, or anyone else for that matter."

"And you must first wish to be helped before you can be?" I relished the phrase. "Perhaps you could convince your brother of the same thing."

"Well, he likes you," she said with a shrug. "He just wants to see you happy." She got up, looking immaculate, and exited gracefully. People actually made way for her as she forded the crowd.

"Hadrian likes me?" I asked the crowded room that had taken no heed of our dramatics.

I don't know what to make of this. If this were a romantic film or book, my wise mentor would reveal himself (probably Coach Tucker or Frank), saying something akin to "Of course he likes you. How could he not?" But this is not so in the real world. I have to ascertain the legitimacy of her nebulous statement myself.

I will, of course, confront him about it. Obviously, Hadrian couldn't possibly like me romantically? Surely I would have noticed?

5/18 SATURDAY
*(Typed, under Folder: Essays)*

I called him this morning, confronting him about said accusation mentioned above. The conversation was made thusly:

"Why are you calling at 5:oo a.m.?" The bleary-eyed voice answered after exactly six rings.

"Hadrian, do you like me?" Cut and dry and easy to understand, that is how I like it.

"What? Of course I like you, Ina, but why're you calling—"

I sighed expressively before trampling his feeble train of thought. "No, do you like me as more than a friend? Do you find me attractive? Do you fantasise about me doing naughty things with you? Do you want to share romantic dinners by candlelight with me?" I asked rapid-fire and increasingly agitated. I just wanted to *know*, and whenever I want to know, I hack at my ignorance with abandon until truth falls into my lap.

"Yeah?"

I sighed again. "I called you too early, didn't I?" I was suddenly weary as I drove in the creeping dawn light.

"Ina, are you—are you asking me out?" The question was small and unsure.

I sighed again. "No, your sister thinks you have...I don't know, a crush on me or some such nonsense. Which is impossible. No one likes me."

"Yeah, she may have mentioned something about you and her not getting on that great..." A second went by. "What did she say about me?" I needed to pull the phone away from my ear, his voice was so strident.

"That you are romantically interested in me. Are you my friend, or are you interested in something more from me?"

"Oh God, Ina. Why are you doing this to me? I just got to bed three hours ago!"

I baulked at the pronouncement. "What were you doing at two in the morning?" I asked, a bit accusingly.

"I was at a party, like everyone else at Hickory High. Some girl was hosting it at Centennial Park, and of course, you didn't even notice when you were invited before exams!"

"I had a few things to deal with in that interim, Hadrian. I'm sorry if some insignificant function failed to jog my memory after nearly dying in the bowels of our own school!"

"Yeah, well. You shoulda come. It was fun." Now, with the gift of hindsight, I can practically hear his hangover growing over the course of the conversation.

"Not too much fun, I hope." I waited for a moment for a response not forthcoming. "At least tell me there are no little Hadrian's possibly invading some poor girl's uterine walls as we speak."

He spluttered at my little joke. It was clearly too early, for he seemed perfectly incapable of speech.

"I *didn't* knock some girl up, Ina! Jesus. Please, call me later. Christ's sake." He hung up on me, and I harrumphed behind the wheel before turning into the Radnor Lake parking lot. He was due for a good grilling after the indignity I endured in his impertinent sister's presence. He also needed a bit more sleep so he won't take everything I say at face value. I supposed a full night's sleep would allow him to remember my admittedly twisted sense of humour, which he usually appreciates very well.

I ripped through the trails at a lightning pace, glad that the steady throb in my ankle had subsided almost completely since Monday. I promised myself that I would never so abuse my body again as I sprinted off the trail to avoid an oncoming trail ranger (Running is prohibited only if you get caught).

I had been so sluggish and unhappy because I had avoided my normal exercise routine for months. Could you believe I only did a bit of hiking or swimming and no weight training at all!? For months. Old habits like early-morning runs and late-afternoon swims have been resurrected, and my life has steadily returned to its earlier equilibrium.

Arriving at the Carnton office computer a few hours later, I wrote Hadrian an angry email detailing just how difficult his sister was to deal with and how I would rather commiserate with a venomous cottonmouth than speak to her in any professional capacity again. I saved it in my drafts for a minute, then reread it, then trashed it. It felt nice to vent, though.

I was called back sometime in the afternoon.

"So what were you saying?" He had obviously only just awoken, and I looked up from my newest project (knitting a cabled skirt, of which I am particularly proud). Lovely, he was more conscious than this morning. I checked my watch before answering him.

"Do you know what time it is?" I asked not unkindly.

"Um, threeish?" he mumbled, uncertain and unsure of the significance.

"Do you know what I do until four every day except on the weekends?" I prodded him lightly, picking up my cable needle to catch my stitches.

"I forgot," he said after a brief pause.

"It's your good fortune that I had my ringer on, and I'm not out with the tourists, Hadrian. It's simply not appropriate to answer a cell phone call in a hoop skirt. Especially when you changed my ringtone to "Baby Got Back". I cannot for the life of me exchange it with something more elegant or at least less embarrassing after you *locked* me out of the user interface." I listened for a moment for his eventual apology, which did not, in fact, tumble out of his mouth forthwith.

"Well, you shouldn't have called me so goddamned early! Just tell me what you wanted, and I'll leave you to your damned job," he said in a very reactionary tone.

I gave the phone a rather aghast expression before replying. "Perhaps you should go back to bed because obviously you need more of it." I pulled the phone away from my cheek and made to end the call.

He shouted out from the tinny speaker. "Don't fucking hang up on me! What the fuck did you want?"

I heaved a deep-bosomed exhalation of complete resignation and weariness. The phone was once again pressed against my ear. "Please don't yell. It's rather disconcerting. I just wanted to know what motive your sister had to infer that you had some sort of crush on me."

He was noisily fiddling with something on the other side of the line for at least thirty seconds. "I don't know, Ina. Do you not want me to like you?" he asked softly.

I shrugged, returning to my knitting. "I already know you like me, Hadrian, or you wouldn't have dealt with me for such a protracted period of time."

He hummed happily at the pronouncement.

"I would be distressed if *anyone* had a crush on me, though. You know that."

"Why?" he asked, concerned.

"Did I not already tell you?" I asked, frowning in disbelief.

"Nope."

Oh. How had I forgotten? Perhaps it was one of those quirks that is never mentioned out loud because the carrier of said quirk believes it is tattooed on their skulls and no one else can even see it unless the quirk is brought to attention. Like my abhorrence of birthday gifts.

"Well, when I was younger, any time I spent outside of my father's sphere of influence, I was around my mother's compatriots. They enjoyed pinching my cheeks and telling me I would end up a charmer just like my mother."

He made a noise to hurry my story to the crux of the matter.

"Well, as time went by, I never did. I focused on my various activities rather than my hormones to my parents' glee and their friends' dismay. They really wanted the gossip, you see."

Another irritated, slightly hungover noise alerted me that my audience was losing interest.

"It also seemed that the only people interested in me were the older men at my father's conference. I've always been tall, you see. Apparently, that gives off the appearance of age or some such nonsense... Anyway, being hit on by men old enough to be my father and sometimes *grandfather* is an excellent libido reducer."

"What? But what about people your own age? Why don't you give them a chance?" he asked, disbelieving.

"No. I suppose I feared being labelled a slut on some level if I dated at all, but I also found every single boy who showed any small interest in me appallingly infantile and disgusting." Freshman year had been a terrifying experience all around in all honesty.

"Why?"

I shrugged again, uncomfortable. "None of them learned how to wash themselves until after age seventeen when they began deluging themselves in Axe products. By that time, I was already off the grid so to speak. None of them were very seductive, either. 'I like your boobs,' they would say, ever so deftly. By Kierkegaard, I hated middle school."

"So your dad didn't keep you from dating?" What gave him that idea?

"No, he only went into disgusting detail about STIs and my mother's horrible pregnancy with me."

Hadrian made a nauseous noise on the other end of the line.

I watched the door for tourists to rescue me from the conversation. I quickly spotted a couple meandering outside. "Look, I have a group coming in, I'll see you later?"

"Yeah—"

I hung up just as the couple walked back to their car. They had just finished a tour with one of my fellows, a towering mountain of a man with a snowy-white beard and a visceral hatred for modern buildings. He lumbered in moments later as I turned off the ringer to my phone.

"How's the new project going? Finished yet?" he asked, sitting heavily beside me, making the antique bench creak unfavourably. I shook my head as he pulled the growing fabric swatch from my grasp to examine it. "Your tension is too loose here. You'll need to rip it out for consistency," he instructed, pulling out the last line and knitting them back, quick as lightning.

"Thanks, Frank." I smiled as he plopped the work back onto my lap.

Frank is my sassy gay friend. Except that he's neither sassy nor gay, but a strange old man who enjoys frightening children with his glass eye and long rants about the evils of Reconstructionism. As you can see, the connotation is strong in this one.

He'd been the one who taught me the ins and outs of the house and environs when I started the summer after freshman year. He also taught me how to build woodworking planes and work the old loom hidden in the back closet. The loom is not for display because it is soaked in the blood of a hundred Confederate generals. Or just two. I can never remember.

"Something bothering you?" he asked. "Tension, sweet pea." He pointed to my loose stitches, and I scowled peevishly. "What's up?"

"Everything," I grumbled. "I don't *want* to stay here anymore."

Father was still a mite frightened for me but tremendously improved from October of last year when I applied for early admission. He doesn't *really* need me at his every beck and call now. Father loves to tell me that he is perfectly capable of caring for himself nowadays.

"I don't blame you. When I finished high school, I crossed Europe with a backpack and twenty dollars in my pocket. Maybe you can take a year off after you finish?" He squeezed my arm reassuringly.

"That sounds like a good idea, I suppose," I groused mulishly. I did not feel very useful or even competent at the moment. Trying to explain something that has been an intrinsic part of my personality since puberty ran down my patience for other people, and that explanation failed to properly convey what I was trying to communicate to Hadrian. I don't really know *why* I shy away from intimacy so very much. I just always have. Romance has *never* interested me outside of fiction.

"Clock out early and I'll handle the masses," he offered, gesturing to the empty gift shop and barren parking lot. I was sulking a bit, and we both knew it. I was in no mood to instruct the great unwashed in the way of life long past, but I always chafed at leaving early.

After an hour of absolutely no business, I rose to undress and leave with a small nod to my compatriot. Frank swooped down to take my project and, without another word, began knitting with ease. He would probably finish it before I left. I swear that man has magic in his veins the way his hands work at wool and wood.

I was down to my corset, drawers, and chemise when Frank knocked upon my chamber door. "Yes?"

"Someone asking for you, In."

I frowned, confused. "All right, I'll—"

The door opened and Hadrian popped his head in.

I cried out in surprise and grappled for my working skirt to cover myself up. "I'm naked!"

He raised an eyebrow. "But you're not showing anything?"

"I'm *practically* naked!" I shrieked like a little girl. I could hear Frank laughing uproariously from the gift shop. Hellfire and damnation to him, then.

"You're less naked than normal!" he assured me.

"I'm in my underwear!"

He laughed at my horrification, walking into the dressing room regardless of my protestations. "I wanted to talk to you," he said finally while I threw on my modern clothes clumsily and quickly over my 19th-century unmentionables.

"About what?" I snapped, flushed and irritated. "Don't you have a job or chores or anything to occupy your time this summer?"

"Nope," he popped, turning to face me. "I wanted to know what you told my sister about me because she's riding on me even more than usual."

"Why is she living here anyway?" I asked awkwardly. "I can understand you trailing behind your parents, but why did she come here as well?"

"Baptist offered her a job in January." He paused. "Hey, don't change the subject. What'd you say?"

"Well, I don't know, but please elucidate." I waved my hand distractedly in his direction as I buttoned myself into the chartreuse monstrosity that was my cardigan.

"Becca thinks you're 'one of the most stubbornly miserable people I've ever met.' What did you say?"

I looked up at him, befuddled. "I have no idea," I said honestly.

He growled in frustration, rubbing his hand across his face. "No idea? Ina, you can't have 'no idea'! You can't have 'no idea' why she disliked you so much."

I watched him pace and grumble for a few seconds, gathering my thoughts.

He turned and pointed his finger at my face accusingly. "What did you do?" It was rather unpleasant, under the spotlight in such a manner, stripped bare metaphorically and, to my sensibilities, literally.

"Let me think, and I'll tell you," I snapped, turning to rearrange my clothes just to keep some distance between the two of us. "I introduced myself. She made a joke. We ordered; she paid. She asked me questions; I answered. She tried to spin the conversation into forcing me to confess, and I did *not* appre—"

"*What* did she do?" he interrupted.

"She and I disagreed on methods of trauma recovery." I made sure to keep it light. Very light.

Hadrian ran his fingers through his hair, muttering almost inaudibly, but I believe he whispered something to the effect of "Did I really think that would work?" He looked up at me, and he stopped his ambulation finally.

"I'm sorry you didn't get along."

I shrugged, unhurt in the first place.

"If you'd only opened up, I wouldn't've had to bring her into the equation."

Did all of his arguments cycle around this tiny bit of insignificant information? I have to admit, construing me as the villain aggravated me slightly.

"You know what, Hadrian? You must think you're a glorious hero out of storybooks," I snapped. Honestly, where this came from, I am not entirely sure. It must have been buried for a long while to explode so ineloquently. He made to protest, but I waved him off without pause as I gained steam.

"You sweep girls off their feet and fix their fucked-up lives with a slain dragon, a charming smile, and a marriage proposal. That is why I *hate* you sometimes, because there are no dragons for you to slay here."

He was shaking his head, but I was not having any of that today. I was feverish in my intensity, almost religious.

"Your insistent invasions into my privacy are not endearing, nor are they wearing at my reserve for diversion. It is only my *patience* with your amateurish enquiries that suffers. You can't fix my life, because *I'm* the problem with *my* life, not an external irritant that a hug or a handful of cash can repair. Just let it go. Forget you ever tried to be my Prince Charming questing to earn your knighthood."

I pushed him out of the glorified linen cupboard-cum-dressing-room and shut the door behind him. I almost wanted to cry but instead slammed my knee into the wall with a resounding bang. An aching knee was certainly a more acceptable expression of rage than a broken toe or burning eyes. I stripped again and, dressed properly now, made to leave, sans friend waiting outside. Frank ignored me completely, as if this happened all the time.

I stared at my dilapidated little car for a few seconds before just running. It didn't matter one iota that my shoes were made more for ballet than sprinting. It only lengthened my stride and softened my steps as I flew for the town proper of Franklin, Tennessee.

I alighted at the old theatre, in rather desperate need to destroy something. People may have been staring at me, I can't tell you for certain (They were probably tourists anyway). I only wanted to express my anger, my irrational feeling that I had been betrayed most soundly by the one person near my age that I trusted at all. I'm glad he refused to text me tonight, as is our flowering summer ritual.

In any case, I shall be very hard pressed to even attempt to repair this most recent devastation against our friendship. Nay, I shall leave him to lounge in his own indolence while I do something worthwhile this summer.

I'm simply too tired of his constant badgering. He never ever lets up regarding anything I'm reticent to tell him. It seems that secrets are abhorrent to him, and the mere idea that I do not wish to flagrantly bare all of my dirty laundry to his gaze is a sin. I'm not a villain because I do not wish to expose myself to further abuse, am I?

If I word vomit until nothing is left, I *know* he won't ruin my life so much as use that information to entrap me somehow. It's a silly theory, I realise, but the only other people I have confided in used that information to tie me close to them for their own benefit. It's why it took nearly a semester to permanently retire myself from public life at Jackson Academy of the Sciences.

My old friends wanted their homework machine to carry over into high school, even if their emotional blackmail was subpar at best, looking back. And my family, well, that is their entire point, is it not? They grasp at every bit of me I share and guilt me into visiting more often *or* providing more comfort to others *or* repairing whatever needs tinkering (including people) *or* acknowledging more birthdays...but I digress.

I mulled over this conundrum while strolling through the idyllic little shops and noting the earthquake buttons attached to the older facades. I ended up jogging back up the mildly intimidating hill to my car nearly two hours after clocking out.

5/19 SUNDAY
*(Dream Journal)*

I was riding out in the Steeplechase, leaping over fences and bushes with practised ease. The black stud beneath me whickered and sped past the field despite my protests. He flew through underbrush and low-hanging limbs with preternatural ease, stopping at the edge of a stream.

He was on the other side, hand outstretched. "Do as I say. Dismount." I tugged the reins instead, and the horse nearly bucked me off in spite before taking an almighty leap forward. As we lurched into the air, the stream turned into cliff side, and we fell into the ocean. It was a kelpie, not a horse at all.

## 5/23 THURSDAY
*(Dream Journal)*

Hadrian promised me anything I wanted. We sailed through the stars together, fighting Wookies and Javert from *Les Miserables*. We had such fun using pool noodles as weapons. I wish we weren't in such a bad way—

## 5/27 MONDAY
*(Typed, Encrypted)*

It seems we were existing under an uneasy truce that had broken before I even realised the calm was impermanent.

Father exploded at me when I returned from work late a few days ago. Of course, he would never actually raise his voice (always the quiet intimidator rather than the blustering imbecile) or his hand against me, but his diatribes are legion...and these most recent lectures take the cake. I am not entirely certain what has unleashed this sudden controlling attitude.

Perhaps this is his actual reaction to my near-death experience, delayed due to shock and relief? In any case, I have no clue, and it is becoming increasingly difficult to divert his attention away from punishing me. I'm no longer allowed to leave the house except when under his purview or to work, and I am chafing under this yoke of injustice, reader!

I had been led to believe that ours was a relationship mellowing into something comradely rather than something between disciplinarian and cringing student. Apparently, I am dreadfully mistaken.

Also, Hadrian has yet to call me, and I'm afraid my own unwillingness to bend prevents me from apologising for whatever miscommunication we have been undertaking recently. I can't recall, and the document has disappeared in the quagmire of my computer files. These bans on my personal freedoms also make it rather arduous to reason out this present friendship difficulty.

I can only just recall our argument over a week past, but it was something more than that, more than an invasion of privacy on an intellectual and physical level. It was about pushing and pulling and giving and taking and overarching tones in our interactions. I'm not at all able to fix that now, however. I'm sure it will resolve itself eventually, as it does. I have too much on my plate trying to reason with an increasingly bad-tempered creature otherwise known as my father to bother with anything else.


5/28 TUESDAY
*(Typed, Encrypted)*

I think I'm going mad with cabin fever and the *hate*. The one day I decide to leave early, my father decides I simply must accompany him to a conference of some sort on the East

Coast. I had been mulish and short-tempered all day but performed my duties without comment and reorganised my schedule.

I simply asked to clean and work inside the buildings instead of testing fate with the incredible dullards that pay to walk and stare vacantly at history they cannot possibly comprehend (Why yes, my mood is still foul, thank you ever so much for asking! And no, it's not because of the corset, *dammit*).

I contemplated telling Hadrian I'm leaving but decided against it. He has failed to notice my existence for the past fortnight so I am sure another few days will go unnoticed along the way. As a coaxing mechanism, Father has allowed me to use his precious electronic reader for the expedition.

To aggravate him, I shall fill it entirely with philosophy and murder mysteries, most of which are well-loved pieces of mine. I'll bring real books for entertainment (He won't actually remember he allowed me to use it. I can promise you that). I have a rapidly expanding shelf of shame (an entirely new phenomenon, I assure you), that is filled with the books that have unfortunately lain unfinished by the waysides. I must finish them soon or the ignominy will drive me mad.

The police called yesterday to inform us that no charges will be filed against me for breaking and entering (Really? I was so worried, literally quivering in my wee little boots!). They also deigned to tell me that the mysterious "prankster" had not yet been found but not to lose hope. It's just another instance of Sherlock completely outpacing Lestrade...either that or Sherlock being left bamboozled and lost by the infamous Irene Adler. Maybe the metaphor is a trifle mixed...

Moving on. I'm glad that I'm taking actually challenging classes (for an infant, that is) next year. By that time, Father will have cooled his protective zeal, and I will have either fixed things up with Hadrian or left him to make friends and lovers in the place "where fun goes to die (i.e. the University of Chicago)" without my dialogue or opinions.

I need to go run. Perhaps when I return, everything will have determined itself without me.


## 5/31 FRIDAY
*(Written, in a worn notebook)*


I think I'm beginning to hate everyone on principle. Everyone I know just lets me down or actively tears at the mortar of my foundations. Why should I expend the energy to hope otherwise? Yes, misanthropy shall be my new byword. Wonderful.

Let me begin by saying that I can only hope that literature conferences are less mind-numbingly boring than ones focused on numerical theorems and trying to one-up each other. I swear the whole institution of mathematics in one giant pissing contest set up to prove who has the best aim, and the new kid on the block always wins.

My father's reputation was almost demolished by some young and cocky thing in an ascot (*An ascot?* What sort of a boy actually wears ascots in public nowadays, let alone to conferences?). He had leaned back in his chair, crossing his arms with the ease of a boy convinced of his own superiority, and spewed vitriol against Father *because of me*. I nearly, no, not nearly, I *did* trounce him the moment lectures were out. Never let it be said that I do not know the adage "blood is thicker than wine," and the wine he was offering was worse than vinegar.

Permit me to elucidate for your viewing pleasure:

Father had finished the PowerPoint I made for him with a familiar flush of pride and accomplishment, and the ensuing questions were easily answered and superficial. The crowd clapped politely as was their wont, and the next man rose to give his presentation. That night was when things went from tolerable to outright horrifying.

We were sitting at the hotel bar, discussing something or another. It doesn't matter. What does matter is that this overfluffed peacock popped his "squat" into the bucket seat beside me. He smiled malevolently, probably a new PhD riding on his first updraft of success. I looked down on him, taking a sip of hot chocolate before turning back to my father dismissively.

"I saw you at the lectures today. You a grad student?" he asked lazily, signalling the bartender. "Rum and Coke." The barkeep nodded and made his way to the bottom-shelf liquor. I smiled privately; no need to break out the good stuff for such a plebeian beverage.

I ignored him for my father's increasingly less-stimulating conversation on violin manufacture. He had already guzzled several celebratory White Russians and was working his way through something with an even steeper vodka-to-additives ratio.

"Is he your professor?" he ventured, and I sighed, extremely put-upon. I would need to claim tiredness to get Father into the lift bound for his room and this nosing-about was irritating.

"I'm tired. Shouldn't we head up?" I asked softly.

Father snorted and shook his head. "*Niet.*"

That was the only word I could confidently identify out of the jumbled mess of Russian and tremendously accented German. Oh, hellfire and murderous intent. It appears I had been speaking too much and failed to note the extra empty glasses next to his quivering right hand.

"You sure you want to take him upstairs instead of me?" the impertinent whelp asked behind me. I went rigid from incandescent rage. I gave him a glare, communicating nothing less than instant, indescribable pain, if not an agonising death.

I snarled and grabbed my father's arm a bit too harshly, for he shouted at me incomprehensibly. I hissed at him to *stand up, and do as I say, or so help me god, I will ensure you meet your sisters and brothers before the night is out.* The boy started at the harsh and spitting Russian issuing from my lips. Father quieted immediately, and I hauled him out of the dining area and into the hotel proper.

As an aside, allow me to explain my standard threat against a drunken Rodger Drew. My father is an expatriate of the former USSR, whose family failed to join him because most of them were dead before he was revealed to be a proper numerical genius. Most of his siblings succumbed to industrial accidents or illness, to the extent of my knowledge, and his parents were the delicate great-grandchildren of fallen aristocracy.

Really, it is very sad and explains why he holds the family he has left to such high standards; he only has so many eggs left in his basket. Now that I have explained, on with the story.

The next morning, I ordered Father room service to be sent up at eight in lieu of a wakeup call. I went out running, still angry from the conversation the night before as an evangelical protesting an abortion clinic setting up shop beside my equally zealous congregation. This was by no means the first time it has been insinuated that I am a bed-warmer or something equally crude by new or ignorant fellows. That *does not* excuse him or anyone else of the assumption, especially given my exceptionally fresh face and the fact that this began when *high school* began.

Two hours later, I returned to shower, dress (a white blouse and calf-length black skirt to counter the apparently whorish T-shirt and jeans from the day before), and check up on Father. He was, of course, still hungover. At least he had no recourse but to sit in the loftiest seat and watch the little ants make their rounds before the podium. He did not have to speak or interact with others that day.

Unfortunately, Father felt it necessary to ask one "friendly question" to each presenter. And wasn't it a wonderful twist of fate that the new kid on the chopping block would present first? I pushed water bottle after water bottle into his grasp, either to sober him up or render his bladder so full as to require an extended bathroom break, I am not entirely sure. Either would work, really.

His name was Gilliam Kronkheit, and I hated him with a passion to fuel a thousand supernovas. He strutted, *strutted* on stage like a cock amongst his hens and spoke with an irritating Jersey accent (made all the more grating by the microphone static). Oh, my loathing was so fierce that, had my father not made an ass of himself, I would have come down like an avenging angel, ripping his ideas and theorems to pieces regardless of whether they were viable or no, I don't care. I could have bullshitted him into tears, I know! It's not something I haven't done before.

Instead, Father, being surprisingly polite, asked whether the coefficients would translate well in a real-life scenario or was this idea strictly true in a so-called "perfect world"? The boy peered up into the nosebleed section, found his questioner, and exploded (well, not really. He was perfectly collected, but you could tell, just tell that he wanted to throw himself on the floor and roll about in the throes of a toddler's temper tantrum). Or maybe I'm projecting. I certainly wanted to hurl myself down and beat my fists against his sternum.

He smiled cruelly and asked if my father, the professor, would rather be sipping Grey Goose instead of Earl Grey. I glared hatefully down at him as my father spluttered at the unexpected ad hominem attack.

Then he took the plunge, and I wished fervently to go home. He mentioned one of my father's less-than-stellar papers, calling it easily refutable and childish. He held that Vanderbilt should force resignation before the man could make a bigger fool of himself than he already had. After running out of professional insults for one of the best of the best in this field, he childishly suggested that the professor *"abstain from seducing his own students and taking them with him to conferences."*

Diogenes, I hate people. Even though he was thoroughly admonished for attacking one of his fellows and going over his allotted time, he still wasn't punished enough because he had sent Father into hysterics. After the conference lectures had ended for the day, I searched out the dead man walking. Of course he would be in the bar, nursing an embarrassing umbrella drink (Which cemented my theory that he was gay as a lark and hitting on ladies such as myself to prove to himself he could actually screw someone with lady parts).

"You are utter necrosis to the academic community, and I hope never to see you again in any professional capacity," I snapped, fingers balled into fists, jaw clenched, and frame looming over his seated presence.

He looked up at me lazily and took a sip of drink. "At least I didn't sleep my way through school."

I wanted to throttle him and ruthlessly crush his sanctimonious attitude. "You have no idea who I am, do you?" I hissed. "I have an IQ of 169 and was solving calculus derivatives by the age of *three*. Just at the start of this month, I nearly murdered a man for playing a *prank* at my high school, *which I just graduated from*. And I *killed* a man in SoHo for trying to take my purse. I do not need to sleep with *anyone* to get what I want because I'm smarter than you will ever be and infinitely better."

He leaned back comically, away from my hissing and spitting.

"Should I wish it, you would be a smear on the pavement, a patch of drying blood without even a prayer of being identified by anyone. *Do not mess* with people you do not know." I cracked my knuckles, leering in a rather deranged way, and he shrank away, obviously disturbed. I was indeed taller than him, heavier, and stronger. My limbs filled with adrenaline and just itching to start a fight. "Do you want to test me again, boy?"

He fled.

I forced myself to relax and ignored the stares of the other patrons as I returned to my room. An hour later, Father called and chewed me out for daring to fight his battles for him. Apparently, the boy decided to apologise most profusely after he learned that I was Professor Drew's *daughter*. Is that more terrifying than attempted homicide? I was forced to listen to him berate me for nearly an hour and punish me for defending my own honour. His pride, I should have recalled, is just as deadly as mine.

I cried that night into my pillow, but I'm not sure why. Was I crying for my father's incomprehension, for my reputation, out of sheer loneliness? I can't tell, and frankly, I don't wish to delve into my psyche anymore. I don't want to know why I do things anymore; I just want things to be simple, straightforward, and childish. I want a fairy-tale ending for *once*... Why can't anything be as simple as children's fairy tales? Sure, your heroine may have to chop off her own finger to open the fabled castle door, but all sacrifices are *rewarded*. All villainy is punished.

It would be better if everything had an obvious cause and effect. Then I would know in advance that I would be punished for something unforgivable and do it anyway rather than being punished for something that helped my pathetic, limping family unit in the long run, I hope.

(Did that even make any sense?)

# June

6/2 SUNDAY
*(Typed, Encrypted)*

We arrived home today, and I am under house arrest until further notice, which has not improved my mood in the least. Father was fiddling with the latch on the boot (or the trunk, if you so like. It is the silliest, most temperamental bit of mechanics we own), and I was at the front door, keys in hand. Immediately to my left was a sheaf of white stuck between the hinges.

A note. From Hadrian. Of course. *Please shoot me now,* I thought, *because I have no patience for this right now.*

All right, at that moment, I could see I had two choices. One, I could take the letter, read it, and deal with it now. Two, I could take it, stuff the thing in my pocket, and pretend I never saw it. Option two seemed incredibly tempting as I plucked it from its resting place, crinkled and stained with the remnants of the last rain. How long had it been there?

"Inanna! Open this damn thing for me, or I'm leaving your things behind!"

Ah, good old dad. I helped him open the latch before returning to the door.

"Inanna, open the door and let me get back to work, or have you forgotten that *I* am the one funding your education?"

"I haven't, Daddy." I forced my disdain to simmer out of vocal range as he brushed past me to his man-cave of mathematics and terribly corny sci-fi. I made my way to my room, my fortress of solitude so to speak (because not a single soul has passed through the entryway but me in the past four years), and put my clothes away, ignoring the letter pointedly exposed halfway out of my purse. It mocked me with its visibility and forlorn appearance.

I ended up opening it in spite of myself.

Ina,

You're not here and not answering your phone, so I'm writing a damn letter. I've been doing some thinking, and I'm sick of this. I really am. You don't tell me anything, and you don't ever apologise for anything you do [which I must contest most virulently].

I'm not trying to be your kni- I'm not an idiot. You think I'm a knight, but you're some tragic heroine who'll spend the last act stabbed in the chest and airing out your suffering to make everyone else feel like shit. So you'll just carry all that shit until it crushes you. No matter what anyone says, I think I know you better than you think. I'm your <u>fucking friend</u>.

It feels like you're dangling me on a string until you want something out of me, and that's bullshit. If you can't see that, then I don't know why I bother with you. I'm going out of the country on Friday, and if you don't <u>talk</u> to me. If you can't tell me why you've been acting so flaky, then, to put it like you would, <u>consider us strangers</u>.

H

Huh?

I sat there staring stupidly at the angriest handwritten letter I'd ever read before realising that the acceptance date had come and gone. I had lost my only real friend without even realising it. I noticed I had started hyperventilating at some point; the sound of my breathing had quickened so much as to make my vision explode into little dots of colour blindness. It was strangely beautiful and heartbreakingly ominous.

I'm not sure when I started crying either, but I do so hate when things are taken out of my hands by forces I have no control over. I hate it enough to scream, but not enough to awaken my father's ire downstairs. And I loathed him, my father and Hadrian both, after another moment of splintered thought. It doesn't matter what I do, I always end up destroying everything I hold dear.

Everything I care about shatters if I hold it too long, and it is always my *fault*. I stayed in my room until stoicism returned with a vengeance some time about 11. Now I am writing it in you because I am going to drink this away if it takes the entire contents of the liquor cabinet downstairs to do it.

## 6/4 TUESDAY
*(Written in a worn notebook)*

I have never been more grateful for a hangover in my life. Not only has it reaffirmed my belief that moderation in consumption leads to a more pleasant experience, the feeling has also dulled the ache of anger and loss, relegated it to a distant memory rather than a new wound. I am happy my companion Jack Daniels could assist me so, even if my room needed a quick clean up and the mountains of rough sketches and angry writings swept under the rug (figuratively, of course).

Thankfully, I am as quiet a drunk as I am a student. Only around people I admire or wish to correct will anyone hear my voice under most any influence. I spent most of my evening between contemplating calling the self-righteous, sanctimonious heathen to chew him out on his decision and cooking something greasy and filled with cream downstairs.

Normally, I am no chef nor do I aspire to become one of those classic fifties mothers in their aprons and rubber gloves, simultaneously cleaning and cooking for a brood of six, give or take, but, when I imbibe, suddenly I believe I am on my way to the French institute, the Cordon Bleu. I wrote down some truly gag-inducing flavour combinations (Cabbage and ice cream; rhubarb and tenderloin with a thyme cream sauce, really self?) on some of the many scraps of paper floating about my room even as we speak.

I reread my recent entries and found the familiar sting of rage and irrational betrayal, but much more contained. I also checked my phone to find that I hadn't even packed it, stupid me.

Now that all of my woes are cleansed out of my system, I can work again. I was off on Monday because Father insisted I stay home for one reason or another, I cannot recall. When I dragged myself out of bed that morning, I swigged the jug of water by my bedside and swallowed down the pills beside it (Thankfully, I plan ahead before I decide to do something as stupid as washing away my sorrows with amber waves of grain).

Father failed to call me down for several hours, probably because he discovered the liquor cabinet (completely devoid of bourbon and whiskey) and decided it was better not to test me.

He learned his lesson during exam week of junior year when he gave me a glass of cognac to calm me down, and I ended up stealing the entire bottle into my room and refused to take any of his usual behaviour lying down (If you find this incredible, you obviously do not have very European parents. My mother was raised on kinder wine and kinder bier and my father is Russian. Of course they would give me champagne during celebrations and casually break the law by the time I was sixteen. They never saw it as an actual criminal offence).

I enjoyed my day of nigh-complete solitude, planning on returning to the real world later (I do so love the word *later*. My parents never tolerated anything less than neurotic punctuality).

And I have never loved work so much as I did today. I was away from home for nearly seventeen hours as I told my father I had to make up for the lost hours last week. Frank took one look at me and told me, in no uncertain terms, that he knew something was up.

"You want to work overtime today? Make up for last week's vanishing act?"

I blushed despite myself, truly mortified. "I'm really sorry about the short notice, but my—"

He waved away my explanation. "I know, I know. Your dad wanted you, so you went. I'm sure you're ready to die after spending all that time with him," he ribbed gently, and I smiled to impress upon him the idea that there has never been any bad blood between us and never would be. He was still my best friend.

"I'm ready to swoon. I swear all he talks about is theories and compounds and quantum mechanics. How I'll survive school with him is a mystery," I complained eagerly.

He laughed as we mounted the stairs to open the mansion for the day. "At least he's still out and about to take care of you. Free room and board is a good thing straight out of school."

I frowned, but answered in any case. "I suppose I'll be fine then, but that doesn't mean I don't want a break."

He threw up his hands in mock surrender when I waved my finger at him "threateningly." "Of course, sweet pea. There's a wedding going on tonight. I'm sure you'll like it."

"Where?"

He unlocked the door and busied himself with disarming the security system. "Belmont, the couple's a bit extravagant, if you get my meaning."

I chuckled, leaning against the doorframe and watching the lights flicker to life, exposing the little models and gratuitous map collection in the Welcome Centre. "I shall wear my best gown, then?" I asked jokingly. Those sort of jobs were mainly heavy labour, moving things in and out of an entrance hall or directing caterers or laundering last-minute curtains still stained from last week's wedding. Arriving in full regalia would be a bit counterproductive.

"Yeah, it's one of their requests. Most of them will probably be men"—because their guides don't dress up, I knew—"because they think girls can't work as hard as boys." He said that pointedly, knowing it would get me riled up. I let him.

"That, my dear sir, simply will not do. I'll show them what a woman can do in a hoop and corset."

He smiled as I disappeared into my changing room. He handed me a new project to work on when I reentered, properly attired. Sometimes, I wish Frank had been my father, or anyone else really. I'm not too tremendously picky. The rest of the day passed smoothly enough, the summer rush filling our coffers and our timetables until quitting time at four.

We spent the next hour or so cleaning, inspecting, and gabbing (as per our usual rounds), and then I left to grab a bite before winding my way downtown for the wedding. It was rather fun to walk through the grocery store looking for skyr (Icelandic yogurt deliciousness) in my work clothes. Also made traffic more bearable to see the disbelieving faces pass me by at a snail's pace on 8th Avenue.

The couple was indeed very strange and wanted docents *in* the wedding photos for some reason. I had set up and taken down all of the accoutrement at the appropriate times, and the manager, a Mr. Browning, told me I could help whenever I wished (Ha, patriarchal system, ha I say! I have flouted you again with my frilly, flouncy skirts of feminist justice!).

It was a mite terrible to sit through the wedding, though. They were all so sickeningly happy, and I wanted to shout at them that it wouldn't last and all things will pass away and not gently into that good night, either. I was mildly distressed, but kept it close to the vest (heh, an utterly unintentional rhyme), so to speak. I never really enjoyed weddings in the first place, but, given the circumstances, I am more inclined to turn my nose at them nowadays...

I have just realised that it is now upwards of one in the morning, dear anonymous author of *Beowulf*. I'll to bed post haste.

**6/6 THURSDAY**
*(Written in a worn notebook)*

You piece of shit, why did you do this to me? If it would make me feel even the tiniest bit better, I would hate you to the ends of the earth...

I don't know how to fix this.


**6/10 MONDAY**
*(Dream Journal)*

He called me a heartless bitch.


**6/13 THURSDAY**
*(Typed, Encrypted)*

Some of my punishments have been levied in favour of inattention. Thank Da Vinci my father's moods come and go like the ebb and flow of oceanic/lunar cooperation, i.e. the tides. If only they were as easily predictable as well, then I would be sitting pretty in the Nile instead of flailing about in the Tigris and Euphrates like an imbecile without a Farmer's Almanac.

Not that I have any free time, mind. I'm gaining a bit of clout in these parts as the single most overworked employee in the county, according to my superiors. It was quite funny when they nearly resorted to grovelling near the end of that particular conversation. Pay and a half is quite a good incentive, and it keeps me out of my father's purview. Why should I bow to their whims because the government implements some sort of policy to "prevent the exploitation of employees"? Ha, more like I am exploiting my employers!

In any case, I have agreed to curtail my hours but failed to inform my father. This leaves me with several hours to spend at my leisure, mostly at the library (which is where I am typing as we speak). Not the most exciting of places to be, but I have placed a limit on how many books I shall buy over the next short while. I haven't been to a bookstore in nearly two months (and I am pouting most judiciously even as I write this down).

I've finished at least two-thirds of my shelf of shame, but I still have miles to go before I sleep.

## 6/13 THURSDAY
*(Dream Journal)*

I was nearly eaten by a bear at an archaeological site. There were dozens of them wandering freely across the lawn and exploring the excavation units. I was among a group of fellows, standing outside of our bus when one broke away from *its* fellows. We scattered, but it followed me with an impressive roar. I screamed like a little girl when something grabbed at my shirt. It turned out to be Hadrian in a ratty duct-taped suit. I hit him with a rolled-up newspaper for scaring me so before I woke up.

## 6/14 FRIDAY
*(Typed, Encrypted)*

Sometimes I wonder what it would be like to travel back in time... I think I would hate it.

But I digress; I had a rather dizzying reflection today and thought I would write it down before trying to implement any sort of plan. I know that Hadrian's father is well and good. He has been since March, but his face suddenly popped into my head while I was touring today, and it got me to thinking. I hadn't heard any recent news from him since April, even if he looked well at the airing of *Dreams* (Which has attracted the attention of several off-Broadway productions and college campuses (I have to visibly restrain myself from dancing stupidly even as I write this in spite of recent events)! Just in the off-chance that you were curious).

I think I shall send him a letter hoping he is well and reminding him that I expect him to outlive me by at least ten years, or I'll be very cross with him. I'll ruminate on this and continue on this vein later.


UPDATE:

The letter, which is short and sweet and not at all intimidating, has been sent, and I am still uncertain as to whether that was a positive or negative thing to do. Is it an attempt to check up on the status of a recently ill friend or some insidious backstabbing thing I fear it is against Hadrian? I don't even know anymore. It's simply too confusing to think in such a convoluted, nonsensical fashion, so I'll desist forthwith.

Work has been going along swimmingly. I was lecturing on the fine art of spinning and finally had the chance to show off my new skill to the odd visitor, cut off from the traversing herds. Unfortunately, the police thought it in our best interests to remind my father that there is a man out there, somewhere, that poisoned his daughter, and he (Father) is now slightly perturbed when I decide to go out and about, *but* not enough to limit my movements. *Hallelujah.*

I cannot think of anything else of interest happening hereabouts at the moment, shall expound upon hypothetical happenings the instant they occur.


## 6/15 SATURDAY

Finished Descartes's *Meditations* today and received a text message from Hadrian's father, I'm not sure which one I am gladder to see. I certainly hated Descartes's reasoning and generally incomprehensible Cartesian attitude, but the text message was very sweet and insinuated that a formal thank-you was in the post.

Hadrian's father: *I do so luv letters Thnx I hope U R well as well.*

Then thirty seconds later: *Hope 2 see U @ the opera on Wed.*

I sent him something back of course.

*Thank you for the thank you.*

And: *I will.*

I am afraid my language does not translate well on such a limiting venue, I must say. I also wonder why their family seems incapable of using lowercase letters in their texts. The opera he is referring to is most likely the encore presentations of Metropolitan Opera shown every Wednesday in the summer at the Green Hills Theatre. I looked up the opera: *Ariadne auf Naxos.* Joy. While an admittedly sweet and lovely opera, my heart will always belong to the likes of *Eugene Onegin* and *Il Trovatore.* I may be a little excited to see one of Catullus's best poems put to music for the first time (for me, at least).

I shall simply occupy my time with a new text chronicling the history of civilisation with regards to alcohol. Hopefully, it shall prove enlightening. I never really liked histories, but my newest acquisition, Montaigne's *Essays*, is taking its sweet time in the hands of the postal service.


6/19 WEDNESDAY
*(Typed, Encrypted)*

That was a singularly painful experience. Here, let me tell you the whole story. I'm sure you'll get a laugh out of it.

I received a letter yesterday, printed on heavy paper and expensive ink. Boy, that man must be as antiquated as I am to have such outdated finery on hand for a silly thank-you notice. In any case, the letter was lovely if more formal than our previous correspondence. He thanked me for my concern and asked how I was doing and whether I would be interested in working for him during the remainder of the summer because Hadrian has expressed no interest in cataloguing his various treasures collected over a lifetime.

My breath caught in my chest just thinking of the possible booty he had collected over the years. I sent off a reply on Monday that held my most current work schedule and a query about attending the opera.

"I am dreadfully excited to help you organise your collections. I hope I shall be of great help to you." It may have been quite simpering in hindsight, but ah, well. Nothing to be done about it now.

He had asked how I had been faring, tactfully ignoring my falling out with Hadrian, and I replied readily with an abbreviated (solely positive) summary of events. Because I know he enjoys all things scandalous and intriguing, I told him an extremely censored retelling of how I was politely asked not to attend any more MIT mathematics conferences for the duration of however long they dictated (They don't want me terrorising any more star pupils, I suppose. Excuse me while I rage at the injustice of it all and secretly thank them for the excuse not to attend any more conferences hosted by their mathematics department). He would enjoy that, I think.

I don't think he received it by today, though, or things might have gone a little more smoothly. Well, maybe he had. He hadn't deigned to attend, nor did his wife or grown-up children, just Hadrian. He saw me as I glared into my contraband candy.

"And you're here why?" He climbed all the way to the centre seat immediately above me to bait me.

"Am I not allowed to watch something I paid fifteen dollars to view?" I refused to crane my neck, to let his height advantage get to me. "I am sorry we have similar taste in seating, perhaps I shall move?" I rose to forestall any disagreement.

He grabbed my arm and loomed over me. "No, sit," he hissed mockingly. "Wouldn't want you to make the effort."

I baulked, hurt and trying to understand why he was being so very cruel tonight. I thought we would be strangers, not hated enemies.

He let go of my arm and stormed off, hiding in the very back, shrouded in shadow yet looking incandescently enraged. I sighed sadly and made my way out of the theatre. This was a very bad idea, and without anyone to act as a buffer, the two of us were bound to get in a confrontation.

"Hey! Where're you going? Don't run out on my account!" he shouted down at me.

I turned to see him standing and still looking enormous so far up the stadium-style seats.

"You really gonna leave me?"

My eyes burned with rage, rage I tell you. Everyone in the theatre, all three of us, were watching our altercation, and I was in no mood to have my self-esteem splattered on the pavement once again. It is not roadkill, damn it.

"I'm sorry, yes," I said stiffly and hurried down the remaining steps, rubbing my eyes as I went. The bathroom was quiet at least, and no one had missed any part of the show but me. There was still five minutes or so until the show began. I cried a little before straightening myself out and returned to the florescent limelight of the real world. Oh, Jonathan Swift, I hate everyone.

I need a nap.

6/21 FRIDAY
*(Typed, Encrypted)*

Apparently, Hadrian spends almost no time at all at home. I never would have guessed. I always pegged him for a homebody type... Anyway.

I was expected there at the Marshall estate, for I always fancy it an estate, at precisely three o'clock this afternoon. The door revealed a cleaning lady bustling about the front hall with her vacuum who pointed out the study without a word. She was too busy listening to the enthusiastic beat bleeding into the air from her ill-insulated headphones.

His father is lovely as always, and my rather distasteful aversion to his features has run its course, thankfully. I am sure that, had this occurred a few weeks before, I would have made up some fabrication to protect my fragile psyche from further harm. Meaning I would not have arrived at all.

I said nothing of my encounter with their son when I found the matriarch and patriarch lounging in the study. No matter how angry he was, I think I understand his rage and forgive him for it. They welcomed me rather sweetly.

"We haven't seen you lately, dear." Julianne, an ice queen in her own right, greeted me, looking just as severe as any other time I'd seen her upon her hand-embroidered couch. Is it funny that my former friend's parents can stand my presence after all I had apparently done to him? I cannot tell if it is ironic or tragic.

"Well, I'm only too glad to help. I can be a bit neurotic about organisation, so you asked the best girl for the project."

Gregory laughed, and I relaxed immensely at the sound. I always enjoy it when people laugh. It portends good tidings and kindness and good humour instead of coldness or callous disregard to all that is right and noble with the world... Excuse my simpering; it's unbecoming of a heartless bitch such as myself.

They led me into a well-lit storeroom/closet of unusual size (I do so love *The Princess Bride*, and only just watched it again instead of *Ariadne*), and I stared at the antique cabinetry and shelves upon shelves of trunks and boxes.

"I'll be organising all of this?" I asked, pointing weakly at the mountains of materialism.

"Did you think it would be easy?" Julianne asked, straightening her spine with an air of derision. "If it were simple, dear, we would have finished it ourselves. Will this be too difficult for you?"

I bristled a touch. "No, it just seems a bit larger than I expected." I stared up at the nearest cabinet hesitantly. It had to be twice my height!

"Said the actress to the Bishop," Gregory quipped a phrase, which is similar to the "yo mamma" or "that's what she said" jokes of today, only straight out of the eighteenth century.

"And how long have you been waiting to resurrect that turn of phrase?" I commented dryly.

"Years, my dear. Years." He grinned mischievously.

"How you put up with him, I have no idea." I looked to Julianne, shaking my head.

"Patience, child, and a great deal of good port." She laughed genteelly at his expense.

"What sort of system should I use? Do you have a preference?"

"System? No, girl, there are more than just books in my treasure trove. I want everything fully catalogued, organised by time period and place of acquisition, then a system of rotation for all my items so they spend at least two weeks out of the year out of storage, and are accorded some unifying theme. Shall we leave you to it then?" He was already turning away, wife in tow.

"Shall I email you questions or just research it on my own?" I called after them. I didn't want to appear stupid or incompetent, even if this looked quite out of my league. Librarians can only teach you so much!

"Call out; someone will let us know if we don't hear you." Gregory waved off my question without breaking his stride.

I turned about the suddenly so much larger-looking room with a sense of impending doom. The closet door clicked shut, and the light flickered ever so slightly. Ominous... Maybe this was a punishment rather than an overture of kindness? Wonderful, I think I shall be ill.

I didn't have my computer, nor were any in reach, but I could spy an electronic typewriter hiding on a low shelf. Great, just great. I meandered through the room, getting a feel for the layout and any general theme/design in the hodgepodge of strange or hugely expensive (sometimes both) artefacts closing in on me. Many of them were already tagged with little bits of string and paper, faded cursive mocking me with its barely discernible curvature. Some were newer. Hmm, I suppose they go through archivists regularly. Utter joy and happiness, I was alight with it, can't you tell?

I grabbed a stack of partially filled forms and found that perhaps half of the cache was noted, dated, and categorised (Even if none of the previous caretakers saw fit to follow a single universal system of organisation). That only left me with the rest of the things in here and out and about in the manor. I was actually feeling confident by the time I finished organising my predecessor's work several hours later.

Viviane poked her head in from time to time to see if I "had suffocated on the dust yet." She also asked me a few strangely pointed questions.

"Say, Ina. Why'd you volunteer for this gig? All of us have been roped into it at one time or another, but you can't exactly get threatened into it like us."

I tapped the pencil I was using to write out provenance information against my lower lip, thinking. "I think it's a wonderful kindness of your father to ask me."

She didn't look convinced, and, even though it was the truth, I wouldn't have believed it either. So, instead, I thought up something suitably personal and in keeping with her view of the work itself.

"And, maybe, it's a bit of penance for the wrongs I've done," I said dryly.

"Really?" she said, sounding mildly shocked. "I wouldn't think you're old enough to rack up this kind of debt."

I shrugged. "Perhaps I'm hoping that the work will tell me how to bring my life back into equilibrium rather than atoning for wrongdoing."

She seemed to understand what I was saying, which was strange because even I didn't know what exactly I was saying.

I was sad to see her go, despite the interrogation; her interruptions were dispiritingly few and far between. It had broken up the monotony ever so nicely. Carson popped by to tell me dinner was ready if I was hungry, but I waved him off, not really listening. I was distracted by the antique 17th-century pistol cradled gingerly in my hand. It was *beyond gorgeous,* I tell you.

Once I embroiled myself in the work, it was quite satisfying and engaging. When I was relieved of my duty (more like forced out of the house), I secretly couldn't wait to do it again. No matter how intimidating a project, taking it apart makes it infinitely more manageable. Remember that, patient reader. Just as you wade through my seemingly wild mood swings and adventures, I, too, am wading through impossible tasks and difficulties. We'll ford it together.

# July

7/1 MONDAY
*(Dream Journal)*

I secretly suspect that writing down these nightmares, in fact, allows me a greater memory of the event in question, which is not my intention in the least. Unfortunately, I find that the habit of writing is too engrained and comforting to simply stop.

We were in a slaughterhouse, and everything was in Cyrillic but also in French, which I am fairly horrible at reading. The cows were being killed with milk jugs filled with butterflies that fell from the ceiling and broke their backs upon landing. They lowed, and I hated it all. I grasped the person beside me, but they were not a person at all. A giant butterfly towered above me and smacked me with armoured wings.

I stumbled back into the line of doomed bovine. My feet stuck to the floor, and I grasped at the cow nearest me but didn't feel the coat beneath my fingers. There were great televisions facing the cows, with visions of diamonds and roller-coaster rides and *The Sound of Music*.

A sledgehammer was swimming through the heat-induced mirage.

"Help me!" I screamed, vision flickering in and out horribly. "Help me, anyone!" The door opened. Ghosts streamed out, stealing cows and replacing them with goats.

"Sheep go to heaven," they sang. "Goats go to hell." The killing floor began to crack with blue light shining up at the sky.

"Hade!" I sobbed, thinking I'd seen him among the ghosts. "Please don't be dead." The floor crumbled. "Please."

Big green eyes.

## 7/2 TUESDAY
*(Written in a worn notebook)*

I was working at Hadrian's house today and it was all very odd. It felt like I was being watched while I went through each room. Not in the same way you feel when you know there are omnipresent security cameras keeping their unblinking eye on the premises. As though I had some sort of hanger-on while taking pictures and noting placements. It was all very eerie, for the house was almost silent. Carson and Viviane were on some sort of vacation in Crete, and Gregory and Julianne were out. I hummed and waited for it to go away.

Though, I'm almost *certain* that one of the doors locked just as I was about to open it.

I decided not to tarry in that part of the house.

## 7/13 SATURDAY
*(Typed, Encrypted)*

I have made a huge dent in the dragon's hoard, huzzah! Feel free to wave tiny paper flags and toss ticker tape to the sky in celebration if you are so inclined, I'll wait.

I also have a goodly amount of money in my bank account, now that I have finally checked it (I have a system where I give myself a budget of twenty percent of my actual gross income per month and round all of my purchases up to completely eliminate the possibility of overdrawing and allow for a decent emergency fund. Father terrified me into frugality).

That, of course, brightens my day because I have enough stashed away to rent a shitty apartment in New Jersey, if I felt so inclined. That should make anyone not out to make a name for themselves in the entertainment/ business world dance deliriously with joy.

Father has mellowed again (I personally think he is becoming more hormonal than *me*, the irascible teenager that I am, as he ages). Admittedly, I am still having rather nasty nightmares as of late, but not terrible enough to disrupt my sleep on a regular basis. Therefore, I must rejoice.

I have taken time out of my schedule to decompress, as well. I still exercise like a fiend to return to my previous excellent working condition, but that is not necessarily relaxing. Exploring of any kind has always been a balm to my soul, not pure physical activity. I pulled out Hadrian's birthday gift and gave it a whirl for the very first time this week (I know...such a sin to deny myself such pleasures for such a protracted period!). It was spectacular, let me tell you. I raided the attics of the Parthenon and it was *glorious*.

The reason I am telling you, of course, is to offset just how miserable Hadrian relishes in making me feel as of late. He does not know of his family's alliance with me. Well, I assume it is with me. We don't actually discuss Hadrian at all when I'm over, but they aren't unkind to me, which I suspect would not be the case if they believed I was a terrifying harlot bent on destroying their family's peace.

Several times, Carson's silence has even slipped up, and, whenever that occurs, he sounds quite aggravated with his little brother. Thus I assume they believe me blameless of Hadrian's all-encompassing antipathy, mostly at least. Hadrian has, however, caught me at various public venues and remonstrated against me among the mob. How very gauche, I must say.

I was in a Starbucks, contemplating their less detestable non-caffeinated products (Did you know the last time I finished an espresso, I stayed up for two and a half days straight, writing manic nonsense and spilling ink *everywhere* my hands were shaking so greatly? I am not allowed caffeine any more, needless to say), when I detected the unmistakable footfalls of a creature incensed. Well, no, I didn't, but I enjoy hyperbole as much as the next person and dramatics as well. But you know that already.

I turned when the clicking heels behind me clattered to a clamorous halt. Ah, Hadrian, you and those Italian leather derbys with an exceptionally loud heel, how could I forget? I had assumed it to be some unfortunate lady about to face plant before she made it to the counter. So, what happened next? Can you hazard a guess?

"What are *you* doing here? You live a half an hour away, but end up in *my* Starbucks?"

I frowned at the floor. *I didn't know that you bought cafés along with everything else you mindlessly consume,* I wanted to say. I didn't.

"I asked you a question. Have you decided to take a vow of silence? Decided to ignore the whole world until it grovels at your feet?"

I turned away, and can you guess my current feelings?

If you supposed a blustering flurry of impotent rage, you are correct! Here is a coupon to some defunct store that went under three years ago! Enjoy.

"I would like a tall herbal paradise tea, please." I was next in line. He fumed behind me. I could feel his glare boring through me like dynamite to be detonated on Mount Rushmore.

He purposefully shoved his shoulder against mine as I made my tactful retreat. He found me amongst the throng eagerly anticipating their afternoon pick-me-ups meant to ward off those pesky feelings of inadequacy and hopelessness inherent with the modern American.

"Really?" he breathed with almost-trepidation as I fetched my drink after several moments of standing together, silently awkward. I wanted to slap him hard across the face but restrained myself. That I also wanted to cry and collapse onto the floor immediately afterwards had no influence on my decision. He was hurting because of me, and I wouldn't exacerbate his pain with retaliation.

I left him to his coffee house, never to darken its door again. When we began meeting by chance in other public places (museums, galleries, theatres, *grocery stores!*), I attempted to leave him be, but my concessions have only further enraged him. Fancy that.

Of course, sometimes he forgets himself and only looks lost when he sees me, which is infinitely worse. He once asked me, after spotting me at the *Frist*, "Why didn't you just pick up the phone?"

"Can't we just be strangers?" I had asked pleadingly, and he just...left. I'm being tormented by ghosts.

I honestly don't know what he wants of me, but we're meeting too often for it to be mere chance. Something is going on. I mean, I only go out of my set routine so much, and every time I wander from that path, he is there. It's enough to drive a girl mad.

I mean a grocery store? *Really?* I know for a fact that his family's chef procures all of the family's produce, meats, etc. herself. He looked as if he had never *been* to a Kroger before that day, and now *I'm* too mortified to ever return. It happened yesterday, and I'm still flushed in the face from the encounter.

I was cruising through the dairy section after work, at ease and listening to music as I compared prices and protein content. I saw something in the corner of my eye, and wouldn't you know it, there's Hadrian, clinging to his cart and looking overwhelmed.

I was so in the zone, it never crossed my mind that walking up to him with his favourite type of yogurt (and it is truly vile. I don't understand why he ate it so often in that little, insulated lunch pail of his) and plopping it into said cart could ever be a bad idea.

He noticed me only when I held the watery, artificially flavoured artifice claiming to be yogurt before him. He was rather intently wishing for one of the cheerfully labelled beers across the aisle, I think. I faltered as his gaze hardened.

"Why would I want that, you bitch?" That really got under my skin better than anything else, the way he pronounced me "bitch" in the off-hand, flippant tone that suggested long internal usage.

"Sorry." I turned away to put the container back.

"And how did you know what I was getting? You've been following me, haven't you," He laughed harshly. "Just like you. Can't leave anything alone, no matter what you say." Inertia sent my upper-half lurching forward when my legs froze beneath me, the sludge flying from my fingertips.

It splattered rather spectacularly before me, bursting forth on the first bounce, twisting midair for maximum spillage, landing squarely on its lid, and leaving the rest of its innards behind as the plastic continued its acrobatics down aisle 13. It really was a sight to behold when you were not currently reenacting a battle-ready berserker set to rip into some unfortunate bugger's innards with your bare hands.

"That is *enough*." My whisper seemed to carry despite the annoying country radio station playing Brad Paisley above our heads and the numerous chattering individuals idling about their payloads nonchalantly. "I have had it to here with these neurotic attempts at getting a rise out of me." I turned to look at him and started to scream.

"Do I care what you think of me? No! I don't care what you think because right now you are worse than dead to me. I will scratch your name out of my life just as surely as you have ripped me out of yours! You're no different than anyone I have ever met, you selfish, insignificant, little princeling! No matter what I do, you will hate me because of a stupid slip of *paper* taped on my door! I never want to see your face again!" I took a breath, glaring at him full-on. He had the classic deer in headlights look about him. I haven't lost control so spectacularly for his viewing pleasure before that moment, I think. "And next time," I spat, "take more care for *when* you send your *fucking* ultimatums."

I pushed him out of the way, produce flying from the basket tucked under my arm. I ended up abandoning my remaining items among the candy buckets in favour of getting out of the public eye as quickly as possible.

Of course, my mother's church friends shop there, my father's students and coworkers shop there, my fellow Jackson Academy of the Sciences graduates shop there! I'm going to be fired from my job and my scholarships repealed out of spite. My life will be shot to hell all because I lost my fucking temper.

Now that I have expressed my rage and let it run away from me, you probably believe my life is completely ruined. No matter what I think now, remember I'm a teenager. That means that everything is a disaster. No exceptions. It will get better because I will not allow it to get worse. I'm merely being insufferably solipsistic and hysterically egotistical at the moment.

## 7/14 SUNDAY
*(Dream Journal)*

I was in school, music permeated the air, and I was in a ridiculous dress. The silly thing was mermaid style, black with a bodice decorated with blue diamonds. I liked the black opera gloves, though. I took gentle, delicate steps in some towering heels heading for the main lawn. It was prom, and everyone was dressed to impress as they danced on the giant dais covering the dewy grass to protect the girls' delicate ankles. Heels and wet do not mix even in dream logic. I was suddenly atop the dais with the rest of the others, magically, and everyone was watching me.

Hadrian emerged from the crowd wearing an expensive white suit and tie. I was whisked away in a stranger's arms while Hadrian stood in the centre of the floor. I looked up at my partner, only to find an unfamiliar face, a good ol' boy through and through. He looked down at me with innocent eyes and kissed my forehead. Something roared off-screen. I was pulled away from my dance and my gloves were ripped from my arms with an almighty jerk.

"Liar!" he yelled and pulled a very real gun out of his pocket. His faced morphed into a familiar pallid, sweaty visage, and he pulled the trigger. The last thing I remember is Hadrian becoming himself and the blood splatter spreading to paint his entire suit red, red, *and so very red.*


7/18 THURSDAY
*(Typed, Encrypted)*

No serious ramifications have manifested outside of the bare minimum (probably because no death threats were issued). Father found out and rather ruthlessly put down any wisp of an idea that such behaviour was acceptable or tolerable in any scenario. No calls ending my employment were forthcoming, even if Frank ribbed me a touch for being so cruel. Vanderbilt didn't care in the least, of course. Yay.

I am always making mountains out of molehills, just as I thought on Saturday. Now, on to the actual reason I thought to put pen back to paper today.

I *may* have spilled more than absolutely necessary last night while working with Gregory. He gave me a splash of cognac to celebrate the itemisation of his entire house and asked me inane questions about animal husbandry of all things. I think, because I was raised in Tennessee by old-world parents, that he thought me somehow automatically an authority in raising guinea fowl of all things!

"No, no. My father is an academic, and Mother has a hands-on personality, but not when it comes to *food,*" I replied lazily, swirling the amber liquid to divine its sweetness before drinking. It was sweet and cleansing (read: burns like hell) on my tongue.

"Really?"

"Oh, yes. Father's always dragging me to this convention or that seminar surrounding esoteric mathematical equations and radical physics theories."

"Your mother, though, you never speak of her, Inanna." He took a long draw, and I followed suit.

"Well, I have no good stories. She's not as funny as my father." I looked at the rhino's head, staring me down from the fireplace, instead of Gregory. It was on my list, a Victorian antique like the rest of the room's furnishings, picked up in a Moroccan bazaar in 1972.

"But you do have some, yes?" he asked when I was obviously not going to elaborate.

"Oh, of course, but they're much too sad for my tastes at the moment. I'm celebrating a job completed!" I smiled, but it was not my best.

"Of course, of course." He gestured to the bottle, and I accepted a touch more out of courtesy. "Any recent foibles surrounding your father then?"

"Oh, so many that if they were quarters they could fill a ballroom." I matched his sip once more. I had forgotten that I, being shorter and female, would become much more intoxicated than he in a wink. Silly, silly girl.

"What sort of stories would you like to hear? Funny drunken Russian stories, convention stories, or incompetent professor stories?"

"What sort of convention stories?" He leaned back and took a sip. I followed suit in a gesture of brotherly kindness.

"One time, when I was five, I was sitting with my parents watching a physics presentation. The man was talking about strings and quantum physics and some such. During the Q&A, I raised my hand. He picked me out of the crowd with the most indulgent look on his face. "Terrible idea," I crowed.

"His entire argument hinged on nobody noticing that his mathematics was twisted out of shape in a very silly way, to my mind at least. He left in tears, and the rest of the room burst into a mix of laughter and applause. It probably seemed precious to the other conventiongoers, but my parents were horrified."

He chuckled and prodded me to come up with more humorous outtakes in my life, some self-deprecating, some self-adulating...

When I got home, I wrote down on a scrap of paper "told Greg about Letter." He also drove me home, I think, but that's not nearly as important as that insignificant bit of dried pulp. The moment I read it (which is just as I was writing this), it all came back to me.

I was thinking about how nice it was to just talk without fear of the consequences when this issued forth from my lips. "Last month—was it last month? Yes, a little more than a month past, I was dragged to a most laborious congress of overinflated egos. Would you believe some twit made base comments about me and derided my father's professional capability as a tenured professor?" I laughed most bitterly, lazily swirling the glass cradled in my palm. I was well on the road to complete intoxication, and he was perfectly sober, damn him.

"He mocked my father before all of his colleagues and was punished, naturally, but I wasn't satisfied. I found him sitting in the bar drinking cheap rum and soda. Yelled at him something fierce, and, would you believe it, he looked about ready to cry? I actually told him 'I killed a man in SoHo,' [retelling complete with air quotes] and he believed it? Am I that intimidating? No, not a bit. The really funny part, though, is that my father yelled and *yelled* when he found out. Howled like he hated me, and then of course Hadrian—" I had bit my tongue, but it was too late.

"Then Hadrian started acting strange about the house. What happened? You seemed so happy together, and the way he talked about you..." He trailed off significantly, and I jumped at the opportunity to unload my guilt and pain.

"He sent me a note, a *note* about how we couldn't be friends if I wouldn't tell him all my secrets. Of course, he would set the ultimatum the day before I returned from being eternally harassed at a fucking conference!" I banged my hand against the arm of the chintz chair and liquid tumbled onto the floor (but no glass, thankfully).

"Oh, sweetheart—"

I continued, unabated. "Is it wrong not to tell someone everything? To keep them from harm? I don't even tell my family everything! Neither of my parents are the confiding type, and that breeds true, I promise. I didn't know that I was being standoffish or bitchy. I just don't tell everything that I feel to the random passersby! I've never told people some of the things I told Hadrian, and yet he hates me for not baring my soul to him. Is it a sin to be introverted?" I asked plaintively, tears, loosened by the good booze in my belly, threatening to fall at the slightest thing.

"Why does everyone hurt me?"

He crossed the space and wrapped his arms around me as I cried.

"Please, don't tell him," I begged into his smoking jacket as I attempted to pull myself together. "He doesn't need me moping about destroying his chances for happiness."

Gregory made a befuddled sound that reverberated in his chest, but agreed all the same.

The next thing I remember is my own alarm clock as I staggered into my room. It was only nine at night when I tossed myself in my bed and fell asleep.

...So, yes, I did in fact spill too much to Hadrian's Faulkner-forsaken father.

7/25 THURSDAY
*(Written in a worn notebook)*

Hadrian went on a tour today. *He* wanted a tour given by *me*, specifically. He waited nearly half an hour for me to finish my first tour of the day. He even ignored the perfectly capable Frank, who sat in the gift shop like a bump on a log, petulant that he was rebuffed by one of the mob, especially one that was currently at odds with his fellow cohort (not that he knew at that particular moment).

The moment I saw him, sitting and staring blandly at the ceiling, I herded my group of small children into the arms of their ever-so-caring instructor (She seemed rather perturbed that I interrupted her smoking break for something so base as the return of her children). I was sure he was here either at the behest of his father, press-ganged into begging clemency for his ignorant cruelty, or as a barbarous act of revenge, attempting to send me out of my livelihood. Either way, I felt rather damned as I went to the docent's podium to better welcome my "guest" (and keep him at arm's length).

Frank stood, glowering at the irksome boy as he crossed the way towards me. "Been waiting for you, lass." He had been in a Scotch mood for the past week or so, adopting the vernacular and frightening guests with the claymore hidden beneath the register ("For thieves," he reassured our boss… Total fallacy, I know for a fact. The thing isn't even sharpened). "Haven't seen another soul since. Ye can't keep him much longer, or he may complain." He was right, of course, but I would wait until he noticed that I was there before conversing with one of the banes of my existence at the moment.

Hadrian chose that moment to jerk his head in our direction, stand, and then stride my way. "I'd like a tour, please." He was almost pleasant, except he refused to meet my eyes.

"Really? I thought you were here for some other purpose, perhaps manslaughter or libel?" I cocked my head as he tensed up, preparing for a fight. Was he going to attack me?

He glared at me instead of throwing the first punch. "Look, I want to talk to you. We can either take a walk around the block *now*, or I can sit over there and scare all the other history geeks who come here. What'll it be?" he asked darkly.

"Eight dollars," I answered, subdued by his anger. *You're not here to apologise but to dish out vengeance*, I thought. Lovely. He tossed me the money, and I slipped it in the register under Frank's watchful eye.

He disapproved of this undertaking and made his views known without the utter luxury that is the spoken word. I had no idea how this would turn out, and Frank feared for my safety, he later told me. Apparently, my bitching makes my exploits more terrifying from an objective point of view.

"Follow me, and we'll make our way through the grounds, then through the house." I walked with faux serenity out the door; Hadrian followed. "You wish to speak with me?" I smoothed the creases of my skirt, fastidiously plucking at my pleating until they were perfect (an impossible task).

"What did you mean at Kroger?" Oh Dante, above or below, what is this boy up to now? "About ultimatums and letters?"

"We're no longer friends, yes? You revoked my right to your secrets in June. For the first time in your life, respect the wishes of others and let me keep mine." I fiddled with my fan instead of looking him in the face, speaking at a rapid pace to keep him from interrupting. The temptation to rip him to pieces was too great.

"No, please. I want to know." It was a soft, remarkably kind way to say it. I almost believed that his cruelty had vanished and my friend had reemerged from his chrysalis of haughty dislike. I would not succumb to his blandishments, however.

"I'm not your toady. So don't test me," I snapped. We walked in silence for a moment. I should have been instructing him, but it seemed unnecessary when he was paying for my time like one would pay a whore for their body, not seeking my knowledge for his self-betterment.

"So, why do you work so much?"

I sighed. Why was he always harping on my working habits, even when he hates me? "Are any of my actions accountable to you?" I inclined my head slightly to create an elegant profile against his slouching figure.

"Are you hiding from your dad or from me?"

I hit the little numb-nut. Well, I wanted to. So, so badly. "Are you avoiding home because you hate your family?" I shot back reflexively.

"Of course not! I— Wait a minute. How'd you— Oh." Well, that was a veritable roller coaster of tonal shift, going from defensive to shocked to invaded to...Oh.

"Because you are as difficult to divine as a shallow pond doused with chlorine. Not even the remains of bacteria exist to obscure my view." *And I never see you when I work at your house for several hours straight.*

"Ina—"

"Please stop your aggravating attempts at prying into a life you have no reason to interfere with. I suggest you leave."

"No," he thundered. "I'm here to talk to you, and you can't kick me off the damn tour!"

I backed off immediately, bowing my head and taking a step away from my aggressor. "Why are you doing this?" I asked softly, staring at the ground, where the blood of so many soldiers turned the earth red with gore, the little spot beneath a window that once had limbs piled so high from necessary amputations, it hid the view. I blockaded my mind with these facts flitting past my consciousness at a swift gallop.

In any case, I am now a rather poor scribe. I was only skimming the surface instead of diving straight down into the depths of body language, tonality, and vocabulary. He immediately quieted, I know, but I said nothing more. He may have attempted to say something, but I am not required to listen to him like Father. I am not required to remember past admonishments so as to provide proof that his disciplinary methods are viable. I abandoned him outside of the house and speedwalked up the steps and through the doors. Frank was sitting in our customary spot, fiddling with a bit of leather and wood, watching me from afar.

"All right, lass?"

"I want whiskey and oblivion." I collapsed against the wood panelling behind us as the bench beneath protested lightly. *Please, I have a wife and kids!* it cried piteously. I ignored it with the practised ease that comes with desensitisation. "I want to go home."

He nodded in commiseration. "Want to check out early?"

"Hell, no. Where would I go?" I sent him an incredulous sidelong glance, my arms crossed defensively. "I have no friends, my father hates me, school is out—and I'm barred from the grounds in any case... What can I do but work?"

"Do something fun? Ya don't have to have people ta have fun. Go to a show or something. Just enjoy your life. I hate to see it go to waste like this."

"I'll enjoy my life when I'm a tenured professor at a first-tier school, preferably Harvard. I'm concentrating all of my suffering into my formative years to give me a strong immunity to it by then."

He wasn't laughing at my sorry attempts at humour.

"What are you making?" I asked to fill the uncomfortable silence.

"Slingshot of sorts... It's slow now; time out, and I'll take up the slack." He waved me off and continued to fiddle with the leather, working the lacquered tool into the stiff kidskin. I went upstairs and cleaned instead.

My life is *so* blessed, isn't it?


7/26 FRIDAY
*(Typed, Encrypted)*

May Faust be damned to the lowest level of Dante's inferno, he came back again. Again, he waited. This time until there were no other guests to take up my time, and, again, paid the admission fee.

I was still smarting from yesterday's assault on my mental defences. I decided to remain completely silent through the excursion. My resolve crumbled as swiftly as a dieter's restraint upon catching sight of their favourite sweet on an unguarded table.

"Maybe I shouldn't have called you a bitch, but you sure act the part sometimes. After bitching me out in May, you shut me out. You never talked to me, you figured out how to block my texts again, and now you won't even argue with me right. You can be so impossible sometimes, and I can't—" He was rambling, and I was pretending not to listen. "Was I really that bad of a friend?"

I sent him a rather scathing look as I fluttered my fan across my face, partially concealing my nose and mouth. The message came across loud and clear: *What do you think?*

He blushed angrily and turned to look about the lawn. "How many people died here?"

I started slightly at the sudden enquiry. "More people than you've met, multiplied by two." He heard my murmur despite my best efforts, as I couldn't just not answer. It goes against every fibre of my tour-guiding being.

"You underestimate how much I get around." Did he mean that to be a double entendre? I wouldn't know because I didn't even think to ask him. "What is that building for?" He pointed to a miserable little shack to the left.

"Servant's outhouse."

This went on for the rest of the tour. He would ask a question pertaining to the house, and I would answer. He would try to intertwine historical with personal inquisition ineptly, and I would mostly evade his amateurish verbal traps.

Why was he doing this? Why was he spending time and money (of which, granted, he has plenty to spare) on trying to weasel out why our friendship failed so spectacularly? He wasn't apologising, and he had said nothing of his father to me, so I suppose this is an act of his own volition.

It is perplexing and stressful to have him lurking about, asking questions and pretending as if he's done nothing wrong. I know that he's angry that I apparently ended our friendship with nary a phone call. That may be why he is trying to divine my motivations. But that is no excuse for this tension and buried betrayal thrown to the surface every time he skulks into my place of work.

I'm going to read Boccaccio's *Decameron* to cheer myself up. At least that is mostly upbeat despite centring on nobles fleeing a plague-infested city and seeking to alleviate the inevitable tedium.


7/27 SATURDAY
*(Typed, Encrypted)*

Again. This must be a sign of insanity, for a normal person does not return again and again in the same way with the same words, expecting different results. Aye, *Gott in Himmel.* Maybe he thinks I will eventually cave if he continues bothering me in this way. It has certainly been disrupting my habits.

Yesterday, I spent most of my shift restocking and making repairs and work orders that had been neglected since last April. Today, I hid upstairs before hours and read the ancient books placed on the shelves for show (One is an interesting treatise on the Galapagos Islands trade routes and their impact on turtle migration from the 1860s).

"I'm not apologising," he said squarely after handing me the money.

I said nothing as we began our next walkabout. He complained that I was overworking myself in every aspect of my life, that he wanted things the way they were, and that my father was a bastard to the *n*th degree... On and on without end. I gritted my teeth and prayed a red cap would magically appear to lure Hadrian off into the woods so his rambling rant would cease to assault my poor eardrums. I interrupted him when no mythical intervention came to my aid.

"And *now* it's all fucked up, because God knows why. Nothing is good enough for Dad now. Never was, and now it's worse because I won't waste my time flipping burgers—"

"Why tell me, then? I'm a shrew, some cruel harpy. That means I don't deserve to be your confidant."

He froze in place, sentence cut short as his mouth snapped shut.

"I'm just a tragic heroine, singing my last song. What does any of this matter?"

He wouldn't, couldn't answer me, and, when he realised it, he left. He actually ran away from me as if I were some monster only just emerging from his playroom closet. I was relieved and dissatisfied simultaneously.


7/28 SUNDAY
*(Typed, Encrypted)*

I was aflame with passionate disdain. Now, I have been dampened by the cold shower of reality. Bollocks.

Something stupid happened with Father—it doesn't matter what—so I ended up coming to my shift teary-eyed and in need of a good bear hug from my partner in crime. Hadrian was already there arguing good-naturedly with Frank. I hope you take the time to fully digest that phrase because I am not saying it again. He has turned my one true ally against me!

I am lost without my lovable Frank to muck about with during shifts so slow that it looks as if we'll have no business at all and starve out on the streets. I can't lose him on top of everything else! How this even happened, I'm at a loss. Frank has always been fully behind me in my disdain for the narcissistic pretty-boy determined to crush my soul.

I almost turned tail, escaping the plotting conspirators against my contentedness, but my nearly perfect attendance record mocked me all the way from the back office, where the time tables were posted.

I just want this summer to *end*. Preferably now, because my sense of personal integrity could not harbour this purposeful renunciation of readily available cash and continued "good behaviour." I feigned ignorance as I opened the door and swung into my changing cubbyhole with nary a glance in their direction.

They continued to speak, lower now and mildly harried, as if their time was near an end (and it was). What they were talking about, I have no idea, but it was sure to infuriate me the moment I strapped myself into my bodice and faced the world.

He had his money out the moment I returned.

"No," I impressed upon him. I was not suffering through another day of this. Somehow, this would end within the hour, or I would eat the bonnie-blue bonnet Mother bought for me last August. "Do you want me to quit?" I asked. "Because I will, if you do."

Hadrian was bemused, and Frank's look of betrayal mirrored my expression not five minutes prior.

"What—"

I held a hand to forestall Frank's arguments.

"Hadrian." I stared him down, and he faltered.

"What?" he asked, a touch chastened and a trifle vulnerable.

I was too angry to take careful note of it. "Promise to leave me be, and I'll quit right now. I am sick of you torturing me." Let the melodrama commence, lovelies. "Say the words, and I'll take the last pleasant part of my life and dash it upon the rocks as if it were an unfortunate, malformed Spartan babe. Either do that or leave."

"No, I don't mean it like—"

"I don't care how you mean it," I said, almost patient. "I want you gone! And if we cannot reach an accord, I will run you off myself." My hands were on my waist (My hips presently hidden beneath hoop and dress) as I stared up into his eyes, challenging him to refuse me. If he had tried, I'm sure the only remains to be had would be a solitary eyeball and an angry note to his parents written *in his life blood...*

I really am not a nice person, am I? Maybe I do deserve to have this heaped upon me until I'm crushed utterly. It could be nature's way of ridding herself of a particularly troublesome, if ultimately insignificant, mammal. It's not as if a happy domestic life was ever in the cards for me. My mental TJV derailed the moment his lips parted once more for speech.

"If your life is that bad, then let me help you." Did he even hear me? Had he taken only a word here and there to formulate such a rebuttal?

"Why? When this entire conversation is an attempt to extricate myself from your life so your hatred may be assuaged, and I may return to my previous activities?" I asked hotly.

"But, Ina. Why? I just wanted—" He shook his head, then continued. "It doesn't matter. Can we just fucking make up already? Why can't we be nice to each other for once?"

"Because you poison everything you touch!" A definite twinge of shrill girlishness exerted its will upon my vocal cords.

"Because you won't let yourself be nice!"

I was comforted by the fact that his ejaculation was just as shrill as mine.

"Not even once!"

"Pipe down or I'm kicking both of you out," Frank warned, and I immediately quieted. Hadrian did not.

"Not until I get her back!" He pointed to me as he whined. What is he? Two?

"That's it. Get out, kid, or I'll call the cops."

I almost expected him to scream, *I own the police!* It would have been perfect. Instead, he looked to me in askance but was away with a flick of the wrist and a warning look.

I collapsed on the wailing antique bench the moment Hadrian was out of view. "Fuck," I breathed, suddenly exhausted.

"You're telling me, sweet pea." Frank took his seat beside me as per usual. We sat in the silent building; no one was coming in for another half hour, at least.

I took another fortifying breath before turning to accuse him. "What were you talking about before I clocked in?"

He shrugged, staring into the parking lot absently. "He wants to win you back."

I started at the pronouncement. "Really? Because he has made no such overture of friendliness to me in the past two months or more! I find that hard to swallow." I was rather incredulous, truth be told.

"Then he's really fucking bad at it. That doesn't mean he's not trying."

I frowned lightly, brow furrowed in unpleasant thought. "Would you mock someone's family, deride their choices, or denounce their actions if you were trying to impress *kindness* upon someone?"

"He's obviously dumb, In. I never said otherwise. What I notice is that he seems to think you *need* help. You need it bad." A volatile phrase.

"Are you taking his side?" An accusation.

"No, just telling you what I think." A refutation.

"I don't need him to be happy." A refrain.

"But you can't go on like this."

I scowled at his presumptuousness. "Really?" I said, mockingly innocent. "Because I have been doing perfectly fine all these years before he stumbled into and out of my good graces."

"But when were you happy? Not working, too tired, or running; just happy?" It was a good question, one that I had thought on often. I can tell you exactly when I was honestly, completely happy. And that opportunity is forever closed now.

"Not for a long while."

"Right, and how are you gonna *become* happy again?" He prodded me lightly.

"I'll not."

He punched me just so in the arm for my stubbornness. "Don't. I think, if you let yourself, you could be happy again."

*Oh, really? How?* I almost asked with doe eyes and all the trappings of trusting naiveté.

"Do you have a book of magic spells hidden somewhere upstairs? That's the only thing I could think of. A bit of black magic or some seeing stones gathering dust in the attic?" It was a bit more acerbic than I would have chosen had I been calm, but it served my purpose well enough.

"Get out of here," he said tiredly. "You need to get out of this house, your house, your own crazy..."

"And what would I do then? Travel aimlessly, achieving nothing at all and dying in some third-world country of an easily treatable illness?" That probably wouldn't happen, but it could, damn it!

"Take some time off," he coaxed. "You were *glowing* after running off to Germany. Take another month or two." He was nothing if not persistent.

"I don't have the money," I combated stubbornly.

"Bullshit."

Well, I couldn't really refute that now, could I? I had nothing to say, so we stayed like that for a while.

"Just let everything *go* for a bit. You're hoarding your own misery, and it's not a good look on you," was his parting phrase before braving the new bunch of fanny-packed, camera-toting tourists.

I stayed in the office the rest of the day and completed all of the taxation forms and balanced the chequebook for our overworked pseudo-secretary.

I admit it freely: it's not in my nature to let things go. I'm a natural accumulator of all sorts of things. I think I inherited it from Father in conjunction with the "good old days" from before I could even remember. When I was born, we had nothing at all. We got better, of course, but it probably left a mark on my psyche, never to be erased.

At least I don't squirrel away newspapers or animals, though.


7/30 TUESDAY
*(Dream Journal)*


I was in a maze and something horrible was chasing after me. Darkness was coming from the east, and I continued south, trying to take wing and fly before I was caught. Was I Icarus? I turned and followed lead after lead until I reached a dead end, my end. I spun, helpless and vulnerable, to view my pursuer. The great ichorous being in black slowed, and I watched it consume the stones, the sun, the sky before descending on me. I let it consume me, dissolving into blackness and oblivion. I woke up into a dream world of surreal colour and light. Hadrian was waiting with something in his hands...

7/31 WEDNESDAY
*(Typed, Encrypted)*

Hadrian has yet to haunt my doorstep since Sunday, but he has left me email messages to the effect that, should I ever need anything, he is always there to "help out." The latest one, which came in just a few minutes ago, is a bit different. I'll just copy and paste.

> Hey luv, [He enjoys creating increasingly problematic pet names when he emails me.]
>
> I'll be leaving for school in a week and a half. Yeah, time flies, doesn't it? Anyway, I'm expecting a ton of letters from you. If not, I'll come back down there and drag you up to Chicago, okay? Ha-ha, but really, I better hear from you, or I'll go crazy wondering what you're up to.
>
> Hade

Well, he's certainly no wordsmith (but I'm sure you already realised that, especially compared with me, long ago). I'm not sure that threat is entirely humorous hyperbole, either. I'm still rather angry that he's decided to forget the strife between us. It's unlike him. He thrives on hashing out his activities to a breathless audience and receiving sympathy or praise for the solving of them.... I think he's trying to give me a taste of my own medicine—trying to irritate me to the point of remarking upon it only to receive a lecture on how horrid it feels to be left out of the emotional loop by "your best friend."

...All right, consider your challenge accepted, Mr. Marshall.

# August

**8/21 WEDNESDAY**
*(Typed, Encrypted)*

Orientation has come and gone, and classes have finished for the day. I must say, I wish I had a roommate. All the other girls seem to be having a great time bonding over whatever it is they bond over. I feel quite out of the loop. At least school has not been a disappointment. I'm finishing out a Bio-Chem presentation for my major (all the other prerequisites have been taken and then some), two 300-level literature courses, quantum mechanics, Place and Period in Mythology, and one "underwater basket-weaving class" (something that is fun rather than required) otherwise known as Intro to Outdoor Education.

Hadrian has been gushing over his classes, the architecture, the food...basically everything positive about Chicago has been touched upon to make me long for the sweet embrace of his university. I have actually been updating the Facebook page he made for me with phrases like "still alive", "out punishing serfs", and, my favourite, "Hadrian is too nosy." The sniping comments under the variations of the latter are always fun to watch, if not comment on in turn.

8/28 WEDNESDAY
*(Typed, Encrypted)*

I want harder classes! Five-page papers? Two classes a day? Socratic seminars? This is child's play! My father was assigning twelve-page papers a week the moment I could type at fifty words per minute. I have decided to take a side job grading papers for a Professor Andrea Godshall (pronounced God's Hall) in the archaeology department. She seems nice enough but dreadfully overworked. She has a huge course load and welcomes the help of *two* volunteers. There is some grad student (I haven't met him), and he'll be helping teach classes with Godshall and grade papers with me.

At least it's something to do. My shelf of shame has dwindled to a *book* of shame: *Serf Anna,* lucky me. I also have a few French novels waiting in the wings the moment I finish it. It's slow going, however. Something is making me drag my feet quite laboriously. Whatever shall I do if I cannot finish this story when I read it to the exclusion of all others? Burn it, I suppose.


8/29 THURSDAY
*(Typed, Encrypted)*

Thomas Jefferson Forrest is surprisingly cordial. I think we immediately struck a friendship before either of us spoke a word, if I dare to be so bold. He's quite striking, even hunched over a desk with reading glasses perched ever so delicately on the brink of his nose. Blond from too much time in the sun and a tough homegrown air about him, he had the appearance of the farmers I meet at the local market downtown. I trod lightly, hoping not to disturb his studies.

"Are you Miss Inanna?" he asked lightly, looking up at me with warm brown eyes and a small smile.

I nodded, silently relishing his deeply Texas accent as I'm an incorrigible accent enthusiast. "And you are Mr. Forrest?"

He motioned for me to sit and handed me a stack of papers thicker than my finger's span. "Yes, ma'am. Call me TJ. Mr. Forrest is my daddy, still. These here are 100-level multiple-choice quizzes. Nice an' easy with an answer key an' ev'rathing. When you finish that, I got more for ya."

I nodded, sure I would do a good job. I ended up correcting the key.

He was pleasantly surprised and commended my sharp eyes and keen knowledge of sociological concepts. I may have preened a bit, I couldn't tell you really. I graded with him, and we talked of many things, mostly class work and PhD requirements.

When my time was up, I shook his hand and made to leave.

"You really don't remember me, do ya?" he asked before I made my escape.

"Should I?" I turned back, examining him closely.

"You took Dr. Morel's class back when I was a freshman. Or was I not mem'rable enough for ya?" I took a moment to calculate exactly what classes I sat in on with Dr. Morel and what year it must have been in order to fit his age and mine...

"Back when I was thirteen?"

"You were thurteen?" he asked, surprised.

"Yes, I'd never taken an anthropology course by that point and thought 'What the heck.' I sat in the...second row, three seats in. And you had much thicker glasses on." I pointed at him, slightly accusing.

"Well, if I ever wanted to get laid, I had to update my look," he replied wryly.

"They were hideous, granted, but you were certainly not the most detestable creature in the room if I recall correctly." I enjoyed meandering through memory lane like this. It was nice.

"Oh, I'd forgotten about the Hoodie!" His eyes lit up nicely.

"Now, he was *disgusting*," I commiserated. We ended up talking together for the next hour, and he invited me to some party tomorrow night, which I now feel obligated to attend. Ah well, at least there will be someone to talk to.

8/30 FRIDAY
*(Typed, Encrypted)*

It's midnight, and I do not like parties. They are too loud with music, too hot with humanity crushing against you, too humid with the exhalation of horny young adults, too raucous period. And too overflowing with insufferable drunkards to do anything intellectually stimulating. I left before things became too "fun", according to TJ. I am not well pleased.

8/31 SATURDAY
*(Typed, Encrypted)*

Had a huge row with Father today, but he has decided to allow me to live on campus. I can't decide if this is a victory or a desecration of his soul. Am I a character crusher like those helicopter mothers I always detested from parenting magazines and fellow overwrought students?

We were in the midst of a really heated discussion centring on my workload. He thought I could squeeze in one more math class next semester, but I was adamant that my schedule was challenging enough for the moment. He disagreed rather passionately. I responded with cruelty and hatred that had been brewing inside my gut for the last *year*.

"What do you even want from me?" I shrieked despite myself.

He froze for a moment, bewildered by the breakneck conversation derailment. "What do you mean?"

"I mean, do you wish for me to reside here with you forever, never living my own life, until you *bury* me? Because that is where you've been leading me as of late, Father." It was intolerably cruel, but I wanted to know if he actually wanted me to succeed outside of his shadow, or if I should relinquish any hope I have of living independently.

He gaped at me. "I would *never*, Inanna! I only want you to excel in the field of your choosing! If you decide to slack off now, how will you be able to complete the path ahead? You will be nothing!" Of course, he would mention "The Path Ahead." It's always been how he bullied me into completing his insane learning regimes in the past.

"I'll go about my business myself! I don't care about *your* inane plan, and I'm not letting you ruin my life with your madness."

He began to reproach me angrily, but I gave him no leave.

"Yes, you heard me right. All these years, I've tried so hard to achieve your approval and love, yet I haven't received it for less than impossible perfection. So fuck that, and fuck you."

I have never, *never*, sworn before my father for any reason. You will understand that he was unprecedentedly gobsmacked. I started to pace, so far into my rant I couldn't stop if I wanted to.

"I don't need your approval or *plans*. I don't need you. I need me. And I need to do something to aid *me* rather than you. I'm tired of bending to your every whim because I don't want to see you suffer. Father, has it even occurred to you that I'm suffering, as well?" I looked to him imploringly. "That I need the attention you so jealously guard? You may still be hurting, but you're drowning me in your erratic behaviour! I'll leave and not return if this doesn't change!"

The hysterical edge on my voice would simply not do. I took a moment to compose myself before fleeing. "If you can accept me as I am, then I'll be extremely happy. If you can't, then we shall part on sour terms. Goodbye, Father." I slammed the door dramatically and exited the house for, perhaps, the last time.

I received a phone call not two minutes into my furious speed walk towards where, I don't even know. "In...I never knew. I love you, Myshka, and I *am* so very proud of you. I just want you to do your best." He sounded so pathetic and small on the other line, I nearly cried.

"I love you too, Daddy. I just can't stand being at home anymore. I'm eighteen and almost out of college. I can take care of myself." *And so can you* was left unsaid.

He let out a long, low sigh. "If I send you to live in the dormitories, will you promise to come back for the weekends? You can choose the rest of your classes, I promise. I'll remain only as a retainer and advisor."

Now, I was crying. My father never makes concessions like that. It is simply not in his nature to concede so much for any reason. Had I broken him?

"I promise."

"Come back home. I'll file the paperwork."

I returned to our doorstep and hugged my father desperately when he met me outside.

I feel horrible even as the ecstasy of imminent freedom creeps through my very being. Maybe I'll put something worthwhile on that silly Facebook after all. I'll tell the world that I broke the indefatigable Professor Drew.

I think I'm going to be sick.

# September

**9/1 SUNDAY**
*(Typed, Encrypted)*

I stare now at my bookcases, layers stacked neatly upon the other to maximise storage capacity. Warm, if a trifle dusty, poplar greets my delicate touch with a familiar fondness imbued onto all well-loved furnishings. All these books have been my best of friends for so long; I know not how I can part with them, even with the reassurance that comes with weekend custody. It cements my resolve never to divorce should I ever manage to marry.

This room of mine has been my sanctuary for so long, I don't know how I will ever cope with a flight for good. I'll just have to bring it with me, I suppose. The walls, too, for I'm sure they don't sell that particular shade of dusky blue anymore. It's far too hideous for modern tastes, you see.

**9/2 MONDAY**
*(Typed, Encrypted)*

My roommate is quite...energetic. She was absolutely floored that she was getting a roommate and helped me "decorate" my side of our cupboard-sized dormitory. She grabbed things out of my bag and tacked them to my wall for a "textured feel." Despite our obvious differences, I think she's growing on me. We both have a vaguely similar sleeping schedule and listen to comparable music. Not a horror show at all.

Her name is Terri Saxe, and she's a junior business major. She may act and dress like a total incompetent, but I already have a theory about her. Her personality is most emphatically *not* a front to distract from the mental acumen hidden beneath. No, it is her natural inclination to jump about in extremely precarious heels and flouncy skirts.

But she knows exactly how to weasel her way into others' circles in order to gain what she yearns for without alerting said others of her intentions. She uses her own nature to her advantage. Terri has managed to win twenty dollars from me in the last hour by betting I couldn't identify all of the classes she's taking this year (One of them was new, in my defence).

I *am* glad to be out of the house. Though most of my things are still there (I will be visiting often, after all), I still feel emotionally disconnected from the utter malignancy that is my erstwhile home. It's definitely a nice feeling.


9/3 TUESDAY
*(Written in a worn notebook)*


Work, classes, dinner, and then more work. Terri noticed my exercise paraphernalia beneath my bed this morning as I rooted about for my jogging gear.

"What do you play?" she asked, peeking from beneath her feather down.

"Anything, really. You?" I replied reflexively.

"Want to come bouldering tonight? Students have a free pass." Her head mostly emerged from the cocoon.

"Just tell me the time." I grabbed my sneakers and pulled down my shirt in a smooth motion. "I'll be there."

"Eight at the Atrium, now leave or go back to sleep." She returned once more to her silken hibernation, and I left to run my circuit.

I was gladdened to have had the presence of mind to leave my things near the door because she was still dancing with Morpheus when I returned. I managed to end my work shifts (TA and tour guide) without bloodshed, turn in my class work early, and finish all homework within my ability to finish by 7:30.

Let me tell you, bouldering is quite fun. I may have been surrounded by strangers, sequestered away from Terri so that I may be examined without reprisal (At least, I think that was the intention). That was not fun, of course, but they seemed nice enough once we arrived at the chosen exercise studio. We walked through the doors, rented shoes, and crowded to the strange hulking menace that is a rock wall.

I never really liked rock climbing. The idea that someone down below holding a single rope had complete control over whether I lived or died is quite nauseating to me (Yes, subject amplification, don't remind me of my foibles). This kind of climbing, however, is completely under my power. I latched onto the wall like a spider navigating its own web and fell more times than I reached my goal, but I enjoyed myself fiercely. It left me exhausted and aching in a wonderful way.

9/4 WEDNESDAY
*(Written in a worn notebook)*

We went belly dancing tonight. I have never twisted my body into such a tizzy before.

The girls Terri introduced me to yesterday are her "go-to" exercise group, as a method to keep morale up and discourage slacking, I suppose. They're nice enough, if incredibly intense about their calorie counting. I swear they have spreadsheets filled with every single thing they've eaten over the past two years the way they chattered on while making our way to the local YWCA.

I have to say, I am impressed by their dedication. Most of them are elder or only children, women, and wholly dedicated to success in the workforce (and every other facet of life available to them). Not all of them are business majors, but their intent is the same. They will be the boss that you never wanted to have. The bitch who will verbally beat you within an inch of your life if you fuck up, yet you can't fault them for their drive and moxie. I'm honestly intimidated by them. They all have more domineering personalities than *me*, and I thought that was only barely possible in the far reaches of organised crime.


9/5 THURSDAY
*(Typed, Encrypted)*

I am not as bored now, at least. I've been thrust into an actual group of friends through Terri. They may all end up as soul-destroying corporate executives or media moguls, but, for now, they're practically kindly. TJ has invited me to a little soirée of sorts after last week's rather disastrous introduction to college partying. He said it was the least he could do after allowing some drunken frat boy to vomit all over my nice skirt (That is so difficult to get out of poly-cotton).

My life has been a whirlwind of class work, assistant assignments, work, and burgeoning friendships with the future rulers of the free world.... Well, life certainly moves quickly after only a week, but goodness if this breakneck pace hasn't popped up in the past. That reminds me, Nota Bene: Run to international office to apply for study abroad next year. No reason to stay in one place if Father is finally purposefully curbing his temper tantrums.

As there are not enough hours in the day to assuage my intellectual curiosity through exercise and company alone, I have already completed a series of excellent biographies and essays by GK Chesterton and the *Summa Theologica* by St. Thomas Aquinas. John Donne is next!

Not much else, life is becoming surprisingly tolerable as of late, Huzzah!


9/7 SATURDAY
*(Written in a worn notebook)*


Had a long, very long, talk with Father today before work. I think everything is going towards a smooth recovery on both sides, and I am immeasurably happy about it.

9/18 WEDNESDAY
*(Dream Journal)*

We were knights searching for the Holy Grail. Hadrian was Galahad and I was Lancelot, but a girl. I think I was still sleeping with Guinevere, though (???). We ended up in Castle Anthrax where we were rescued by John Cleese and Eric Idle. I don't even know, self. I just don't know.

9/21 SATURDAY
*(Typed, Encrypted)*

So, I slept with one of my roommate's friends today...

9/22 SUNDAY
*(Typed, Encrypted)*

So, for my own peace of mind, I've decided to recount yesterday's events for the sake of a record for future reference. Given that this was my...sexual inauguration, it seems only right.

I was with Terri's posse, drinking champagne to celebrate a birthday within the group, I forget who. In any case, I was slightly to the side and slightly awkward at the onslaught of so many women in the tight quarters of a single dorm room. Terri did nothing to include me in her conversations, and I failed to make conversation last longer than two minutes between myself and anyone unfortunate enough to stand near me. It seems outside of a structured environment, I am terrible at human interaction. Who would have guessed? (Me. I would have guessed. I am not so oblivious not to realise my own flaws).

Andy came to sit with me, swirling the strawberries at the bottom of her clear SOLO cup.

"You remind me of Shakespeare's dark lady sonnets," I said, in lieu of a sensible conversation starter. I stared at my second cup of champagne. I definitely needed more.

"What did Shakespeare have to say about his dark mistress?" she asked instead of leaving me.

"But if thou catch thy hope, turn back to me, And play the mother's part, kiss me, be kind: So will I pray that thou mayst have thy 'Will,' If thou turn bay and my loud crying still."

She looked at me oddly. "And here I thought you were going to talk about my hair."

"I like your hair," I said stupidly, "but I like that you're better than me more."

The rest of the conversation is a bit of a blur, but I definitely remember enthusiastically agreeing to visit her off-campus apartment and kissing in the cab.

Of course, in the morning, she reminded me that this was definitely a one-night stand or, at most, a friends-with-benefits situation.

It was AMAZING. She even let me kiss her before I walked back to campus. I am so delighted. It was such a lovely night, and I didn't catch any inappropriate feelings in the course.

9/29 SUNDAY
*(Typed, Encrypted)*

So glad I put my foot down when it comes to classes. Not that I couldn't use the additional intellectual stimulation, but my schedule has simply run away from me. Next semester would be intolerable if I were taking twenty-one credits. Friday nights are devoted to symposium with TJ and his companions (I'll tell you how those pan out in a moment), the other weeknights are brimming with yoga, belly dancing, bouldering, etc. with Terri's workaholic playmates, and weekends are filled with theories and proofs with Father. I only have mornings to myself (if you discount working, that is), which is...nice. I'm always much more contented when I have so much to do and so little time to mope like a child.

TJ is very...cool, I suppose. We work together on Godshall's essays and assignments and, at the end of the week, do something fun. I call it a symposium because of its obvious parallels with the ancient Greek activity of drinking water-cut wine, lounging on couches, and talking about everything under the sun, but the rest of the group complains that it reminds them of taking seminar classes. TJ has a wide assortment of friends, a collection of the most intriguing philosophy questioners, anthropology studs, psychology observers, and odd humanities students in all the land (including the long-since graduated and the odd newly inducted freshmen).

On the first night, I wondered why none of the dozen or so milling young adults were in the science department or any other academic strata, for that matter. It was soon made obvious when the wine was passed about and everyone settled either on the shag carpet swatches or the compressible, old, and hideous couches pulled out of Goodwill dumpsters. I clung to TJ just in case one of the insidious pieces of furniture decides I would make a tasty side dish to accompany these "sedentary academics," of course. He led me to a rather impressive chair set a touch apart from the circle of quietly decomposing upholstery. I sat beside it, accepting my Target-brand mini bowl half filled with red wine without a word.

"This here is Inanna. I'm sure you've seen her 'round campus." TJ graciously invited all of his guests to introduce themselves to me, which was very gallant of him. I counted out the major distribution and gender/race/socioeconomic background in my mind as the group gave their little spiel instead of catching names. I think a few moments of potential embarrassment are worth it, though. First impressions only happen once, after all. When TJ motioned for me to introduce myself, I baulked a bit before relenting.

"My name is Inanna Drew. I am completing my biology-chemistry and literature degree. I hope to teach and write when I finish my education."

A few nodded, many sipped importantly from their bowls, examining me intently. Perhaps they were judging me, but I was too nervous to care (Such a funny paradox, no?). Once the discussions were underway, however, I was in my element. Though some conversation was beyond me, I merely took that time to sit, sip, and people watch.

To my right was a boy who obviously, painfully never managed a successful date, yet studied the motivations for infidelity in American men for his thesis. A greying communist across from me watched everyone with hooded, suspicious eyes. A woman who casually threw out show-stopping vocabulary sat opposite of TJ. Only one of them was younger than twenty-two, and I enjoyed showing off my varied knowledge to a group almost exclusively focused on the ins and outs of human nature. I most definitely don't come back time and again because I have a crush on TJ, no matter what Terri says to her friends and mine. I'm not even sure I understand crushes outside of the purely theoretical.


9/30 MONDAY
*(Written in a worn notebook)*

I was working in the library's study rooms with Terri when TJ passed by. He waved, and I dropped the books held so precariously in my grasp to wave back.

He laughed, opening the door to help me reestablish order in my personal Sodom and Gomorrah. "Maybe y'all shouldn't be readin' three books at once, In. 'Cause goodness if it don't make a mess."

I made a vague noise of agreement as he placed the books onto my pile of "read" documents before making his way out.

"You're blushing, In." Terri smiled knowingly as the door shut. "Can't you make up your mind?" she asked playfully.

"I'm sorry, Terri. Is it my fault you are the token heterosexual in your group of friends?" I asked hotly. Just because he had nice arms didn't give her leave to tease me mercilessly.

"It's your fault if you start working through my girlfriends while pining after Mr. Archaeology. One at a time, sweets."

Ah, the joys of youth.

# October

## 10/3 THURSDAY

Slept with another friend of a friend today... This is becoming a habit.

## 10/9 WEDNESDAY
*(Written in a worn notebook)*

TJ was making out with one of the girls from the symposium in Godshall's office this morning. I am a little hurt but mostly outraged that they were acting so indecorously in an *unlocked* office belonging to TJ's *employer*. Not their best laid plan, I must say. I'm also angry I never noticed the amorous looks they were continually sending each other in hindsight.

"*How in the world didn't I pick that up?*" I asked the hallway. It provided no usable answer, and I was left with the very awkward duty of reminding the lovebirds that life does indeed go on (Even if your tongue is all the way down your lover's throat). I shut the door, knocked loudly, and listened to the couple desperately try to right themselves.

"Please be a bit discreet next time, if there is a next time," I said blithely, then strode to my seat, picked up my assignments, and looked TJ in the face. "Should I leave? The moonlight is lovely this time of the month, after all."

"Naw, naw, weel jus be leavin'." Wow, it was like someone thrust marbles into his mouth the way he garbled his English with embarrassment.

"Bye!" I waved them off, and they slinked off to do Byron knows what. I have to call Terri and point out how unaffected I am after being confronted with the object of my unending pining in a most indecorous position... Ah, well. Back to work.

10/14 MONDAY
*(Written in a worn notebook)*

TJ is incredibly, hilariously awkward around me, and I revel in his insecurities. I'm tempted to insinuate that the tent he'd made in his pants was one of the most...*uninspiring* I'd seen. Not that I've actually seen a penis in real life, but I want to be on the other side of a teasing conversation, dammit.

10/15 TUESDAY
*(Written in a worn notebook)*

First one again. Why do girls have to be so pretty? And have such nice hands? And smell so nice?

10/19 SATURDAY
*(Typed, Encrypted)*

Hadrian is on vacation, apparently. Though my fall break is another week away, he visited me this evening while I was working on Godshall's Mayan Archaeology class. I was, as per usual as of late, sitting in the bowels of the social sciences complex listening to the usual basement sounds attempting to drive me to distraction. The door opened a full hour before Godshall promised she would return (and she's always *exactly* six minutes late). Hadrian's outline shone in the bright hall light, contrasting with the pathetic little lamplight and abysmal colour choices (Dark blue? For a room without windows??) of my own personal purgatory. I swear to myself every time that I shall never work nights ever again, yet there I was once more.

Hadrian stayed, frozen in the entrance, and I was reminded of the many times we butted heads a year ago for some reason. I waved, red marker in one hand and a cuppa (decaf Lady Grey) in the other.

"Glad you're not making out with your boyfriend down here."

I blinked, a trifle bit bemused. "What boyfriend?"

"Your roommate said—"

I groaned obnoxiously, and he fell silent.

"Ignore her. She thinks she's funny." I looked down at my stack of papers morosely. "Well, come in. The light is ruining my night vision."

He shut the door, and we were bathed in the great muffling darkness that inhabits all underground dwelling places.

"What brings you by my neck of the woods?" I asked from my little oasis of off-yellow incandescent glow.

"I think I owe you." He scuffed his expensive patent-leather shoe against the cheap 1977-chic textured carpet.

"Hmm. What did you say?" I asked, feigning greater distraction than necessary. *This*, I thought, *would surely be interesting*.

He stalked to the desk (tripping on more than one mysterious object littered every which way in the process) and slammed his hands on the wood. "I hate it at school."

I frowned, sympathetic despite myself. I know how much he enjoys using his education as a social scene. For him to dislike it, something must be terribly out of place.

"I can't stand it up there...I miss you too much." Now that was a surprise.

"I missed you too?" I asked, unsure and desperately distracted despite myself. I did miss him, but he sent me so many emails and text messages and other modern fiddle-faddle as to be pathetically annoying rather than something to be missed... I've also been dreadfully busy as of late.

"Are you still mad at me?" His eyes begged for kindness, for some sort of reprieve from the guilt no doubt gnawing away at his innards *that very second*. Too bad, buster. I want to torture you a bit before officially forgiving you of your ass-hattery.

"You metaphorically tore my heart from my chest, tossed it into a churning garbage disposal, and spat on it for good measure...so, no, why would I be the least bit perturbed?" I asked, all innocence.

"I'm *sorry*. I was mad. I thought you were just avoiding me after what happened at school."

"Why would I avoid you?" I asked, genuinely confused. "It wasn't you who poisoned me, was it?"

"No," he said, mildly scandalised. "Of course not. But I thought...You avoided me after you left the hospital, randomly called me just to piss off my sister, then screamed at me. What did you expect me to think?"

"I didn't expect you to assume that attempted murder would make me shy away from you," I said honestly. "Did something happen while I was delirious?"

"Yeah," he said with a soft laugh. "You said you loved me." We stared at each other for a long stretch of time, mulling over the statement.

"Ah," I said finally. "I wonder why I said that."

"So, you don't love me?"

"What happened when I left the building?" I asked instead, still heart-stung and unwilling to answer such a question honestly. He sat on the corner of the desk, taking a moment to rub his hands on his thighs, a self-soothing gesture I hadn't seen him indulge in since his father left the hospital. He looked up at me, eyes lit from below and deeply shadowed by the limits of my little lamp.

"I heard you. From the car. You were crashing through the woods about half an hour after you left. I'd called, but you hadn't answered, and I guess I was gonna look for you. Thought you were being a little shit for making me wait." He smiled just a little at the memory. "But I heard you cussing out a tree in German, so I went to the woods instead." He grabbed a pen and began playing with it, balancing the tip on the pad of his index finger and flipping it in the air. Flip. Flip.

"You know why your hands were bleeding?" Flip.

I shook my head.

"You were clawing up an oak tree. I think you tried to eat one, too." Flip. Flip. "Freaked me the fuck out, trying to drag you back onto the path. You know it's a good thing that the woods are so fucking small, or we'd both still be stuck there. Pretty damn sure."

I reached out and stilled his frenetic movements.

He smiled into the darkness. "I think you recognised me after a bit, but you were still in 'anything but English' mode. Talking and talking, and you could hardly walk straight." He snorted. "Had to pick you up and carry you to the car."

"That must have been frightening."

"Understatement of the year." He shrugged. "Couldn't get a single useful thing out of you. Just something about apocalypse and 'Ich liebe dich.'"

I squeezed his hand.

"You really don't remember?"

"Not a thing after leaving the old contagion ward."

"You scared the shit outta me," he added, apropos to nothing.

I pulled him roughly to the side, gripped him in a tight hug, and said, "I promise not to be poisoned with witch's salves ever again. All right?"

He relished in the rare act of physical contact between us. Especially as it was initiated by myself. He was awkwardly pressed into my shoulder but didn't seem to mind being half sprawled over my ordered paperwork.

"I'm sorry," he offered after a long pause.

"Promise not to drop notes off at my doorway anymore?" I asked, confident he would concede.

"I can do that," he said, earnestly.

I smiled and patted his head. "All right, but I absolved you of wrongdoing ages ago."

That happy smile curled into a coy one as I finished. His features smacked of shock and disbelief as he separated from my person. "What?!"

I laughed again. "Yes, and I have two more classes worth of essays to grade at the moment, so you may stay here and entertain me with stories of school—as I occasionally nod or laugh—or leave and see me later."

He stayed, bless him. It certainly made the next hour and twenty-three minutes (as Godshall actually broke with tradition that night) infinitely more bearable.


10/21 MONDAY
*(Typed, Encrypted)*


No matter how glad I am that we are no longer at odds, it cannot blot out the sheer mortification that possessed me tonight. Needless to say Hadrian is no longer allowed to accompany me in my group exercises. I didn't even invite him.

He appeared out of nowhere, and I could give no counsel to sway him. Competitive group swimming is not nearly as fun when a friend of yours is lounging on the haphazardly organised deck chairs, waiting for you to finish so that we may "do something more interesting." The girls complained in the locker room that he was leering when I wasn't looking. Let me take a moment to lament my ill fortune...

All right, my wailing finished, I can continue. I asked him not to be so lascivious, and he said he was obviously only ogling me. Yeah, right. I really must convince him to work off his frustrations on someone not in my social circle. This could become ridiculous should I allow the two strata to overlap in such a fashion.

10/22 TUESDAY
*(Typed, Encrypted)*

What happened today? Nothing too interesting, I suppose. I saw Hadrian for maybe five minutes between classes and work and crushed the egos of several philosophy students during a harried lunch period. I think I have been banned from certain parts of the school dining hall now...


10/23 WEDNESDAY
*(Typed, Encrypted)*

I had an actual hour to myself today and Hadrian completely monopolised it. At least his conversation was not totally uninspired. I learned why he had tried to join the infamous Jackson Academy of the Sciences mathletes all those months before.

"I liked the quiz-bowl team at my old school and thought that mathletes were basically the same thing, right? Only less trivia and more complicated math problems."

"You had a quiz-bowl team?" I asked, amazed. He preened a bit, explaining that he was quite good at relaying random facts at breakneck speed. The rest of the conversation revolved around the friends we had made and lost since the end of high school. Which were many and varied on his part.

He seemed particularly interested in my Socratic seminars, and I teased him for possibly having a crush on the venerable TJ. He punched my arm with adorable gentleness, so I punched him back. He complained endlessly that his pectoral was going to bruise, and that I had to "kiss it better" before he died of internal haemorrhaging. Really, he's adorable when he acts so oppressed.

10/25 FRIDAY
*(Typed, Encrypted)*

I was in an unaccountably good mood today. Maybe it was because I had all that wine with lunch. Maybe it was because I had skived off for the first time in ages. I know, very naughty of me, but I shall make up for it in excellent papers and homework. Comparisons of Ancient Greek and Edwardian literature is just too boring sometimes. Which is truly a shame, because it had started out so well…. But in any case, I was very happy to be alive today. Hadrian and I drove to Centennial Park to feed the ducks and cluck about Grecian architecture.

"I have a gift for you." He handed me an envelope as thunder rippled through the sky. I thrust it into my pocket without a single care, pulling my body out of the car and motioning for him to join me.

"Ina, it's about to rain." He shook his head admonishingly.

I smiled because that was the point of my merriment. "Where's your sense of adventure?" I asked laughingly before shutting the door and leaping away into the shadowed sunlight. The next thunderclap split open the heavens for me, and I spun in place, beaming in ecstasy. I love the rain. I laughed, cackled really, and danced about like a bacchant ready to rip into the closest target. A hand caught mine and pulled me close. "See, it wasn't that difficult to enjoy yourself, was it?" Hadrian and I danced stupidly and awkwardly in the rain, and I could not ask for a better gift than that.

Lightning flashed and the sounds of ripping atmosphere begged for attention like favoured musicians playing for an adoring audience. I took no heed of danger; I was happy with hair clinging to my back in a single snarl, clothes soaking me to the bone, and a song in my heart.

The flashing lights were pyrotechnics, the thunder merely percussion to the orchestra of human nature. Had it been night, the fingerlings of pure electricity would have lit the sky past normal daylight. Instead, they burned the retinas of any fool who dared to behold them as Ham beheld his father.

Hadrian set the pace to a waltz and directed us back to the car, clearly unhappy in the dangerous weather but unwilling to leave me to my most certain doom.

I pushed his fringe out of his eyes. "Don't be so scared, it's only a little electrocution."

He looked at me as if I were mad. "You are such a fucking space cadet," he grumbled, as I resisted his efforts to steer us to safety.

I laughed at his silly internet speak, twisting his arm with a strange, blinding delight. "Nay!" I shouted over another bout of sudden earth-shattering din. "I am unrooted and godless!" I spun out of his grasp just in time to see a bolt roar down not fifty metres off and strike a poplar, setting it alight like a Roman candle on Independence Day.

"All right, enough! Back in the car!" He tugged and yanked me, backpedalling to the car where we soaked the leather straight through. We smelled wet and clean. Purified by nature itself...and I think I may still be slightly intoxicated! My language is much too flowery for sobriety, my dear reader.

10/28 MONDAY
*(Dream Journal)*

I was on a beach, speckled with the odd boulder, staring out at the churning surf. I was waiting for something, waiting for it to begin. The sand beneath my bare feet felt like smooth glass beads shifting and rolling beneath me while I stayed still. I was almost floating, ethereal and windswept in a shining moment of anticipation. The sea boiled and acquired a ghastly violet cast. I waited. The sea smoothed to the appearance of glass and shone gold in the clouded sunlight. I waited still. The sea pulled away, taking with it the water, the sand, the boulders, and me. I didn't cry out. I had expected to end up tossing and turning in the frothy waves. I waited still. A form filled my vision, green and vaguely human. I held out my hand, and we slipped beneath the waves into the sweeping current below. I looked again, and it had changed to Hadrian, holding my hand tight and smiling like a shark whose prey had swum into its mouth. He gobbled me down in an instant, but I wasn't afraid in the least. Just irritated.


10/29 TUESDAY
*(Written in a worn notebook)*

I suddenly want to see the sea. I want to watch the sun fall and rise according to that tumultuous, mysterious monstrosity. I want to thrust my feet in the sand and allow myself to be sucked into the riptide and become consumed completely. To touch the cold black bottom and push and push until my head breaks the surface and everything is light and warm and alive again. It would truly be marvellous...

Enough of my idiosyncratic madness, I have news. Hadrian had been bothering me intensely since he returned to Chicago (Even if he was only there for a few days, he has sent me more emails than I even thought possible), so I suggested he sign up for a Skype account. I had hoped a bit of face-to-face time would dampen his enthusiasm, especially if I were disgusting from a workout or otherwise bedraggled during the intercourse.

He didn't reply, but not five minutes later, I was barraged by Skype alarms saying that "HadriansWalloxo" wanted to be on my contacts list. He has only just finished blathering to me about his day, and I am exhausted.

That had been a bad idea, In. Very bad, indeed.


10/31 THURSDAY
*(Written in a worn notebook)*

I fucking hate birthdays sometimes.

# November

**11/11 MONDAY**
*(Written in a worn notebook)*

I'M GOING TO ICELAND! This is the best anniversary of the death of millions of men for no reason at all ever!

**11/12 TUESDAY**
*(Written in a worn notebook)*

I just realised that you have absolutely no clue what I was on about last night, so I have, in my eternal benevolence, decided to elucidate. I applied for a summer internship studying archaeology arranged by TJ in lieu of an apology for rampant and repeated misuse of Professor Godshall's office (or perhaps as an incentive to keep quiet?). In any case, I shall be excavating a little but mostly doing lab work and library research (my favourite kind). I do believe I shall be hugely contented for those lovely three months. Life is quite nice, really.

**11/17 SUNDAY**
*(Dream Journal)*

Sex dream. Sex dream with HIM. And Hadrian. Sex dream with *Hadrian* of all people.

Very confused, not at all aroused.

**11/20 WEDNESDAY**
*(Typed, encrypted)*

Skype is intolerably exhausting. I've been burning through my laptop's batteries as if they were peppermint humbugs at Christmastime. This really does have to stop, or I shall scream myself into insensibility.

I also found a slightly crumpled envelope in my coat pocket this morning. There was a note in it, but water had rendered it unreadable. I wonder what it had said?

**11/23 SATURDAY**

So staying on campus led to all sorts of sapphic shenanigans over Thanksgiving break. I suppose boys are nice, but, from what I've heard, they're not good enough lovers on average to be bothered with.

# December

12/15 SUNDAY
*(Typed, Encrypted)*

I apologise for the inattention: class work, friends, paid work, and Hadrian have taken up most all of my time as of late. Finals, it seems, are a mite bit harder than anything else in university thus far. In any case, classes are over, and I was rather morose. I'm not sure why... Well, yes, I knew exactly why, but that gave me no excuse. Everything horrid in my life has happened over a year past, so why should I choose to mope in the faint dustings of snow this Sunday morning?

I'd been sitting in the cemetery when I called him. "Hadrian?"

"Well, isn't this a surprise. You're usually telling me to get off the phone. This must be serious." He was obviously in a good mood, with a pleasant lilting tone to match. I'm sure he was smiling.

"Are you busy?"

"I actually just got out of church, so no. Nothing's going on but brunch. What's up?"

"May I visit or some such after your brunch?"

"You can come to brunch if you want. We always have plenty." He was always saying things like this. It wasn't so much the words as the intonation, as if he were coaxing a wild animal into a cage to be rehabilitated.

"I can feed myself perfectly well," I said, gruff but fond. "And I wouldn't intrude on your family like that."

"You know you're always welcome," he wheedled. "Everyone likes you."

I laughed pointedly.

"Right, not everyone, but most of them!"

"I'll pass for the afternoon, I think. I have a few errands to run. Good afternoon."

"See you then," he replied and hung up.

I went back home and baked a batch of cherry turnovers and chocolate-chip cookies. Usually, I'm no chef, but such activities can prove to be a constructive force. The exact art of measuring and heating and cooling to produce a perfect product is soothing in its predictability...and maybe I was also concerned. After all, cooking, if some television personalities were to be believed, can act as an effective coping mechanism and stress reducer.

I'm not so sure, but the treats came out well enough and none of them burned. It looked like I would be later in coming than I anticipated, but I didn't care. The treats would be an apology of sorts or a sly ploy meant to distract so that I could speak without interruption. I also washed my car; it sorely needed it. I knocked on his door two and a half hours later. He opened the door himself, beaming at my initiative.

"You decided to show up, congrat— What is that?" Hadrian peered forward at the basket tucked under my arm.

"Hot food. I hope you haven't yet glutted yourself so thoroughly as to refuse dessert?"

"Of course not!" He followed the food, of course. I walked inside and made my way into the smoking parlour. I really adored this old house, even if I hadn't visited since summer. So lovely and delightfully outlandish. There was a fire burning hickory in the marble fireplace. I smiled as we sat down.

"So, what's up?" he asked cheerily.

I pulled back the handkerchief (if one could call the monstrous table runner a mere handkerchief) instead of answering. He took a deep breath and nearly swooned, closing his eyes and licking his lips. I handed him a turnover as I picked one out for myself with my other hand.

"We shouldn't eat them in here..." He was staring longingly at my outstretched pastry, not taking it for fear of leaving crumbs on the carpets.

"You are such a pampered product of wealth." I rolled my eyes and put the food briefly away to relocate to the kitchen. It was deserted and immaculate. "Did you have brunch out?" I asked while pulling the morsels back into the open and revealing the canister of hot chocolate also hidden inside.

"We ate in. Mrs. McAllister is just inhumanly fast. I've never seen a woman so bent on cleaning up and clearing out as her." He took a bite and dissolved in buttery ecstasy. "God, that's good!"

I smiled. "It's the only sweet I can make other than cookies." I held up a chocolaty bit of heaven, and he snatched it from me in an instant.

"I love you, Ina. Marry me," he said in utter seriousness, even if the effect was slightly offset by the cherry filling smeared on his cheek and the chocolate melting on his fingertips.

I laughed and wiped the crumbs off of his rapidly souring expression. "I don't think you would like that. I'm far too infuriating to take in large doses."

He shook his head to arrest my mothering. "I'm pretty sure you didn't come over just to feed me, but I appreciate it!" he backtracked. "I would love it if you fed me all the time!"

Maybe that was over doing it, Hade. I bit into my turnover, musing over the steaming cherries floating on my tongue. I swallowed swiftly.

"My mother was nearly in the Olympics, did I tell you?" I poured a cup for each of us.

"Then she had you?" he ventured.

A perfectly reasonable assumption. Many aspiring athletes were probably waylaid by the pesky responsibility and inherent weight gain involved with parenthood. But no, that was the wrong answer.

"Then she snapped her spine while training for the Beijing Olympics. Father would have shot the horse himself if Mother hadn't ordered him not to."

He looked shocked. "She was a rider?"

I nodded. It was her best, her ultimate talent. She'd already earned a bronze in dressage a few months after I was born. She raced her horses at Steeplechase every year.

"She seemed to do everything: equestrian, shooting, swimming, sailing. She could do anything she wanted, and she was shattered, utterly. Mother thought that she could domesticate anything." Bitterness seeped into my tone as I stared down my turnover.

"She can still— Well, at least she's not...you know." Wrong thing to say, really. Really. Had he forgotten?

"But I never had a mother before the fall," I burst out. "I had a strict instructor and life coach, not a stereotypical caregiver and confidant. All she seemed to do when she was home was reinforce my father's rulings and give me even more work to do. I was so busy, I'm surprised I even learned what free time was." I paused to look at my audience; he was captivated by my candour.

I continued as he took another bite. "There was a reason I had few real friends as a child, and the ones I had would later viciously mock me for my mother's disability." I hadn't meant to let that bit slip, but words tend to tumble ass over tea kettle when they are finally loosed upon the world.

He patted my knee, wonderfully silent.

I looked down at my shredded pastry, conflicted. "But I had a mother, suddenly. She doted on me and actually *listened* to me." Maybe because she had time or maybe because my thoughts were worth listening to, I'll never know. "I had someone to nurture me, not tutor me. We would spend hours talking and singing and reading together. It was heaven."

"I'm glad you could fix your relationship with your mum, Ina. I'm sorry if—"

I waved him off. Now was not the time for him to talk. "Then she decided to try an experimental surgery designed to repair the nerve damage. Stem cell research." I marvelled morbidly at the thick red staining my fingertips. "I feared that I would lose my mother when she regained the use of her legs. I begged her not to do it out of selfishness." I took control of myself before my voice could break, before the tears could burn behind my eyes.

"She died on the operating table of complications on September seventh of last year."

He gasped softly, and I grasped for another of the cool, unappetising dainties. Cherry sauce smeared like cannibalistic war paint.

"We used to bake cookies before we had 'adult conversations', Mütti and me." It sounded much more tremulous than I intended. "I miss her."

He gathered me in a hug, and I cried in his terribly cavernous kitchen, set aside from the rest of the house out of an outdated fear of flames licking the side panelling of your freshly lacquered living room walls. I wanted to howl like an animal, bleed out my sorrow until there was none left, but I restrained myself to heavy wracking sobs against Hadrian's once-clean button-down shirt.

"I'm sorry," he said right back. "I swear, I didn't know. I'm so sorry, Ina."

"H-how could you even miss such a thing?" I wailed. "*Everyone knew*. It was in the *news*."

"I thought your dad just got custody or something. I asked, but they just said it was about your mum and changed the subject. They were trying to protect you." Perhaps there were some decent students hidden in Jackson Academy after all. "It's okay," he promised into the mess of my hair. "It's gonna be okay."

"I'm sorry. I'm so sorry I tortured you so." I heaved between cries. "I just wanted everything to *stop*. I was so sick of you trying to make it *better* when it could *never—*"

He hushed me again and again, but it didn't seem to help. Wasn't this supposed to help? Shouldn't I feel so much lighter and more at ease after telling someone? Was it not working because he isn't my love interest?

Is he the villain in the story, not the hero?

*(Dream Journal)*

Mütti is in her hospital bed, lulling the nurses into a false sense of security before she leaps out of bed and dances out of the building, complete with musical accompaniment. She was giggling and smiling at me, gossiping about the first day of school and the books I was reading.

"Don't succumb like *Serf Anna*, Liebling. You're a strong and independent woman," she lectures, still smiling. "You need no man. They only cause the worst of pains, at all times."

"What about—"

"Especially the ones you love. Cast them aside before they may break you."

"Come home, Mama?" Why did I call her Mama?

"Promise to cast him aside; he loves you so very much." She gripped my hand and kissed it softly before laying her head once again against the hospital pillow and dying.

I woke up screaming.


12/16 MONDAY
*(Typed, Encrypted)*

Why don't I feel any bettered by the revelation I made to Hadrian?

Carson interrupted our touching embrace not five minutes into my hysterical attack.

"What—" He cut himself short, and I wrenched myself violently away from Hadrian, stumbling to my feet. "Um, is everything okay in here?"

Hadrian reached out to grab my arm, but I escaped his grasp, stole away my handkerchief, and made my escape with a muttered, "You may keep the pastries."

On my way out, I could hear Hadrian's incredulous screech of "Oh my God, Car!" all the way from the second hallway. Though there were footfalls after me, I did not slow for the life of me. Once safely ensconced in a moving vehicle, I allowed my mortification to seep into my higher faculties.

"Idiot," I snapped at myself. "Why are you such an idiot?!" For the love of all that's holy, why on earth would I act so incongruously with my former modus operandi?

I had only wished to elucidate, to clear the air and leave it at that, pride intact. No, instead I ruined everything with my hysterics.

It isn't even that I have failed to trust him. Of course, I trust him very well. I would have continued to hate him if he were not upright and trustworthy. In the beginning, even, he was only trying to be polite and left me be when I made perfectly clear that I was adept at my peculiarly solitary lifestyle.

It was only after the funeral that I truly felt my own loneliness. I allowed it to consume me and shored it tight into my heart. There were others about me, circling not like sharks or vultures but as herds circle their young and injured. They tried to protect me in their own way as I dismantled everything I liked about myself because it reminded me too much of what I had lost.

My mother is dead.

I told him, and I've told you.

Why is there no lifted burden? Why haven't I felt stronger, lightened by the tears and confessions?

Is it too late? Have I run so fast, that closure has similarly fled my grasp?

Should I have confided in someone else? Was he a poor choice?

But he couldn't be, could he? He's been here this whole time, a strange, alien presence to draw me from myself. Isn't he the perfect candidate? A friend, steadfast and loyal, despite the *Pride and Prejudice* beginning?

After all, when we are good, we are very good indeed, which I have not properly portrayed in these writings. He *listens* to me. Really listens. And I can make him laugh so hard his sides begin to seize.

When my musing slips into the excessively maudlin, he is there to clown his way into making me smile, if only a little. When he is swayed too far by public opinion, brought low by the feelings of the mob and their fickle tastes, I reveal my ultimate trump card. That nothing in life is permanent, nor does the opinion of a few people forever stain a reputation. Little embarrassing stories of the people who snubbed him or a sharp word against his imagined hurts do him far more good than coddling ever could.

He never apologises, though. Not even when he did something very nearly unforgivable. He waits and waits and waits, then reappears and asks for life to return as normal. It's infuriating and confusing in droves. I don't even understand how the habit came into being. What brought this on? What made him like that? I can't understand it. Certainly, I am prideful as well, but he can be so ridiculous...

We're both ridiculous. Too alike despite outward appearances. Both smart children born into smart families that expected the sun and stars to fall from our pens and lips. We are all products of our upbringing and perhaps better for it, but I still cannot see how this attempt of mine has failed.

If this were fiction, I would be happily packed off to my next adventure, not still wallowing in self-doubt and lingering vestigial feelings clawing under the skin of my torso at odd intervals. Or I would have thrown myself from some romantic cliff side into the raging, frothing sea on a storming summer night ages ago. Either or, really.

Did I confess wrongly? Was it not enough? Should I share more, air out more secrets to ease my troubled self?

Can I even bear to look at him after all of this to try it again?

--

Coming back to this after taking a moment to regain some composure, I wonder if, perhaps, this did not go according to the tried and true ways of human interactions I have seen because such confessions always are between lovers or family. As we are neither, perhaps—

I'm acting in an altogether too silly way. Of course, he couldn't. I couldn't. I can't even imagine trying. It all seems too arduous an undertaking, too momentous a wall I have erected to even think of dismantling it, even for the relief that comes of a good bloodletting.

Besides, he could never.

No. Never.


12/18 WEDNESDAY
(*Written in a worn notebook*)


Father was out today. In a rare moment, he claimed he needed a bit of fresh air. That means he's consuming more than his daily allowance of high-calorie foods that litter the urban landscape about the house. But I decided I needed company, despite my misgivings.

Hadrian arrived within the quarter hour, rosy-cheeked and glowing expression. He is still blindingly pleased that I haven't pushed him away after revealing my great secret. I'm sure I don't understand his motivations, but it is a little pleasing to see him so glad to see me so often.

It will wear off, though. Always does.

We sat on the obscenely flowery couch in the living room and watched a film, some new version of *Pride and Prejudice* that I enjoyed in a vague aesthetic sense and in the spirit of mockery, obviously. I pointed out the incorrect interpretation of canon, poor acting, and historical inaccuracies for his benefit, of course.

By the ending credits, we had consumed well over two bowls of popcorn between us and a half-finished bottle of Maltese white wine I'd used in dinner the night before. Neither of us is anywhere near intoxicated, obviously. I wouldn't be nearly so coherent if I were, and the wine has just made Hadrian quiet his constant chatter for once.

I'm going to show him something.

1:26

*(Written in a worn notebook)*

I've been up all night thinking, trying to figure out how this actually came about. I'll just start from the beginning and hope for the best, shall I?

After I was done writing in the kitchen, Hadrian ventured into my domain, wondering why I hadn't returned to the couch for another film.

"Just recording notes." I shrugged, putting away my frayed collection of loosely bound papers. "Would you like to come upstairs?"

He looked surprised, almost shocked as the credits rolled behind him. He didn't *bound* up the steps to my room, but it was a near thing, really. I opened my door, and he traipsed into my living space, cool as you please.

"Your room smells like lilacs." His eyes were closed as he breathed in deeply.

I pointed to the vase on my desk: lilac blooms and roses surrounded in baby's breath. "I find it relaxing." Memories associated with scent, after all, are the most potent of all sensory triggers.

"So do I."

I watched him for a bit, exploring these four walls as a tiger surveys its new territory, assessing and very present. I've no clue what he was thinking. Maybe that it could do with a fresh coat of paint or a few new knickknacks. It's been rather sparse as of late, but I digress time and again, don't I?

"So what's up?" He smiled, relaxed and sure even in my domain.

I commended his courage with a nod before dropping to the floor and making my way under the bed as soldiers crawl beneath barbed wire in basic training. There was a rather painful wrenching sound as I pulled the siding out of the wall with a practised hand. Behind was my box. When I didn't immediately emerge, prize in hand, Hadrian wriggled beside me, obvious askance on his face.

It stays down there. I contemplated bringing it into the light, but decided to keep with tradition, keep the thing under wraps. It is a secret comfort after all. The ritual of retrieval and exploration kept the pretence that this was a secret, special, and separate magic that did not exist outside of its hiding place.

The highly embellished façade (decorated with the elaborate girliness my mother gleefully indulged in) slides out of place and Hadrian stares. It's not a small box by any means, but it is filled to the brim with things, pieces that still make my mother's memory tangible.

The flowers on her nightstand the night she passed are pressed and preserved in plastic sleeves, the notes she would write me on occasion are laminated with care, her obituary and the funeral invitations I made stared back at me as I pulled more and more bits of materiality out of the box. Her favourite book, her last needlepoint project (she had started crafting after the accident). Inside a pastel book were her birth, marriage, and death certificates. Even her immigration papers were all laid out for Hadrian's perusal. He was conspicuously silent.

"I love my mother," I said, waiting for him to at least look at me. He brushed his shoulder against mine for no discernible reason. "I couldn't just let her go. Like she never lived."

He exhaled, and the newspapers fluttered. They floated for a moment off the ground before I snatched them away and pressed them gently back into their proper places.

"So you scrapbooked?" It was like he didn't believe me, as if I were incapable of something so outrageously feminine and homely. I may have been slightly offended when I pulled the lovingly decorated hand-bound book out of his grasp.

"I created something enduring for the sake of her memory. Is that not a valid way to deal with grief? To create out of adversity?"

He backpedalled furiously. "Of course, I just meant—I never thought— Just— I'm sorry."

I waved him off, pushing away the irritation with a practised hand. I swept the little bottle of ashes back into the hidey-hole.

Obviously, he was unprepared for my decision to take some of Mother's poetry and, after scanning and hiding the digital copies away, burning them in an archaic send-off (a sacrifice to the god she'd had an absent faith in). If he couldn't meet my milder madness with anything less than incredulity, how could he hope to cope with that? He had her marriage certificate under his hands before I could reply. He was staring it down with great intention and verve.

But he baulked at the mother's name. "That's not right, is it?"

I smiled fondly, pointing to the birth certificate on the opposite page. The "It's a girl!" sticker beside it was a bit gauche in hindsight, though.

"Mothers in my family are notoriously vindictive in their naming habits." I smiled grimly. "I got off easy with the name of an obscure Sumerian goddess. My mother's name was Thallium Schmitt. She changed her name immediately after high school. She was positively ecstatic to become saddled with Nancy Drew."

He laughed a little, and I chuckled along amicably enough.

"Well, no wonder. Who wants to be named after a poisonous metal?" He nudged me again, possibly in camaraderie.

We went through the pink and lacy scrapbook, and I told funny stories of Mother's little foibles and idiosyncrasies. After over an hour of collecting dust in the comforting darkness, I made a rather crucial offhand remark. A bit of outright sentimentality that led to...a wholly unexpected turn of events.

"I am so glad I have someone to share this with. She thought you were hilarious. She insisted that you had some crush on me, and I told her she was mad to think it even possible—"

He pulled me into a clumsy, cramped half-embrace and said, "She's smart, then."

"—that I could date such a little brat," I said over him. "I mean, yes, you grew out of it, but—"

I froze, stunned, stumped, surprised, and startled like a Douglas-damned deer staring down an imminent, screaming automotive send-off.

"What?" It was a whisper. Maybe I only mouthed it because he said nothing in rebuttal. No clarifying statements were to be had at that moment. I quailed, still wrapped in one arm and utterly trapped in this suddenly claustrophobic holy space. I hadn't realised we were sitting so closely, like the bosom companions we were.

What was I doing with a *boy* (even granting long-standing friendship and recent emotional intimacy, I still couldn't say I have allowed anyone else so much personal freedom for so little in return), under my bed, telling funny stories and letting him wipe away my tears? What sort of idiot was I?

I wasn't some weeping heroine a man could sweep off her feet with a well-timed proposal for fuck's sake. I am *not* the serf Anna or any of the other millions of fainting maidens waiting for their personal Jesus to arrive on his white stallion of strange, ill-conceived metaphors (Revelations, people! Why did I read it?).

"You know how much I care about you, right?" Resounding silence can be intensely deafening. Huh. Who would have guessed? "I kinda love you."

I stared at my mother's note, the one that prompted this current predicament. I'll translate it from the German here.


Inanna Doll,


I hope you're putting my advice to good use and setting that new boy straight. Though he seems to be working a bit hard to get your attention. Turn the tables on him, lovely. If you want him, don't let him do all the work. You're lucky. Most boys don't offer themselves up on a silver platter like this one!

Have fun driving your incompetent English teacher mad, darling. I'm sure Minka [the family cat from her childhood] knew more English than this cretin understands in the simplest of connotations. Don't let him bother you.

Love, Mütti

I didn't crease the plastic or crush it under spasmodic fingers, though I sorely wished to. Why did he have to tell me *now*? Why, when I was utterly laid bare, vulnerable and trusting, would he throw this in my face and force me to recognise that *yes, perhaps* I had noticed some winsomeness or overt friendliness in the past, but that had been Hadrian *manipulating* me into doing as he pleased, not expressing true *attraction*. That would be absurd.

"Truly?" I whispered, heart ready to shatter.

"Yeah, I just figured you didn't—" He looked away from me, slightly embarrassed. "You really didn't notice? I thought I was pretty obvious."

But I was mistaken. "No."

He stared at me, shocked. "I thought you just...that you didn't want to hurt my feelings—that you just wanted to be friends."

*I do, I do. Herodotus's eyes I do,* I thought.

"And I'm fine with that," he added when I remained paralysed in the dusty atmosphere. "I love being your friend." He is painfully sweet. "Can you say something? Anything?" Begging.

"I didn't know," I said finally.

"Well, is this a good revelation or a bad one?"

Oh God.

"I mean, nothing has to change. Unless you want it to. Obviously."

Everything hurt.

"Please say something. You're freaking me out."

"I—" I swallowed and thought about the many times I've used the noun "I"! In everyday speech, essays, this journal. So completely self-involved in the most childish way possible. How it pleased me to make myself a martyr of life. One who never falters or suffers until freedom is won with bloody teeth and clawed fingertips.

"I might have noticed," I managed.

"Do you not...like me back?"

No. Yes. Could I even tell any longer? What were my own inner workings that were fighting so desperately against present circumstance? How could I suddenly be so indecisive? I had *known* that he couldn't like me. Yet here we were, under my bed and shoulder to shoulder, sharing secrets like children in the early hours, whispering promises we didn't intend to keep with clasped hands and shoulder nudges.

"I like you." Half-truthful whispers with the dust motes as my witness. I now pronounce us Dumbstruck and Lovesick. He leaned, touched his head to mine. Pleased.

"I like you too," he said indulgently.

"Why, though?" It seemed I was trapped in a cycle of only the simplest of phrases.

He flushed. "Because you're smarter than me, and you can bench press your own body weight? I mean really, the only things I have on you are social skills and stunningly good looks."

"You forget the crippling levels of personal wealth," I quipped dazedly.

He laughed. "Yes, I'm also the filthy rich son of a pirate," he amended.

Thinking back on the statement, I can't help but laugh.

But then I peeked at him and immediately flushed in embarrassment. I was bowled over by the myriad of possibilities racing through my head. How to evade his advances, destroy his attraction, and make things *normal enough for me.* So I could function without this terrifying presence looming over my head.

"I'm serious, Ina. Be my first mate?"

I stared with eyes wide as silver serving platters bedecked with an elegant tea service. Then he leaned, pressing his shoulder against mine and kissed me lightly on the lips.

What.

"That was weird."

He frowned at me.

"I—"

"Good weird or bad weird?"

"It didn't feel right."

"How would you know what felt right?" It occurs with hindsight that he may have assumed that was my first kiss. Dear.

"Well, my gaggle of incredibly athletic friends-with-benefits kiss better than you."

"What *gaggle* of friends-with-benefits? You only hang out with those scary upperclassmen girls."

"And I've slept with half of them," I shouted, a little. "I've been sleeping with women this semester, and let me enlighten you as to the *wonders* of sapphic entanglements because you would not *believe—*"

"You're a *lesbian?*" Oh, and here we *went.*

"*I don't know,*" I said hotly.

"How can you not *know?* Why didn't you *tell* me?"

"I like being chatted up by girls. I don't know what it *means* because I still don't want to marry any of them," I explained.

"No one wants to get *married*; we're teenagers."

"Well, I don't want to date, either. I just don't have that romantic inclination, believe me. I've tried very thoroughly."

"So, you're a lesbian player or something? What? Why didn't you ever *tell* me?"

"Because I knew you'd act like this," I said divisively, and he went still. "I knew you would assume I was slutting around or— Or *whoring* myself out because I was *lonely* and *confused*." I glared at the wainscoting. "I'm not, Hadrian. I know what I like. I always knew I didn't precisely *fit* into the categories available to me, and with patience and experimentation, I've pinned down what I actually *like*. What makes me *happy*."

"Sleeping with girls makes you happy."

"Sleeping with people I *trust* and not being expected to...to *feel* things I cannot."

"So, you can't have romantic feelings." He was staring at me. "And you don't sleep with men."

"Well, I haven't. Yet," I said awkwardly.

"And you don't want to sleep with me either, I guess?" Now he was getting prissy.

"I didn't *think* about it. Besides, men, historically, aren't worth the investment, sexual-satisfaction wise, according to second-hand accounts and academic studies like—"

"*Jesus*." He covered his face with his hands. "Jesus, just stop, okay? I get it. Men suck. You don't want me. We can still be friends, right? Is that what you're saying?"

"You're my *best* friend," I said finally. "I'm trying to be honest with you, because this last year and three months have been filled with *unimaginable* pain for me, and you're still here. That. That is more important than romantic love could ever hope to aspire to. You fed me and held my hand and...I don't know. I don't know what you want me to say."

"I want you to *love* me," he said all in a rush. "I want to move in with you and sleep with you and hear you say you *love* me."

"But you'll *settle* for my friendship?"

"I wanna be with you!" He was staring at me. "I just. I want to see you *every day*. I want to be in a *relationship* with you."

"We are in a relationship!"

He rolled his eyes.

"What do you think a friend*ship* is, Hadrian?"

"Not enough."

"I've told you secrets I'm never sharing with anyone else ever. I stood by your father's bedside even though *it was a razor threaded through my intestines* to see him like that. How is a friendship not enough? Your friendship means the world to me and sleeping with you wouldn't change that in the slightest. We could live together after college if we wanted. I am *telling* you exactly how I feel *right now*. There's no hard and fast rule to fucking *adulthood*, Hadrian."

He was quiet, but not for long.

"Do you love me?"

"Yes." It wasn't exactly a hard question. Hadrian had become family, with all the bumps and bruises those relationships entailed.

"Then okay."

"Okay what?"

"Okay, you sleep with girls now. Okay, you don't want me like I want you. Okay, we're gonna be okay. Right?"

"Right."

We were going to be fine, him and me.

# May

5/31 THURSDAY
*(Typed under Folder: InaIsSoCrazy)*

The newly minted Dr. Inanna Drew here. It seems Hadrian has found my stash of old diaries on my computer and elsewhere scattered about the house while packing. We're moving to the city that offered the best benefits-to-notoriety ratio, Boston, so that I can try my hand at postdoctoral work.

He's insisting on collating all of my "memoirs," as he calls them, mixing and matching in our document treasure hunt. He was hilariously disturbed by the bile dripping off every other page, especially the stuff directed at him. I *may* have purposefully misinterpreted his actions and body language, but high school is a cruel mistress to us all. I have also left so many things unexplained, but perhaps it is better that way. No one really pays attention to the complaining of an angry teenager. Though I'm not sure what he'll do with them, I am sure he won't do something as gauche as publish my silliness, will you?

# About the Author

Born and raised in Nashville, TN, K. T. Swift works as an archaeologist by day and a writer by night. When she's not writing technical reports and cataloging artifacts, K. spends her free time writing fiction and cooking weird and exciting dishes. She also loves travelling and has tooled around in Europe for the last four years.

Website: www.ktswift.wordpress.com
Facebook: www.facebook.com/kt.swift.5
Twitter: @KTSwift27

# Also Available from NineStar Press

# Connect with NineStar Press

Website: NineStarPress.com

Facebook: NineStarPress

Facebook Reader Group: NineStarNiche

Twitter: @ninestarpress

Tumblr: NineStarPress